WONDER HORSE BOOK SIX

KASHMIR

An Arabian Horse Novel

Victoria Hardesty and Nancy Perez
Authors of Action and Adventure with Arabian Horses

 PUBLICATION
CONSULTANTS
We Believe In The Power Of Authors

PO Box 221974 Anchorage, Alaska 99522-1974
books@publicationconsultants.com, www.publicationconsultants.com

ISBN Number: 978-1-59433-978-3
eBook ISBN Number: 978-1-59433-979-0

Manufactured in the United States of America

OTHER BOOKS BY

Victoria Hardesty and Nancy Perez:
Prince Ali – Wonder Horse Book One
La Duquesa – Wonder Horse Book Two
Desperado – Wonder Horse Book Three
Desert Rose – Wonder Horse Book Four
Freedom – Wonder Horse Book Five

ACKNOWLEDGEMENTS

We thank Shanna Carta for sharing her part of Kashmir's story with us. It was her idea that we use Kashmir as the main character in one of our books. The first part of Kashmir's story is what happened to him. Shanna accepted an Arabian gelding that was mad at the whole world, and a horse nobody else would take. They are best friends now.

We thank Tonii Ventimiglia, the Queen's Court Advisor for the Hesperia Wranglers organization in Hesperia, California. She explained the steps the young girls go through as they compete for titles from Tiny Miss through Queen. She explained the benefits for the young ladies who compete at the local level, State level, and the National level. The Rodeo Queen's program has much to offer young ladies, including scholarships to help them with their college educations. It develops self-confidence. It isn't just a beauty contest. The girls are required to know a lot about horses and ride well.

We also thank Virginia Jablonski for her help in understanding what Animal Communication is and how it can help animals who've suffered abuse and neglect. She spends a lot of her time working at home and on the road helping animals who have suffered from their connections with humans.

In addition we thank our Beta Readers Rebecca Gordon, Sharon Zarogoza, and Connie Neri. They go through the entire manuscript to keep us from getting off track and "walking in the weeds" and help us with spelling and punctuation errors too.

As writers, we are sincerely thankful for our family members support during the writing process. Sometimes it makes for late or non-existent dinners, laundry piles up a bit, and vacuuming gets put off when a writer is on a hot streak and has something to say. Thank you, Michael and Ray, for your help.

CHAPTER ONE

Kashmir was born under a cloud of deceit. His owner bred her mare to his sire without the knowledge or permission of the sire's owner. The relationship she had with the owners of the stallion fell apart long before Kashmir took his first breath. There was no way his owner could get the stallion owners to sign off on registration papers for the colt. The value of any purebred Arabian diminishes by this lack of proof of their heritage. Kashmir's owner owned him because she owned his mother when he was born. She could never prove he was a purebred Arabian, so many doors were permanently closed to him.

Meannella Dimes, who lived up to her name, but went by Ella, approached the stallion owners with lots of knowledge about Arabian horses, training techniques, and a highly exaggerated list of accomplishments. She "talked the talk" of a professional Arabian horse trainer; unfortunately, she never "walked the walk" of one. Ella also had difficulty paying her bills, which led to evictions and lock-outs from other facilities. She had no facilities of her own, so she and her horses and training horses went from facility to facility often. It took a while for the stallion's owners to figure things out. They were happy when they finally got their stallion home. They were upset enough about the situation they refused to talk to anyone about it for years.

When he was a cute baby, Ella fussed over him and handled him a lot. As soon as he grew out of the sweet baby stage, things changed. He was a colt that became a stallion. She refused to allow anyone else to handle him. She isolated him in a stall, so he had no contact with other horses, even geldings. He spent so much time isolated; he became angry and difficult to work with, even for her. The more difficult he was to handle, the less she wanted to handle him. The result was Kashmir spent most of his life alone in a stall with no contact with people or other horses. His manners did not improve. His depression turned to rage. Whenever someone new came near him, he went into attack mode, either charging them or trying to kick them. That situation went on for fourteen long years. Kashmir watched other horses groomed, tacked up, and taken to the arena for exercise and practice or turnout time while he stood impatiently in his stall. Horses are herd animals. They instinctively group together in nature. He wanted to run. He wanted to play. He wanted the company of other horses.

Kashmir noticed the care and love shared between humans and their horses. He got none of that. When he was out of his stall, which was seldom, it was always wearing a stud chain across his gums with the strong arm of Ella Dimes on the lead. If he took a misstep, she punished him by jerking on the lead. Sometimes it caused his gums to bleed. Ella attempted to teach him about saddles and bits and bridles when he was a young horse. Her personal fear of him made the training difficult at best. She lost interest quickly and put him back in his confinement. Kashmir wanted someone to love and care for him. He wondered why. Was there something wrong with him? Why did others deserve affection and love, and he did not? His despair only fed his anger.

* * *

Katie Barclay was born to Rodeo. She had no choice. Her mother had been Miss California Rodeo Queen while she attended college.

Her dad was a nationally rated Heeler in a roping team. Her father drove livestock around the country between his competition in rodeos and roping practice. Neither her mother, Shanna, nor her father, Clint, owned a decent pair of shoes. Cowboy boots and jeans were all they ever wore. Katie's first shoes were a tiny pair of pink cowboy boots, and her first pair of long pants were denim. She took her first horseback ride at the age of six weeks, firmly held in the saddle in front of her mother, going on a long trail ride with her father. Her first complete word was "horsie."

Katie grew up knowing she would be a Rodeo Queen like her mother. Shanna encouraged her, helped her study, taught her how to ride, and began teaching her how to run the barrels and bend poles by the age of four. Katie was more comfortable in the barn than she was in the kitchen or living room of their small house. The only place in the house she loved was her bedroom, which her mom decorated with horses of every description. Pictures, books, and figurines of horses littered every flat surface in the room. "My Little Pony" covered her bed. Even her bedroom curtains and the rugs on the floor had horses on them.

Katie's first horse was a pony named Tootsie. Katie took riding lessons from her mother on Tootsie and longed for the day she could run barrels or bend poles on her in competition. Tootsie was in her late teens when Shanna and Clint found her. She was well broke and very gentle. She'd been used in a children's pony ride for several years, then in a lesson program for younger children for another ten years after that. She was a sweet pony that genuinely liked children. She developed a special bond with Katie when Shanna and Clint brought her home to their barn. Tootsie had never had just one child before, and she loved Katie dearly.

Katie spent most waking hours with Tootsie. She brushed the little horse from top to bottom every day, spending lots of time brushing out her long thick tail and mane. Shanna got down on her knees in the barn to show Katie how to braid Tootsie's tail and enclose most of it in a tail bag to keep it clean and orderly and still have something to swish off the flies with. Shanna showed Katie how to clean and braid Tootsie's mane in long braids that gave her something she could shake from side to side to shoo off flies from her neck as well. She also showed her how to comb out the mass of forelock and bind it in a rubber band just below her ears to keep it neat and tidy.

Shanna showed Katie how to care for her tack. She showed her how to use saddle soap to clean the leather and how to apply neatsfoot oil to preserve it and keep it in good working order. Katie shined her saddle until it gleamed and kept it covered with a saddle cover on the lowest saddle rack in the barn when she wasn't riding.

The year Katie turned six-years-old, Shanna helped her with the paperwork to enter the Little Miss Rodeo competition. Katie wrote her own speech about why she was the right candidate for the position. She practiced that with her mother until she remembered it word for word, and it didn't sound like she was reading it from a piece of paper. Shanna had earned the title years earlier, so she was the perfect person to teach Katie what would be expected of her if she won the award.

Shanna taught Katie the horsemanship skills and knowledge she needed to be a successful candidate. They went over the chart showing the parts of the horse in detail until Katie knew every part marked and how it functioned. Shanna went over proper nutrition for a working horse until Katie understood that as well. Katie practiced measuring feed for Tootsie and checked it with her mom. The two went over all the tack in the barn tack room until Katie only had to see something to be able to identify it and explain how and why someone would use it.

Shanna took up training barrel horses when she made the decision not to proceed to the Miss Rodeo USA competition. She needed a way to help support herself and her family. She and Clint rushed off to Las Vegas and married the day she would have begun the grueling schedule for contestants. Eleven weeks later, she discovered she was pregnant. Shanna was young and healthy, so she continued training horses until she could no longer get her swollen belly behind the saddle horn on her saddle. Four weeks later, Katie came into their lives. Six weeks later, Shanna was back in the saddle again, holding onto Katie on trail rides.

Shanna taught Katie how to run the barrels on Tootsie. When Katie began getting good times on her runs, she encouraged her more and more. Katie stretched and pushed Tootsie for faster and better times. Shanna knew Tootsie wouldn't be capable of the times required in competition in another year or so. She and Clint started looking for another horse for Katie. They wanted a small horse, not a pony. When Katie's toes got closer and closer to the ground on her turns around the barrels, Shanna knew Katie would need a bigger horse than Tootsie soon. Clint found the perfect horse for Katie to transition up to within a few weeks. Blaze was an American Quarter Horse/Pony Of America cross that was half again as big as Tootsie. He was a stout little gelding weighing out at about 750 pounds, a bit over 13 hands tall. Clint and Shanna bought Blaze and brought him home, but didn't tell Katie he would become her horse. Shanna thought Katie had enough on her plate with the competition, and she was very comfortable with Tootsie. Shanna didn't want to throw in a change like that this close to the competition.

The day before the Little Miss Rodeo competition began, Shanna and Katie laid out her new clothes for the event. She had a nice fitting pair of jeans, new boots, a beautiful plaid blouse cut in Western-style, and a brand new white cowboy hat that fit perfectly. She had a white Western-style jacket embroidered with a floral pattern across the back and front yokes and at the end of the sleeves in a color that matched the blue in the plaid blouse. It was the perfect color to accent Katie's beautiful blue eyes. Katie bathed and shampooed her hair so Shanna could pin it up in curlers for the night and went to bed early.

Katie tossed and turned in her bed that night. The curlers were uncomfortable. She worried she'd forget her speech. She worried she'd miss the correct names for the parts of the horse. She worried about everything until about 2:00 a.m. when her fears dissolved in exhaustion, and she slept. She woke with a fresh attitude.

"Mom, I'm going to win this competition, you know," she said as she walked into the kitchen the next morning for breakfast. "I want to win every year from now on until I get to be Miss Rodeo California. Then I want to be Miss Rodeo, USA."

"I know you have it in you," her mother said, glancing up from the pot she was stirring on the stove. "I'm glad you want to do this. I had so much fun when I did, and I learned so much about myself in the process."

"You?" Katie asked. "How did you learn more about yourself?"

"I knew I had the confidence in myself to do anything I wanted to," her mother explained. "Just winning that crown taught me that I could do anything I set my mind on. You will learn that about yourself too, I'm sure."

"How does that work, Mom?"

"I learned that if I applied myself and worked really hard, I could be the Young Miss Rodeo for a year. I decided I wanted to become a trainer. I decided I wanted to go to college. I decided I wanted to get married and have my own family. I did all that. I'm happy with everything I did and all the things I learned. I also know that I can get whatever I really want and am willing to work for," Shanna explained. "When you get older, you'll understand it too."

"Mom, why didn't you go after Miss Rodeo USA when you could have?"

"That's a complicated question that you will understand a lot more about when you get older. I will give you a simple answer. I was in love with your dad. If I won that crown, I would be away from home most of that year. He was not happy with that, and neither was I. We decided to get married instead. Now we are lucky because we have you."

"I love you too, Mommy," Katie smiled as she dug into her breakfast.

After breakfast, Shanna took her daughter to her room to help her get ready for the competition. She washed her face and had her brush her teeth after breakfast. Shanna added a bit of blush on her cheeks, and a smidge of blue eye shadow on her eyelids to accent the color of her eyes. She brushed on a bit of mascara, applied a rose pink lipstick on her lips, and turned Katie around to see herself in the mirror.

"Are you sure this isn't too much goop on my face?" Katie asked.

"No, I'm sure. You look beautiful to me! Now let's get your hair combed out."

Shanna took the curlers out and brushed Katie's brown hair into long spirals that gleamed in the light. "Time to get dressed," she told her as she grabbed the armful of new clothes from Katie's bedroom. Katie stood in her mother's bedroom and dressed carefully. When she finished dressing, Shanna added her new white cowboy hat and arranged her curls a little. "What do you think now, young lady?" Shanna said as she turned her daughter around to view herself in the full-length mirror on the closet door.

"Wow. I think I look great!" Katie exclaimed and blushed a little.

"I have to agree with you," her mother told her. "Now it's time to get going. Be sure you have the cheat sheet on your speech. You can review that in the car while we drive over to the community center. Just relax. You're going to do just great."

Katie had been practicing her walk with a book balanced on the top of her head. She walked with grace as they left the house and got into Shanna's truck for the drive. She crossed her fingers while she studied the paper in her slightly shaky hands.

CHAPTER TWO

Kashmir was hauled to yet another facility and put into a box stall lined with wood shavings. Ella made sure the water bucket was full and dropped a half flake of hay in his feeder before walking out and latching the door. She moved her other horses into stalls, including four new horses she acquired by leasing them from their owners for her new lesson program. That promise got her box stalls for all of her horses and decent outside housing for the leased horses. She would be responsible for their feed and cleaning their stalls daily. If the lesson program turned out as well as she projected it would be to the facility owner, she would never have to pay board for her horses.

As soon as all the horses settled into their new home, Ella left the facility. She told the owner she had work to do on the internet to publicize the new lesson program at the ranch. She returned at the end of the day to feed and water her horses and have another short conversation with the owner. Ella spent the rest of her evening on her computer, posting notices about the beautiful new facility she was working from. She advertised the lesson program she hoped to get off the ground and working.

Ella was back at the ranch every morning early to feed her horses. A few calls trickled in on her cell phone. She spent time with each potential customer talking up the benefits of the facility and her ability as a trainer for lessons and horse training. She spent time every day talking with the facility owner, exaggerating the number of calls she was receiving. She also told the owner how she did her business at her previous facility. She, of course, exaggerated the number of students she trained. The facility owner was sucked into Ella's world for the moment and believed what she said.

A month went by with Ella always being at the new ranch early in the morning for feeding. She didn't leave until she fed her horses again in the evening. Then she called the owner one day with a problem that she couldn't make it to the ranch that day. The owner was sympathetic to her situation and promised to make sure her horses got fed that day.

Soon it happened at least twice a week, once on a weekend day. For several weeks, Ella called the facility owner and let her know; then, she stopped calling. She didn't answer her cell phone when the facility owner called her. Ella always had a good story when she returned to the ranch. The dog got hit by a car, and she had to run the poor thing to the vet and waited during unsuccessful surgery to save it. Her family was utterly destroyed by losing the dog, and she couldn't talk on the phone. Her father-in-law was terribly ill, and his wife had doctor appointments for herself, so she had to stay and care for him. The excuses were always serious and, most times, tragic.

The owner called the last place Ella worked and talked to the owner there. She got an earful from the woman who actually tossed Ella and her horses off her property. She found it interesting that Ella used the same excuses for not showing up. How many times can your father-in-law die? How many dogs that you own can get hit by cars requiring surgery and still not survive? How many times does losing a dog devastate the entire family? The owner of the ranch began thinking about Meanella Dimes and her many promises. The lesson program was almost nonexistent, only one or two new students since Ella moved her horses in. There were no new boarding customers either because no one put their horse in training with Ella. Now,

Ella was not at work, and there was none of her feed left to feed her horses, so the facility owner fed them again from her feed supply. She began to put two and two together and realized she'd been lied to and taken advantage of. She made one more call to Ella's cell number and left a short, curt message.

Four months passed. The facility owner couldn't reach Ella by phone or by mail after many tries. In desperation, she took her case to court for back board fees owed. Ella failed to show up for the court hearing, so the judge awarded ownership of all Ella's horses to the facility owner. She was at liberty to sell any and all of them to recover the amounts due to her.

With the court order in hand, the ranch owner returned to the ranch and moved all of Ella's horses into an enclosure together. She needed the box stalls and individual outside stalls for other paying customers.

Kashmir finally got what he'd been asking for. The owner turned him out with mares and geldings in a herd. The problem was he believed he was the herd stallion, and that gave him the option of breeding any of them as he wished. His mother didn't approve. She was the herd Alpha mare. When he first approached her, she turned on him with teeth and feet. She kicked him clear across the enclosure before she walked back to her place in the herd. He didn't understand at first. He kept trying. The other horses, encouraged by the herd mare, chased him away with teeth and feet too. The feed crew tossed hay over the fence for the horses. The mares and other geldings got to it first and kept Kashmir backed into the far corner until they finished eating. There was rarely enough for Kashmir left. He began to lose weight. He was scarred and scraped up by teeth and hooves. He was in a worse situation than when he was locked up. At least there, he got his food and free access to water.

The owners of the horses Ella leased for her lesson program showed up at the ranch to check on their horses. They had not been able to contact Miss Dimes either. The ranch owner gave them each the option of paying her cost for caring for their horses, or she would sell them for whatever she could get toward the board bills due to her. One by one, the owners of the leased horses paid the bill and took their horses home.

The ranch owner sold all the rest of Ella's horses for enough to cover the balance of her costs. Her only problem was she still had to feed Kashmir, and nobody on the ranch wanted to deal with him. She offered him for sale and dropped the price several times, but no one was interested. He was too much trouble.

CHAPTER THREE

Katie won her first crown and became Little Miss Rodeo. Her speech went very well. She was obviously photogenic. She was smart. She passed her horsemanship test easily. She excelled in every part of the contest. She was the standout for the Judges. It was a unanimous decision for them.

That year, Katie never missed an event. She rode Tootsie in every parade, at every rodeo, and even competed well in barrel racing on her. Her dad and mom attended every event she did and couldn't have been more proud of her.

Near the end of her first year as Little Miss Rodeo, she told her parents she wanted to compete for the title again. Clint and Shanna took her into the barn and introduced her to Blaze. Katie didn't want to change horses, but she'd grown several inches that year. She was too tall to be riding Tootsie much longer. She accepted Blaze and began working with him. Six months later, Shanna introduced Katie to a four-year-old girl. "Katie, this is Megan. She's been looking for the perfect horse. I think she will love Tootsie. What do you think?"

Katie was shocked. She'd never considered Tootsie would ever leave the barn. She expected to spend time with her every day after she'd spent time with Blaze like she had been doing for months. The realization that she would probably never see Tootsie again brought tears to her eyes. "Mom, do we have to?"

Shanna saw the sorrow in Katie's eyes. "Let's take a short walk. We need to talk, okay?"

Once they were out of hearing from Megan and her mother, Shanna began, "Katie, you are growing up, and you are getting too big to ride Tootsie. Tootsie needs a little girl of her own, just like she needed you when we got her. If we keep her here, you won't be able to ride her at all soon, and she will just stand around. That's not good for her. Why don't we give her a chance to be happy with another little girl of her own?"

Katie's eyes began leaking tears. "But, Mom, I love Tootsie."

"I know you do, sweetheart. Sometimes if you love something, you have to let it go so it can be happy too. I think it would be better for Tootsie if she had Megan to love on her and ride her instead of her just standing around, don't you?"

Katie nodded her head as the tears streamed down her face. "Yes, Mom, but it's so hard to say goodbye, not knowing if I'll ever see her again. Are you sure we have to do this?"

"Katie, I remember when I outgrew my first pony. It was very sad when my parents found a little boy his size for him. I didn't want to say goodbye to Patches either. I saw the little boy riding Patches around the neighborhood. At first, I cried, but I came to realize Patches meant as much to him as he had to me. He loved Patches too. I had a new horse to think about. I got over it and wished them well. I know that will happen for you if you give it some time. Why don't you dry your eyes and get to know Megan a little? Maybe you can show her the special things you learned about Tootsie. You know, the special places she loves to be scratched, and the way you brush her down and braid her tail and mane. Maybe we should give them the saddle and bridle you used on her. You've outgrown them too. They will fit Megan just right, and Tootsie is used to them. They still smell of you, so Tootsie will know you are still around because she can smell you on them."

19

Katie sniffled back her tears and wiped her face with the back of her hands. "If we have to," she stuttered, and she turned back to the barn.

In a few minutes, Katie was busy showing Megan everything she should know about Tootsie. For a little while, she forgot to be sad. She pulled out Tootsie's saddle and bridle and showed Megan how to put them on. She took the reins, let Megan's mom put Megan in the seat and walked the pony and the little girl around the barn a couple of times. Megan was delighted with Tootsie. Katie remembered how much fun she had riding her when she was little. That made it much easier when they loaded Tootsie in their trailer for the drive home. Katie stood at the end of the driveway watching the trailer jounce down the road until it disappeared into the distance. Her tears began to flow again. She went to her room, took off her clothes, pulled her pajamas on, and climbed into bed. She pulled the pillow over her head and let the tears flow silently until she fell asleep, exhausted.

Katie came into the kitchen for breakfast the next morning with swollen red eyes, but they were dry. She sniffled a little and said nothing while eating breakfast. She finally looked at her mother. "Mom, I know this is the right thing for Tootsie, but I will always love her, and I will never forget her."

"I don't think you should ever forget her, Katie. Tootsie was your best friend. I think you should always remember her. But you should remember that you've given her a new life with a new young person who will also love her. I know you did the right thing letting her go."

"I know, Mom. I wish it didn't hurt so much."

"I wish I could take all your hurts away, Katie. I know I will have to let you go someday too. You will grow up and want to live a life on your own. I hope you remember this then. I love you, so I will let you go so you can fly on your own wings. But that won't stop hurting me any more than knowing you gave Tootsie a new life by letting her go stopped hurting you. Life is all about changes. Everything changes. That isn't necessarily a bad thing. Sometimes it is because of love."

CHAPTER FOUR

Katie entered and won the Little Miss Rodeo competition for two more years. She took Blaze into the barrel racing events for Junior Rodeo and won more often than not. Her mother was a champion barrel racer at her age and was now a trainer. That didn't hurt her chances at all. She got her training from a winner. Her winning also helped her mother. Shanna got calls from the parents of other girls who wanted to compete. They wanted Shanna Barclay to train their daughters' horses and train their daughters as well.

At age nine, Katie was eligible for the Young Miss Rodeo competition. She could enter that competition for four years before she would qualify for the Rodeo Young Queen competition at age thirteen. Katie became Young Miss Rodeo by unanimous decision of the judges at nine. She won again at age ten, eleven, and twelve. During that year, she hit a growth spurt and shot up to five feet six inches. She was too tall for Blaze. Her toes nearly touched the ground when she rode him. Even she knew she needed a bigger horse.

Clint found the perfect horse for Katie while on a stock delivery trip in Wyoming. The horse was a buckskin gelding with AQHA registration papers. His sire was one of the top performance horse producers in the breed at that time, a beautiful Palomino. His mother was a champion barrel racer herself, and a lovely bay mare. Clint knew both parents of the buckskin gelding when he saw him the first time. Go for Cash came home with Clint after he talked it over with Shanna. They decided to surprise Katie and put Cash in Blaze's stall before she came home from school.

Katie's parents were both sitting at the kitchen table, having a cup of coffee when she got home that day. She kissed them both and scurried off to her room to change into her barn clothes. She planned to run a few barrels on Blaze before doing her homework that day.

She came back to the kitchen and opened the door to the refrigerator for a snack. "What are you doing home so early, Dad?" she asked.

"I finished up my stock run and came home to spend some quality time with your mother," he said between sips of steaming coffee. "What are your plans for today?"

"I planned to run a few barrels on Blaze, groom him and put him up. I have an essay to write for Social Studies tonight. I have to write about the agricultural revolution. You know, where farm machinery took the place of horses and mules on the farms and allowed farmers to work more land with less livestock and people. Did you know that put small farmers out of work? They had to sell to bigger farms, then learn how to fix those machines to earn a living. That kind of stunk for their families. They had to move back to town and all."

"Would you rather live on a farm that was miles away from anyone else, or would you rather live in town?" Clint asked her.

"I don't know, Dad. I guess there would be benefits to either one," Katie said as she thought about the question. "Maybe I would prefer living in town. If I were a boy, it would be easier to play football if you had friends close by. But if you loved to read, there would not be as many distractions if you lived on a farm."

"If you got sick, the doctor is much closer if you live in town," offered her mother.

"You're right, Mom, but I wouldn't like to live the way most people do with their neighbors breathing down their necks. You can't have horses like that. Here, where we live, we have 20 acres, so our neighbors are not close. But if you need help, they are only a short jog away. And I think people are friendlier when they're not crammed so close to each other."

"I wish you could have talked to my grandmother," Shanna said. "She could have told you tales and then some. She married my grandfather in 1915. They bought a small farm in Kansas. My grandfather ran that farm with a pair of mules. They had chickens, pigs, a few cows, and the mules to care for. They raised a family of six kids on that farm. My grandmother was in charge of the "kitchen garden," where she grew fruit and vegetables for the family. She took care of the chickens because they laid the eggs and made chicken dinners. She raised the six kids, did the cooking, and took care of her husband. I can't figure out when she had time to sleep," Shanna laughed. "In between other chores, she made all the kid's clothes and her own dresses herself."

"How did the kids get to school?" Katie asked incredulously. "Or did they even go to school?"

"Your great grandmother was a reader, so she taught all her kids to read. She also taught them to "cipher," which is what they called addition and subtraction in those days. It was simple math, but it was something they needed to know to work on the farm. She got to town every other month and brought back new books from the lending library. She used those books to teach her kids."

"Holy cow! Mom, your grandmother must have been some woman. If she did all that and it didn't kill her, she must have been strong like a warrior."

"Honey, my grandmother was the most gentle lady you ever met. She did what she needed to is all. She never thought of herself as anything special. She was just a farmer's wife."

"Mom, she had to be so much more than just a farmer's wife."

"My grandfather lost the farm in the 1930s during the dust bowl that struck the middle of the country. When he couldn't raise enough to feed his family or his animals, they had to walk away from their land and settle in town. He got a job for the railroad at first. Then he went to work for a carpenter who was building houses. He and your grandmother bought a small plot of land, and your grandfather built them a home. The only tools he owned were a knife, a hammer, a shovel, and a screwdriver. He built their entire house with those tools and your grandmother's help.

"Honestly?" Katie stammered. "How did they do that?"

"Where there is a will, there is a way," Shanna told her. "That was one of my grandmother's favorite sayings. You are named after her, you know. Her name was Kate."

"Mom, Dad, this is great stuff for my essay. Thanks!" Katie dashed out the back door to the barn.

"Wonder how long it will take her to charge back in here?" Clint smiled over his coffee cup.

"Not very long," Shanna said. "She is a quick study. It won't take long for her to figure there's a new horse in Blaze's stall."

They were right. Katie dashed out to the barn and picked up Blaze's halter before opening his stall door and hurrying in. She put the skids on when she realized she was not looking at Blaze, and Blaze's halter would never fit the horse she was staring at.

"Where in the devil did you come from?" she asked the new horse, not really believing he would answer her. She stepped out of Blaze's stall and went searching for him. She finally found him and started to go into the stall to halter him when it struck her that it was really odd there was a different horse in Blaze's stall. How and why did that happen? She needed to find out. She hung Blaze's halter up and rushed back to the house.

"Mom! Dad! Did you guys know there's a buckskin horse in Blaze's stall?" Katie looked puzzled.

"Yes, as a matter of fact, I do know because I put him there," her dad answered. "You've outgrown Blaze. Last time I watched you run a barrel pattern, your foot was dragging the ground all around that barrel, and I'm pretty sure it took points off your time. You need a bigger horse. What did you think of Cash?"

"You're so funny, Dad. I love cash. But that doesn't explain what that buckskin is doing in Blaze's stall."

Clint laughed out loud. "I'm glad you love cash. His name is Go For Cash, and he's your new barrel horse. I found him in Wyoming on my last stock run, talked to your mother, and brought him home. He's a beaut, isn't he?"

"Yes, he sure is, but…" Katie almost whispered. "Does that mean I have to say goodbye to Blaze?"

"No," Shanna said. "I have a couple of new kids coming in for training. He'll be perfect for them. He has a job here, so he will stay with us."

Katie sighed with relief. She got her new horse and didn't have to say goodbye to her Blaze. That was the best of all worlds.

Clint set his now empty coffee cup down on the table. "Why don't we go and see how he works for you?" Katie's dad pulled his 6-foot 4-inch frame out of the kitchen chair and hugged his daughter. "Let's head out to the barn and take a good look at your new horse."

CHAPTER FIVE

Clint grabbed Katie's hand as they walked to the barn. "I got your new horse from some people I know in Wyoming. They breed only the best. I know he's broke to ride, but not sure how far along he is in his barrel training. I talked it over with your Mom, and she thinks Cash will be perfect for you from now through High School. He's 15.2 hands, so we don't have to worry about your feet dragging anymore," he chuckled. "He's sure a handsome devil, isn't he?"

"Dad, to tell you the truth, I was so shocked he wasn't Blaze, I didn't notice much about him but his color."

"Well, then, let's get him out in the barn aisle and let you take a good look at him. I thought he was an excellent looking horse, myself," Clint said. "I thought he would be perfect for my little girl."

Clint put the halter on Cash and walked him out into the barn aisle so they could walk all around the horse. "I love the golden color of his coat, don't you?" Clint smiled at Katie. "I saw him in a turnout at my friend's place and had to take another look at him. He's got such great conformation too. Don't you agree? His registered name is "Go For Cash," but you can just call him "Gopher" if you'd like.

Katie stared at her dad with her mouth open for a second. Then her eyes rolled, and she snickered, "Nope, Dad. I'm going to call him

Cash because that's what we're going to bring home!" Katie stroked his neck and shoulder and found the itchy spot on his withers. Cash leaned into her hand as she scratched him. If he'd been a cat, Katie thought he'd start to purr.

"Dad, he's beautiful," Katie smiled. "I think I can ride him until I graduate from high school. That would take me to the Miss Rodeo California competition. But we have to see if he has the speed and agility for barrels. I want to win!"

Shanna put Cash in training for barrel racing the next day. He was slow at first, and he didn't get the idea right away. When he finally put in the burst of speed Shanna asked him for, she was amazed at his speed and agility. Katie watched his first training runs and was encouraged. He was faster than Blaze, and he was bigger too. She spent extra time after his training session, grooming him in the barn to get to know him better. He was sweet and wanted to please. He was easy to work with. And he was very affectionate with her in particular. He also loved carrots. To her, that was a perfect sign. She knew she had her horse.

Katie ran into her friend Maryann Wilcox in the hallway between classes at school the next day. "My parents got me a new horse!" she exclaimed with pride.

Horse talk always interested Maryann. Her face lit up, "What did you get?"

"Oh, you should see him! He's a big beautiful buckskin, and his name is Cash. You should ride over after school to see him. I know you'll love him. He's so sweet. My mom is training him to run the barrels."

"That's a great idea, Katie. Do you mind if Brody comes along with Rosie?"

"The more, the merrier! Maybe we can all go for a trail ride together. I've been out on him once with mom. He's great on the trail."

"You sure you don't mind being seen with two Arabs?" Maryann laughed.

"Your Quesa and Brody's Rosie are beautiful horses. They're just a bit small for what I have in mind for Cash. Remember, I do Rodeo, and there are no Arabs in Rodeo," Katie laughed back at her.

"Oh, you stuck-up Rodeo Queens are all the same," Maryann chuckled. "The only horse worth having for you is those huge, ground-pounding American Quarter horses. They barely lift their feet off the ground. You should try riding an English horse sometime. I could put you up on Quesa if you're not scared to try it," she teased.

"Young Queen," Katie corrected her. "I'm not the Rodeo Queen yet. I'm going to try out for the Young Queen position again this year. Year after next, I hope to be the Rodeo Queen! And, I'm not scared at all. I'd love to take a spin on Quesa sometime."

"Princess, Young Queen, Queen, Little Miss, Miss, you are all the same. The only thing you think of is Rodeo."

"Not! Aren't we going for a trail ride? That's not Rodeo."

"Sure," Maryann laughed. "I'll talk to Brody, and we'll head over to your place when we get home from school. I really must see this new giant horse of yours. I admire buckskins. Arabian horses don't come in that color."

"We'll see what my giant Quarter horse thinks of your tiny little Arabians then," Katie giggled. "Hope they don't scare him."

"Hey, we'd better get a move on. The bell's about to ring. I don't want to get to class late." Maryann dashed off, leaving Katie chuckling to herself as she charged off in the opposite direction.

Maryann's mother, Rose Wilcox, dropped Maryann off with Brody at Hartley ranch after school. "Please don't wear your good clothes on a trail ride. And don't forget your riding helmet," she cautioned her daughter.

"Mom, I have clothes in the barn to change into. I won't ruin my good ones. And you know how Aunt Ginny feels about the helmets. She would never let us leave the ranch without wearing them," Maryann reminded her mother. "We'll be back before dark. I'll see you then. I can call you about 15 minutes before we get to the barn." She flashed her cell phone at her mother so she would know she had it.

"I love you, honey," Rose said as she shifted her Jeep into drive.

"I love you too, Mom," Maryann said over her shoulder as she ran toward the main barn.

It took only a few minutes to brush down and tack up La Duquesa and Desert Rose. Maryann and Brody mounted and left through the rear gate of the ranch, across the open desert toward Katie's ranch. The ride took 20 minutes. Katie was standing in the barn, holding her new horse when they arrived. Maryann and Brody dismounted, tied their horses to the hitching rail in front of the barn and walked around Katie's new horse admiring him.

"He's a looker, for sure!" Brody said after walking around Cash with an observant eye. "I can't find one fault in him. And I love his color. He's got more gold in his coat than most. It sure stands out against the black on his legs and face. What are you going to do with him, Katie?"

"He's going to be my new equitation and barrel horse," Katie explained. "My mom is already training him for the barrels. She says he has quite a bit of speed, and she thinks he'll only get better with practice."

"I think he's beautiful," Maryann said. "I love that buckskin coloring. But, if we're going on a ride, we best mount up and head on out. We only have a couple of hours before dark."

Katie explained to Brody and Maryann that trail riding was part of the training Cash needed for him to be her horse in the Young Queen competition. "This gets him used to the stuff we find when we go out. You know, that horse-eating scrap of plastic stuck on a bush, or that deadly chewing gum wrapper that blows across the trail, or that dog that jumps out of the brush barking. I need to get him used to all that stuff, and the best way to do that is get him out on trail rides with other horses. Would you two mind doing this with me at least once a week? I'd really appreciate it."

It didn't take much to convince Maryann and Brody. They were always up for a ride. "Hey, you and Cash could ride to our ranch some of the time, too," suggested Brody. "My Uncle Mike would love your horse. He's a Quarter horse guy."

For the next two months, the trio rode for close to two hours together every week. Rosie and Quesa were in great shape after all the endurance riding they'd done to help Nathan and Freedom ride the Tevis Cup Ride. Cash never spooked once at anything. If he saw something new, he stopped in his tracks and looked at it, sniffed at it, and ignored it, and walked on by. All three riders were impressed with him and how sensible he was.

Then something went terribly wrong. The three riders split up about a mile from Katie's home. Brody and Maryann headed south toward Hartley Ranch and quickly lost sight of Katie and Cash. Katie had to cross over two dirt roads to get home. The first one was no problem. The problem came up as they passed the second road three-quarters of a mile from the ranch. Katie and Cash had to descend into a shallow ditch before climbing out after crossing the road. The electric company worked in their area that day, bringing in new lines for several new homes under construction. They put up a new electric pole and guy wires to keep it upright securely. Cash tripped on one of the guy wires and nearly fell on his knees. Katie had been lost in thought and didn't see the accident coming. She tumbled off Cash and landed badly, crashing her head into a large rock dug up by the workers. Her helmet cracked nearly in half. The blow knocked Katie unconscious. Cash spooked and streaked for home and the safety of the barn. His leg was cut and bleeding.

Shanna was in the kitchen preparing dinner when she saw Cash fly past the kitchen window. Katie was not riding him. She dropped the dish in her hand. It shattered on the tile floor, but she didn't notice. She was already running for the back door, screaming for Clint.

Clint was in the back of the barn, getting feed ready for the evening feeding when Cash galloped into the barn in obvious distress. He dropped what he was doing and rushed to the horse, grabbing the reins. He talked to the horse to calm Cash down. Shanna ran to the barn. "Where's Katie?" she cried.

"I don't know, but the horse is bleeding. I need to check him out," Clint told her.

"Where is Katie? Shanna cried again, looking down and noticing the blood pooling at Cash's foot. "Oh, my God! He's hurt! What happened to my baby?" Shanna began to sob uncontrollably.

Clint, still holding Cash's reins, pulled her close with one arm. "I don't know. Can you call the kids she was riding with and see what they know? I have to tend this leg and get the bleeding stopped right now. Can you make that call? We're going to have to double-team this, okay. I'll take care of the horse. You see what you can find out about our girl.

Shanna sucked in a deep breath and pulled her cell phone from her pocket. She dialed Maryann's number.

CHAPTER SIX

Maryann and Brody chattered all the way back to Hartley Ranch. They just dismounted when Maryann's phone rang. She answered. Brody watched her, curious who would be calling her when most of their friends knew they would be out trail riding. He saw the color drain from Maryann's face as she listened to the caller on the other end. "We'll head back out to where we split up. I'll call you if I see anything." Maryann hung up the phone. "We need to go now. Cash came home with a gash in his right foreleg, and he came back without Katie!" She mounted her horse as Brody mounted Rosie. Maryann called Aunt Ginny from her cell phone as they rushed down the trail to explain what happened. Aunt Ginny said she would let Rose Wilcox know as she ran to find Uncle Mike, tack up two horses and follow behind them.

Clint cleaned the wound on Cash's leg and put pressure on the wound to stop the bleeding. When that was under control, he applied an antibiotic salve and wrapped the leg, and put Cash in his stall. Shanna had her horse ready to go. Clint said he would follow her as he dashed to the rear of the barn and got his own horse out. Clint saddled his horse and did a running mount following Shanna.

Shanna found Katie first. Katie lay on her back with one leg bent in a nearly impossible angle beneath her. Katie's head was turned slightly to the right. A large, dirt-encrusted boulder lay to the left of her head. It was apparent she'd hit that boulder with the back of her head. Her eyes were closed. There was no sign of blood, but no immediate sign of life either. Shanna got off her horse, praying, "Please be breathing Katie. Please breathe." Shanna got on her knees beside her daughter and saw Katie's chest lift slightly as she took a breath. Shanna was shaking as she dug her phone out of her pocket and called 911 for emergency help.

Clint galloped to a stop as Shanna began speaking to the emergency operator. She gave the location and a brief summary of the problem. "Please get here quick! She's breathing, but she's unconscious. I think she hit her head on a rock. Yes, she was wearing a riding helmet! It is still on her. We haven't moved her. We just found her. No, we won't move her! Please tell them to get here!"

Shanna got to her feet as soon as she hung up her phone. She put her head on Clint's chest and began sobbing uncontrollably. Clint stood and held her as they waited for the emergency crew to arrive. That's where Maryann and Brody found them. A few minutes later, Aunt Ginny and Uncle Mike found them as well.

"Oh, Katie! What happened?" Maryann spoke out loud, not expecting an answer.

"The paramedics are on their way. They told us not to try and move her," Shanna told the group while her eyes remained glued to the prone figure of her daughter. She was shaking uncontrollably, like a dry leaf in a wind storm. Her husband, Clint, held onto her firmly around the waist to support her and offer moral support as they waited.

Katie suddenly coughed, and her eyes flickered and opened. It took a moment for her to focus on the six people standing over her. "Ouch, my neck hurts, Mom."

Shanna dropped to her knees beside her daughter. "Katie, listen to me very carefully, okay? The paramedics are on their way. They should be here very soon. You fell off your horse, and it looks like you hit your head on a rock. Don't try to move! Please stay right where you are until they can check you out. You might have hurt your neck or your head. Are you listening to me?"

It took a few seconds for Katie to comprehend what her mother was telling her. She lay still. "Yeah, Mom. I'll stay put. But I'm cold."

Clint took off his jacket and gently pulled it over the girl's body, being careful not to move her at all. "This will keep you warm until the paramedics get here," he said as he stood back up next to his wife.

"Thanks, Dad," Katie whispered and closed her eyes. Shanna began to cry again. Katie opened her eyes and said, "Mom, I'm going to be just fine. That electric pole was not there when we went out. I think Cash tripped on the wire, and it scared him. It wasn't his fault. I will be okay. They can check me out, but I'm wearing my riding helmet. I'm sure I'll be fine. I have a little headache, and my ankle hurts, that's all. Don't cry, Mom. Rodeo Queens don't cry! You've been telling me that for years. I'll get up and rub some dirt on it and be fine."

The red and white flashes of the firetruck's cab lights slashed the darkening sky as the sun dropped below the mountains to the West. They pulled up close to where Katie lay, leaving their headlights on the area so they could see as they worked. Two of the paramedics handled large flashlights as two others got on their hands and knees in the dirt and began their physical examination of Katie.

One of the paramedics stood up and asked for her parents. Shanna and Clint stepped toward him. "How is she?" Shanna asked.

"She needs a couple of x-rays for sure. Her pupils are working as they should. I don't think she has a serious brain injury, but the doctors will need to check it out. We'll put her in a neck brace and on a backboard to get her to the hospital. We'll take it easy on the dirt road until we get to the pavement, then we will turn the lights on and step on it. If she has a brain injury, the faster we get her to treatment, the better she will do. Mr. and Mrs. Barclay, you will have to follow us to the hospital. Depending on what the doctors find, they may keep her for observation overnight. I'm no doctor, but I can tell you that riding helmet saved her life. She hit hard and split that helmet open like a cantaloupe. Had she not been wearing it, we would be calling for the coroner right now." The man went to the back of the firetruck to pull out the things they needed to move Katie and get her to the hospital.

When the paramedics laid Katie out straight so they could get her on the backboard, she cried out when they moved her leg. One of the men felt the leg. "It's not broken, but probably strained or sprained. We should put an IV in and get pain meds loaded before we take off," he told the others. The men worked with quiet efficiency and finally got Katie loaded in the back of the ambulance strapped to the backboard with the neck brace in place. The lead paramedic came back to the group. "We're ready to take off. We'll see you two at the hospital," he said to her parents. "She'll be fine in a few days."

The group of six left standing by the side of the road watched as the trucks pulled away and turned back down the dirt road toward town with the cab lights flashing red and white through the still night air. Clint thanked them for joining them and promised to call when they had news. The group mounted up and headed off in opposite directions. Clint and Shanna were closest to home, fortunately. They walked into the barn, pulled saddles and bridles off their horses, and put them in stalls to eat their dinner before taking their truck and driving off to the hospital.

The ride back to Hartley Ranch was quiet for Maryann, Brody, and the adults with them. No one had much to say. The accident could have happened to any one of them, and they all knew it. Maryann worried for her friend.

CHAPTER SEVEN

Clint and Shanna waited in the emergency room while the doctors had x-rays and CAT scans taken of her head, neck, and leg. When the orderly pushed Katie back into the emergency room, one of the doctors had the nurse call her parents in to stay with her while he reviewed the tests. A few minutes later, he joined them in the bay where Katie lay sleeping from her ordeal.

"She has a slight concussion. That riding helmet she was wearing saved her. We've given her pain medication. Her leg shows no bone damage, but she is painful near the ankle. She didn't break anything, but sprains and strains can be even more painful. I want her to wear a walking boot for at least a month. If she doesn't cooperate, we can always put a cast on. I know these pretty young girls don't like those clumsy-looking walking boots. Just tell her it's that or the cast which she can't take off at all," he smiled at Clint and Shanna. "She's fortunate. She had parents that insisted on the right kind of protection. I saw the helmet. The paramedics brought it along with them. She'll have a headache for a few days, but that's better than making funeral arrangements for her right now. I will give you a prescription for the headaches. I want to keep her overnight for observation. You can pick her up in the morning. You should have her seen by her regular doctor within three days. We also gave her something to keep her calm, so she will probably sleep until morning. You two should get on home. We'll take good care of her for the night," he smiled, then turned and picked up another patient chart and walked down the corridor to his next patient.

Clint took his wife in his arms. "A concussion and a sprain. I'm relieved. It could have been so much worse. She's going to be fine as frog hair in a week, you'll see."

Shanna came to the hospital early the next morning. She got the room number for her daughter from the front desk and took the elevator up to the floor and followed the signs to her daughter's room. Katie was sleeping when she arrived. She quietly sat in the side chair and watched over her until she woke up.

"Where am I?" Katie sputtered to her mother. Her head spun side to side, looking around with a puzzled look glued to her face.

"You are in the hospital, dear. The doctor wanted to keep you overnight to be sure. You look great. How do you feel?"

"Ugg, my head aches, and my leg hurts," Katie admitted. "When can we go home?"

"As soon as the doctor sees you and releases you, I guess."

"When will that be? I want to go home to my own bed," Katie said emphatically. "I'm not sick. I don't need to be here."

"If nothing else, being in a hospital will teach you patience," her mother laughed. "The doctor will be here when he gets here. There's nothing we can do to hurry that up. But your breakfast tray is on the way. Maybe you'll feel better if you have something to eat."

The nurse's aide delivering breakfast trays appeared in the doorway about two minutes later. She put the food tray with the covered dish on the bedside table and helped Katie adjust her bed to a sitting position so she could eat. The nurse's aide disappeared down the hallway just as Katie pulled the cover off her breakfast.

"Oh, yuck, Mom. Do they really expect me to eat this? Two itty-bitty pancakes, two tiny pieces of bacon, I think, and what looks like scrambled eggs? I can wait until I get home."

"We don't know how long the discharge is going to take. You might want to eat that now. I can get you something else to eat when we get you home," her mother admonished her.

Katie huffed as she picked up the plastic fork and began eating the eggs. "Are you sure these are eggs, Mom? They taste like paste from grade school." Katie made a face. "I'll try the pancakes." She had no better luck with them. She looked over the tray and discovered a small plastic sleeve of pancake syrup, ripped the corner off, and poured it on the pancakes. "That's a little better but not as good as yours!" she said. She realized she was hungry. She hadn't eaten dinner the night before, and suddenly she was ravenous. Katie ate every bite of food on the tray, including a piece of stone-cold toast with a dab of butter and a slather of grape jelly.

"Do you think they have a cafeteria in the hospital, Mom?" Katie said as she looked over the empty breakfast tray. There was nothing edible left on it, and her hunger pangs were still crying for more to eat.

"What? Are you a bottomless pit again?" her mother laughed. "If you still want more to eat, I can check at the nurses' station. I'll be right back."

Shanna returned to her daughter's room ten minutes later with a carton of orange juice, a large glazed donut, and a breakfast burrito from the cafeteria. Katie thanked her mother between bites. "This is more like it, Mom. I think I'll survive another day."

Just as she finished up every crumb, the orthopedics technician arrived with Katie's new walking boot. He put her leg in the boot and showed her how to adjust it as he fastened it.

Katie was horrified. "Mom, this is huge and ugly. How am I going to go to school with this thing on? I can't be seen in public this way!" she nearly cried. "How am I going to get dressed with this hunk of junk on my leg? You know I have my speech to give for the Young Queen competition in two weeks. I can't wear my new outfit over this thing. How am I going to pass my equitation exam wearing it? I can't ride with this!" Things were starting to close in on Katie. Her new situation was falling on her shoulders, and it pressed on her heart.

The Young Queen competition was two weeks away. She worked hard on her speech. Katie got her new outfits together. She practiced her equitation exam questions. She practiced possible equitation patterns with her horse. She was ready just yesterday. Today it felt like her world was falling apart. The tears spilled over her eyelids and streaked her pale cheeks.

"It's not the end of the world, sweetheart." Her mother tried to soothe her. "If you don't make it this year, you can try again next year. You will still be the beautiful young lady you are, and you will probably ride even better next year than you do this year."

"Mom," Katie sobbed. "I need to be the Young Queen this year, so I have the best chance at taking the crown next year. You know that. If I lose the year, I'll be behind the other girls. I can't miss an entire year. I've worked so hard! I haven't missed one single event all year. I've competed and won against my age group all year long. Missing the year is a disaster. I'll never make that up."

"Katie, I will take you to see your doctor the day after tomorrow. Before you get upset, let's see what he has to say, okay? Maybe it won't be all that bad. Give it until then before you give up on your crown."

Katie nodded her head, but in her heart, she knew what he would say. Her dream would not come true. She would lose her crown and not be able to get the one she really wanted. Depression settled around her shoulders like a warm blanket in the winter, except it didn't feel warm, and it didn't comfort her one tiny bit.

CHAPTER EIGHT

Shanna took Katie to her doctor, as promised. Dr. Kettleman examined Katie, looked into her eyes and ears, asked her to watch his finger as he moved it across her line of sight, and examined her leg. He already reviewed the x-rays and CAT scan results from the hospital.

"You are one lucky little lady," he told her. "You wouldn't be sitting here in my office if you had not been wearing your riding helmet."

Katie looked at the floor and nodded her head. She looked up at the kindly gentleman and asked the most important question. "When can I ride again?"

"Let me explain it to you this way," he began. "When your head contacted that rock, your helmet protected you, but your brain bounced around inside your skull a bit. You've probably bruised it, but not seriously this time. I'd rather you not ride for at least four weeks. Then, we need to consider your ankle. You were lucky there too. You sprained it, which means you stretched the tendons and muscles beyond their capacity. They also take time to heal. Had you broken the bone in that location, you would have had surgery to pin and plate the bone back together last night. You would be in a cast above your knee for at least eight weeks, then in physical therapy for another three to four weeks. That would be nearly three months before you could ride again. I want you to wear the walking boot for four weeks and come see me again. If we find you've healed in that time, we can take the boot off, and I'll clear you to ride, but only if you promise me you will wear a riding helmet."

It was the worst news for Katie. Four whole weeks with no riding. It might have been four years as far as she was concerned. Her dream was evaporating in front of her eyes. The Young Rodeo Queen competition was less than two weeks away. She couldn't possibly pass the equitation pattern test. She couldn't ride for another two weeks beyond that. She'd never gone more than a day without riding. Riding was as much a part of her life as breathing was. How was she going to get through four weeks without riding her horse? How would she survive this? A darkness enveloped her. She went through the motions until her mother drove her home. She went straight to her room, crawled into bed and pulled the covers over her head, and wept for lost dreams.

Dr. Kettleman gave Shanna an out-of-school note for the balance of the week. He also gave her a prescription to help Katie's anxiety. He could see how distressed she was. Shanna dropped the note off with the school administrator's office on the way home from the doctor's office. She also made arrangements to pick up school assignments for Katie the next day. Shanna worried about her daughter. Katie took the news she would not be able to ride for four weeks after the accident quietly, but Shanna knew it hit her pretty hard. Katie was out of the Young Rodeo Queen competition for this year. Shanna knew how much Katie had her heart set on winning again this year. She left her in her bedroom that night, hoping Katie would be the happy young girl she'd always been after a night to think things over, but she doubted it. Shanna was worried.

The next morning, Shanna made an elaborate breakfast for Clint and herself and Katie, hoping that would encourage Katie out of her room. She had always been the most cheerful over breakfast. That didn't happen. Shanna had to drag Katie to the breakfast table. Katie never said a word and picked at her food, pushing it around on her plate but not eating much. She went back to bed immediately after not eating her breakfast and pulled the covers over her head again. Shanna was sure she could hear sobs through the closed bedroom door but decided to leave Katie alone for the moment. She went on with her chores and riding the horses she had in training. She checked Cash out and rebandaged his leg. He showed no sign of lameness. She had the vet out to be sure. The vet told her he would be ready to ride in a few days.

Cash's leg healed quickly. He nicked a blood vessel that caused the bleeding they first noticed when he came home without Katie. The wrap came off his leg two days later, and he showed no sign of lameness in the leg. He was young also. The cut was nearly invisible within a week. He missed Katie but didn't know how to express that to the people who took care of him. He waited and watched for her in vain.

Maryann called Katie after the doctor's appointment. She spoke with Katie's mother the day Katie came home from the hospital, so she knew what happened. Katie answered her phone.

"How are you doing?" Maryann asked cheerfully.

"I'm okay," Katie answered without further explanation.

"Your mom told me you have to wear a walking boot for a month. I'm so sorry. She told me you had a concussion too. Are you feeling okay with all this?"

"No, I'm not. I'm out of the Young Queen competition. That's the end of that. I'll never be able to make up for an entire year. It's over for me."

"Katie, that's not true! You are the prettiest girl applying for the position. You are the smartest and the best rider of them all. You'll miss this year, but you can come back strong and take it next year for sure."

"No! That dream is dead. It's all over for me. Don't call me again!" Katie slammed down her phone and crawled back under the covers sobbing.

Maryann was shocked. She didn't know what to say. She would talk to her mother about it. She was afraid for her friend. She felt there must be something she could do. She didn't know what that could be. Maybe she should talk to Becky. Becky was good at things like this.

Maryann called Becky Howard. They had been best friends for a couple of years because of the Arabian horses. Becky lived in San Juan Capistrano, which was a hundred miles from the High Desert where Maryann and Brody lived. Maryann used to call a visit to Becky's house a trip to the land of green. The climate in San Juan Capistrano was so different from Maryann's desert home. San Juan Capistrano sat on the Southern California coastline, so they got a lot more moisture than Maryann and Brody were used to. Trees grew taller, and grass grew everywhere, flowers and shrubs decorated homes, businesses, and much of the community. It was a different world. But people problems were the same everywhere, and Becky was great working with people problems.

"I have a good friend with a problem. Can we talk?" Maryann asked Becky when Becky picked up the phone call.

"Sure, give me all the details, and don't leave anything out," Becky replied.

"Okay," Maryann began to fill her in on Katie's situation.

"So, Katie came off her horse less than a half-mile from home, and she would have died if she hadn't been wearing her riding helmet. And she has a concussion and sprained ankle so she can't compete in the Young Rodeo Queen competition, and she thinks her life is over? Do I have that right?" Becky asked.

"That's it in a nutshell," Maryann admitted. "It seems so trivial to you and me, but Katie lived the whole Rodeo thing since birth. Her mother was the Miss California Rodeo Queen. She could have gone on and probably won the Miss USA Rodeo Queen title except that she and her boyfriend, now Katie's dad, didn't want to spend a year apart, so she didn't. Instead of competing for Miss USA, they got married and had Katie. They are a sweet couple. Katie's mom trains barrel racers, and her dad drives livestock, mainly horses, around the country. He is a world-class Heeler in the Team Roping events. He's pretty high in the national rankings from what Katie says. He makes a lot of money roping steers. They own a big ranch out near us. Katie started as the Little Miss Rodeo here in the High Desert. She's been a part of that since she was five years old. She's our age, fifteen now, so she's been on the rodeo circuit for ten years. Taking a whole year off must seem like forever to her."

"I could see how that would be a shock, especially if she doesn't feel injured as bad as the doctors say. It could be that she needs a couple of days to think about it and get used to the doctors' restrictions. If she's usually a cheerful person, on the whole, give her a few days and check back in with her. Things could turn around once she has a day or two to think about it. There are other ways to enjoy horses and the whole rodeo thing without being the queen, princess, or whatever they call it. You could remind her of that. In four weeks, she can get back on her horse, then beat the pants off the other girls in barrels. Didn't you tell me she just got a new horse? Didn't you tell me her mother is training that horse for barrels? If that's the case, with another four weeks of training, that horse should be ready to kick some booty and take some names in the arena. You could remind her of that too."

Maryann thought about what Becky said. "You could be right. I will call her again the day after tomorrow and see how she feels. I am going to miss one of my riding buddies, though. Now it's just Brody and me. It was more fun having Katie with us."

CHAPTER NINE

Maryann waited two days and tried to call Katie again on her cell phone. The call was intercepted and transferred to Katie's voice mailbox. Maryann was going to leave a message, but the voicemail box was full, and she was disconnected. Did her friend Katie block her calls? She'd never had that happen to her. She was surprised but still concerned. She called Katie's mother for an update. Katie's mom told Maryann there was no change. Katie was still in her bedroom, refused to come out for meals, refused to go to the barn to see her horse, and looked like she was in mourning with puffy eyes. Her usually meticulous daughter had not even taken a shower since the accident. That was not like her at all. Her mom and dad were worried.

"Why don't Brody and I ride over there tomorrow. It is really easy to hang up a phone but much harder when your friends come to see you in person, don't you think?" Maryann suggested.

"It's certainly worth a try," Katie's mom agreed. "I'll have some cookies and milk ready for the three of you tomorrow afternoon."

Maryann and Brody rode over to Katie's home after school the following day. They pulled the tack off their horses and put them in the guest stalls while they visited. They expected to be there for a while. Maryann knocked on the back door. Katie's mom let them in. "She's still not talking with me," she explained. "She stays in her room with the shades drawn, and the door closed."

"I'll go and see if she will let me in," Maryann suggested and walked down the hall toward Katie's bedroom. She knocked lightly on the bedroom door. She got no response. She turned the knob and pushed the door open a few inches and peeked around the door. "Katie, are you awake?"

"Go away!" Katie hissed at her friend.

"What do you mean?" Maryann asked, perplexed by the violence in her tone.

"What do you think?" Katie spat out. "I said, go away! That means get out of here. I don't want to talk to you or anyone else."

"Katie, I know you're upset," Maryann said. "Brody and I came over to see if we could cheer you up. Your mom has milk and cookies in the kitchen. Why don't you join us before Brody eats all the cookies?"

Katie picked up a book sitting on her side table and held it up like she intended to throw it at Maryann. "I said, go away! I don't want to talk to you or anyone. I don't need cheering up. Just leave me alone, or I'll throw this at your head right now!"

"Alright, already," Maryann said as she pulled her head out of the way and pulled the door closed. Katie was one of her closest friends. Her attitude shocked Maryann. She never expected her to act violently. She stood at the closed door for a few seconds before walking back down the hall and meeting Brody and Katie's mom in the kitchen.

"This is so not like Katie!" Maryann told them. "I thought she was going to throw a book at me. She's obviously not ready to talk about anything right now. Maybe we should give her a week and try again."

"If she doesn't come around soon, I'm going to take her to a therapist for that," Katie's mom told them. "She feels like her life is over now that she can't compete in the Young Queen competition. I will wait until that passes and see if she perks up a little. I know she's been pretty driven about those yearly contests, and she likes winning."

"Katie has always been goal-oriented. When she sets her goal, she never fails to meet it. I've seen it with her schoolwork too. When she sets her mind on something, she works really hard to get there," Maryann told the others. "I've never seen her not reach any of her goals before."

"Yes, but threatening to throw a book at a friend of her's is not a good way to handle it," Brody said. "That could get someone else hurt."

"You are right, Brody. I will talk to her about that. I went to the school and signed her up for home study for the balance of this year. She refuses to wear that walking boot to school. But she still needs to finish up her classes. She and I will talk about that tonight. I have her schoolwork for her to do, and she owes you an apology, Maryann," Katie's mom told them. "I will give you a call tomorrow after school and let you know how that conversation went. I appreciate you coming over here to see her. Friends are so important."

Maryann and Brody rode back to Hartley Ranch without talking much. "I can't believe she was going to chuck a book at you," Brody said as they turned into the back gate.

"Heck, I couldn't believe it either," Maryann laughed. "I've seen her toss a softball in PE. She's got a strong arm, and she'd deadly accurate too. That book could have broken my nose."

"Well, she's disappointed right now, and her ankle must hurt," Brody said. "Her leg was pretty twisted when she landed on that pile of rocks. She's lucky she didn't break something. I just don't understand why she thinks her life is over because she can't compete in some dumb contest and wear a shiny gold doohickey on the front of her cowboy hat."

"Hey, don't forget those Queen sashes and those fancy fringed chaps they wear," Maryann giggled.

After Shanna and Clint finished dinner and cleaned up the kitchen, Shanna gathered up the school materials and walked down the hall to her daughter's room. She knocked on the door and opened it, turning the light on as she entered.

"Please go away," Katie wailed as she ducked her head back under the blanket.

"No, I'm not going away. I'm here to talk to you about your schoolwork," Shanna stated flatly. "You are going to pay attention."

"Mom, I don't want to talk," Katie answered, muffled by the blanket.

"Pull that blanket off your face. I'm going to talk, and you are going to listen to me. Do you understand?"

Something about the tone in her mother's voice reached Katie. She sat upright, propped on pillows, and pulled the blanket down to her waist. She stared at the bump her feet made in the comforter that covered her bed. "I'm listening," she mumbled.

Shanna handed her daughter the materials she picked up from the school that day. She explained the assignments for each class as best she could. She told Katie they would be taking her assignments back to the school for a two-hour meeting with her teacher once a week until school was out for the summer. Katie would get full credit for all of her classes if she completed the assignments each week. She could work at her own pace, on her own schedule, but the assignments must be completed and turned in every week until school let out.

Shanna turned to leave the bedroom when she finished explaining the school assignments.

"Mom, if I do this work, will I still graduate with my class when I finish High School?"

"That's up to you. You've been a straight-A student all your life. You can go back to school with your friends when school starts up again later this summer if you want to. I enrolled you in home-study, so you don't have to walk into class in that walking boot. That's the only concession I'm making here. Your education is important to me, and it should be to you. If you still want to go to college, you'll have to pass your high school classes first. And it also might be a good idea if you stop threatening your friends. Maryann and Brody came over here to see you, and you threatened to throw a book at her. What a nice friend you turned out to be! Do you know Maryann has tried to call you every day since the accident? She calls me to see how you are doing. Don't be a jerk. Friends are too valuable to throw away like that."

Katie's pale face turned red from shame. She couldn't look at her mother. She was ashamed of how she treated her friend. Tears rolled down her cheeks silently. Katie continued staring at the bump her feet made in the comforter as her mother turned off the light, walked out of the room, and closed the door behind her.

CHAPTER TEN

The following morning, Katie listened until she heard both her parents leave the house before she went down and made herself some toast and cereal for breakfast. She cleaned up the dishes and stacked them in the dishwasher before heading back to her room. She picked up the stack of papers her mother gave her the previous evening. She began to read and do the assignments. She worked on her schoolwork until she heard her parents head off to bed. She got up and quietly made herself something to eat from the leftovers in the refrigerator. She cleaned up her dishes and went back to her room to study and work on assignments until she fell asleep with her textbook on her chest.

Within two days, Katie had all her assignments done for the week. She decided to reread one of her horse books. Katie repeated her pattern of listening for her parents to leave the house or go to bed before going to the kitchen for a quick meal. She read one complete book every day. She ticked the days off her calendar until she reached the day of the Young Queen competition. Katie was terribly depressed that day. She should have been there to give the perfect speech she'd written nearly a month before, answer questions, show her equine knowledge, and share her equestrian skills with the judges. Katie cried most of the day. She ended the day crying herself to sleep, hoping she would not wake up in the morning.

When the sun began to drench the desert in the soft glow of morning, Katie woke up and opened her shades to witness the dawn. She noticed the streaky cirrus clouds in the sky above the mountains east of the ranch painted in vibrant colors of pinks and golds. They made a striking contrast to their background of deep blue. She dressed quietly, sneaked down the hall to the back door, and stepped out into the fresh morning air. She took a deep breath and turned away from the ranch for a walk. She had to clear her mind. Her world felt turned upside down. The goals she set for herself for most of her life were unattainable. She still had two weeks of wearing the darned walking boot. Well, she'd walk with it, then.

Katie thought about her situation as she struggled with the walking boot. If she couldn't have what she planned and worked her whole life for, what was she going to do? What would her second option be? She tossed a couple of ideas around in her mind and finally settled on one. She would be the best-educated cowgirl on the planet. She would throw herself into her school work, read books by the hundreds, and learn to write well enough to impress college professors.

The boot walking was giving her a backache within a half-mile. The discomfort was taking over her thinking. She decided to turn around. She was young and healthy, but the persistent ache pushed out her thoughts and became an annoyance she could do without. She was back in her room before she heard her parents in the kitchen pouring their coffee.

Katie began that day. She read each of her textbooks two chapters beyond the study assignment and completed all the test questions at the end of each chapter. She read one book every day, if possible. She often fell asleep with an open book on her chest. Once she reached the end of a textbook chapter, she answered all the test questions in the Section review areas and began on the next Chapters. She carefully printed out the Chapter questions in separate notebooks for each subject, with her answers and the Section Review questions the same way. Within three weeks, she completed the problems and the final review questions for each subject. She began writing book reports on every book she finished in a separate notebook. She included, in the end, the main points she thought the author made in writing each one. She took her time writing the book reports to ensure she was using correct grammar and punctuation in writing, and that her writing was clear and concise. Her book reports improved as she practiced writing them.

When Katie had her teacher-conference the following week, her home-study teacher was surprised at the work Katie completed in one week. The teacher graded her assignments while Katie was with her. She was pleased with how well Katie understood the material and how far she had gotten in the textbooks. Katie even studied portions of the books that would be a simple review by her teachers during regular classwork. She gave Katie the assignments for the following week and excused her.

Katie continued working at the pace she set for herself, including the reading time with books she got from the library at school. Within six weeks, she completed all the assignments and took the final exams for the year while the other students had six more weeks of schooling. Her teacher began giving her assignments for the following school year.

Shanna and Clint had breakfast before heading out for their chores for the day. "I know Katie has not been to the barn to see her horse since the accident," Shanna told Clint. "That's not fair to Cash. I used him for the last two weeks on another student. She's doing well with Cash. Her mother asked about buying him for her daughter. I don't know what to do," she said sadly, and she stared into her coffee cup.

"We bought Cash for Katie. We thought she would use him for competition. You spent quite a bit of time on his training. It's not fair to the horse to leave him standing in his stall. That horse needs a person of his own. Apparently, Katie has changed her mind about what she wants to do, and the horse isn't in her plans. I agree with you that's not fair to Cash. Maybe we should consider that offer," Clint said.

"I can get a good price for him," Shanna said. "I can get all that we paid for him and some for the training I put into him. I will talk to Lexi's mom tomorrow when they get here for Lexi's lesson. If this works out, we can keep him in board for a while so Lexi can take her lessons, and let him go home so she can show him."

"It makes me sad to do it," Clint said. "That's one fine horse. I could see my little girl competing and winning on him for several years. But it's just not fair to Cash to stand around waiting to see if she comes around and changes her mind. I can always look for another horse for her if she does."

Lexi's mom couldn't write the check out fast enough the next day. Cash became Lexi's new horse. They planned to leave him at the ranch for two weeks while Lexi took tune-up rides then take him to the next Rodeo for Lexi to compete in and take him home. Katie did not even notice when the trailer hauled "her" horse off the property. She was busy studying in her room.

CHAPTER ELEVEN

Shanna got a call from a dear friend of hers around noon several days after Cash left the ranch. It was her friend Betty. Betty owned a boarding facility and bred and showed her horses for years. "I have a problem that you might be able to help me with," she told Shanna after their initial catching up conversation.

"Oh, yeah, what do you think I can help you with," Shanna laughed. "You never need help!"

"This time I do," Betty said. "I had a supposed to be trainer suck me into a deal a while back. I gave her box stalls for her horses and outside sheltered paddocks for her lesson horses. I did all that for big promises about the lesson and training program she was going to set up here at my place. Well, it was all garbage, but it took a while for me to figure it out. In the end, the supposed trainer left and left me with nine horses to feed and care for while she disappeared into the sunset."

"Oh, no," Shanna said under her breath. That was a boarding facility owner's nightmare. Getting stuck with a bunch of horses you have to feed, no matter what, while you make no money on the facilities, can break an owner in a hurry.

"What did you do?" Shanna asked her.

"The only thing I could do," Betty told her. "I took it to court. The judge awarded the title to all the horses to me. I've been able to sell all the horses but one. I'm stuck with him. He's a problem to deal with. That's why I'm calling you. If you will take him and work with him, I'll sign him over to you. You are the only person I know that might be able to turn this horse around."

"That sounds ominous," Shanna said. "What's his problem?"

"He's probably been abused. I'm just guessing from how he acts. He's an angry gelding. I don't know his history. I don't know what happened to him before he came here, but I did talk to the person that owned the last place this trainer had him. She was not very encouraging, either. It seems like this horse has been locked up for a while, maybe years even. He's difficult to manage, and it seems to me like he's plain angry at people. I thought of you. You are so good with horses. I thought you might have a chance to turn him around. He's a purebred. The only problem I see with you is that he's a purebred Arabian, not a Quarterhorse. Would you come to see him and take a look? You are about my last hope."

"Of course, I'll come over and take a look. Betty, I can't promise anything, but I do have an empty stall right now. If I think I can do something with him, I'll let you know. Will you be there around 10 this morning? I can make it by then."

Shanna, true to her word, showed up at Betty's with her truck and trailer. She walked around Betty's place, admiring her horses before they got to the stall that held Kashmir.

"Don't be surprised if he charges you," Betty told her. "He scares the life out of strangers here doing just that. He charges them and backs off watching them to see how they react to him. I can't tell if it's all a big show, or he really wishes he could knock people down and stomp on them. My stall cleaners have trouble with him, and some won't go into the stall to clean. The feed crew tells me they toss the feed in because he charges them too."

"Is he a stallion?" Shanna asked.

"The trainer told me he was a gelding when he got here, but he has stallion tendencies," Betty told her. "When I put him out with the other mares and geldings, the first thing he tried to do was mount his mother. She wasn't having any of that and kicked, chased, and bit him into a corner. The other horses in the group did likewise. He didn't get his share of the feed, so he lost weight and condition. He looked like garbage in a week, all scraped up, but he finally settled into his corner and left the other horses alone.

"Oh, that poor baby. He was never socialized. That's his problem. He doesn't know his place in the herd and doesn't know how to act around other horses," Shanna told her. "He needs a bit of education. Let's see how he reacts to an offering." She walked over with a carrot in her hand. She offered it to Kashmir. He stood at the back of his stall and stared at her. He wanted that carrot but was afraid to come close enough to get it. Shanna waggled it with her hand, trying to entice him to come take it. Kashmir refused. He stood and watched her from the back of his stall. There was something different about this woman. He needed to think about it. She was inviting him to take a treat. He wasn't sure he should take it. He wanted it. But, he had a different feeling about this woman. She had a glow about her. It was a beautiful glow, but he couldn't make up his mind if he wanted to enter that glow to get that carrot. He stood his ground.

CHAPTER TWELVE

S hanna agreed to take Kashmir home while thinking she was crazy for doing it. He was an Arabian horse. Her experience was with the ponies her daughter rode or quarter horses she trained. What was she going to do with an Arabian? She and Betty got a lead on Kashmir and walked him to her trailer. He was a complete gentleman the whole way. He walked into Shanna's trailer as if he'd been doing it all his life. He was quiet and under control the entire time, even after Shanna shut the trailer door and drove off.

Shanna opened the trailer when she got back to their ranch, unhooked Kashmir from the trailer, and walked him into a stall in the barn. He was cooperative the entire time. She offered him the carrot again, and he took it. Kashmir was intrigued by this woman with the aura he didn't understand. It didn't hurt him, but it was there. He didn't know what to make of it. Shanna checked his water and tossed some feed into his feeder. She stood and watched him for a few minutes before she took her next training horse out to work.

The back of Kashmir's new stall had an attached corral that allowed him to see what the woman was doing. He walked outside his stall into the paddock. He watched when she brought her training horse into the arena adjoining his paddock. He watched her as she worked the horse on the barrels. It excited him. It looked like fun to him. He watched the other horse run at full speed toward the barrels, turn around them, and head for the next barrel. He was excited! The horse was running at top speed. The turns were tight. The horse and rider came so close to the barrels they almost touched them with their bodies, and then they were around them and heading for the next barrel. When they finished running around the three barrels, they headed back to where they started. The woman praised the horse for what he'd done. She hugged his neck and talked to him. Kashmir wanted that. He needed that. He wanted praise so much it ached in his heart. Why couldn't he get approval like that for anything? He'd die for that kind of recognition, any type of attention. He'd seen enough for one morning. He walked back inside his stall and hung his head in the corner. A tear slowly dripped from one eye.

Shanna got a phone call that morning as she groomed the horse she finished working. It took her by surprise. She stopped brushing the horse and sat on a tack trunk in the barn aisle as she spoke on her phone.

"Are you sure?" she asked. "When did you find her? What hospital did they take her to?"

Shanna called Clint when she got off the phone. "You'd better come home now. I have some bad news," was all she told him before she put the horse in his stall and walked back to the house.

Clint arrived in his truck, slid to a stop, turned off the engine, and sprinted to the house.

"What did you need me home for?" he asked Shanna.

"It's your mother," Shanna said softly. "She's in the hospital in Oklahoma City. They are not hopeful. We need to get there right away."

Clint rushed to the bedroom and pulled out his suitcase. He began stuffing it with clothes and toiletries. Shanna met him in the master bedroom. "What are we going to do with the horses and the ranch while we're gone?" she asked.

"Katie is 15 years old. She's shut herself up in her room for months. She's just going to have to take up the slack for right now!" he almost shouted at her. "My mother is in the hospital. My dad died a year ago. I have to get there. She's going to have to cowgirl-up and help us now."

Shanna nodded. "She's old enough to take care of things here for a few days. I'll talk to her." Shanna pulled her suitcase out of the closet and began filling it with things she knew she would need. As soon as she finished packing, she said, "I'll go talk to Katie. I will ask Ginny Hartley to check in on her every day. I know Ginny will help."

Shanna went to the kitchen and made the call to Ginny Hartley. She told her what she knew and that she and Clint would be gone for several days, maybe longer. Shanna knew Ginny would check in on Katie. She only hoped Katie had not wholly ruined her relationship with Maryanne and Brody. They might be a big help to Katie while Shanna and Clint were gone. Clint's mother's life was hanging by a thread. They didn't have much time, and it was a long drive to get there.

Shanna went to Katie's room next. She opened the door to Katie, studying one of her textbooks. "Katie, we have an emergency. You will have to step up and help us out."

Shanna went on to explain that Clint's mother was in a hospital in Oklahoma City and was in serious condition. She and Clint were driving to the hospital. Katie would be in charge of the ranch in their absence. She hoped Katie would be responsible and take control for them. She had no one else she could call on for that.

Katie was stunned. Her grandmother? In the hospital? This was another blow to Katie. She loved her grandmother. She didn't get to see her often, but she remembered her from visits to Oklahoma and her grandparents few visits to the ranch where they lived. Her grandmother made the best cookies in the whole wide world. She would miss their monthly phone calls. She would miss the smell of grandmother's perfume. She would miss the aprons her grandmother always wore in the kitchen and the stories she told about her father when he was a boy. She couldn't lose her grandmother now! She just couldn't!

"Mom, I'll take care of everything. Don't you worry. Take care of Grandma. I want to see her again. Tell her I love her, will you? Tell her I miss her," the words tumbled out of Katie's mouth as tears streamed down her cheeks. "Please don't let anything happen to Grandma."

Shanna held her daughter, shaking as tears flowed. "I promise we will do everything we can."

Clint barged into the room, "You have all the phone numbers, don't you, Katie? You know who to call if you need help? Your mom has already called Ginny Hartley, so she knows what's going on. You can always call Ginny. We will call you from the road. We have to get going. I'm so sorry to leave this on your shoulders. I love you, sweetie." Clint hugged his daughter, then pulled his suitcase out in the hall and dragged it to the back door. "I love you!" he said again as he ran through the door to his truck.

Shanna hugged her daughter. "I'll call you from the road as we go," she said. "Ginny will be there for you if you need help. If you are not comfortable at home by yourself, maybe your friend Maryann will stay with you, or you could stay with her. We have to get on the road, honey. I'm sorry to dump all this on you at one time. We love you." Shanna dashed out to the truck with her suitcase in hand and tossed it into the bed before Clint put the truck in reverse and backed out of the driveway.

Katie was still in shock as she watched her dad's truck pull down the dirt road toward the highway. When it disappeared from view, she felt suddenly alone. She had been alone at their ranch before for short periods of time. This was different. She was in charge of the ranch, and she had no idea when her parents would be home. It was overwhelming all of a sudden.

Katie slowly walked back into the house and looked around. What would it be like if her parents were suddenly not there? Would she be able to handle it? She had no idea. She called her friend Maryann and asked if she could stay with her for the night.

Maryann was surprised by the phone call from Katie. Katie explained what happened and asked if she would stay the night with her. Maryann asked her mother. Her mother gave permission and said she would drive her over. Katie breathed a sigh of relief. She would not have to spend the night alone tonight.

CHAPTER THIRTEEN

Maryanne and Katie didn't get to sleep until 4:30 the following morning. It was an off school day for Maryanne, so it didn't matter to her. She and Katie talked most of the night. It cleared the air about their friendship, and both girls felt better about their special relationship afterward. They raided the refrigerator several times during the night for snacks, laughed, made fun of each other, and got back to where their relationship had been before Katie's accident. Maryann fell asleep on the couch in the living room. Katie covered her up and spent a couple of hours in her own bed before it was time to get up and feed the horses.

Maryann was sleeping soundly on the couch when Katie sneaked through the living room to the kitchen to the outside door at feeding time. She quietly closed the back door and walked to the barn to get the feeding done. Katie got the grain buckets ready, loaded up the hay cart, and began at the back of the barn. She tossed the hay into the feeders and topped it off with the grain ration each horse was supposed to get.

As she was tossing the hay into Kashmir's feeder, he tried to take a large bite out of her arm! She jerked back, pulling the hay with her, and landed on her butt in the middle of the barn aisle. Katie, covered in alfalfa, was shocked that a horse tried to take her arm off while she was feeding him. "What the heck...." was all she could say as she sat in the middle of the barn aisle looking up at the new horse she never met before.

"Who the heck are you, and what do you think you are doing?" she snapped at the bay horse in Cash's old stall.

"Who the heck are you?" the horse snapped back. *"Where is the lady with the golden aura?"*

Katie sat in the middle of the barn aisle in shock. Had she just heard a horse speak to her? Was she crazy? Did she not get enough sleep? Was she still asleep and dreaming? What the heck was going on? Why did this stupid horse try to take her arm off while she was trying to feed him? Who was the lady with the golden aura? She must be losing her mind!

Katie thought about it. The horse didn't speak, in the human sense of the word, but she clearly heard what he said, that is, if she had not entirely gone around the bend. She patted the stall mat she was sitting on. It felt like it always did. It was cold but not as cold as the concrete it covered. It was hard, but not as hard as the concrete. She looked toward the front of the barn and could see the early morning glow of the sun rising in the eastern sky painted on the windows on the western side of the house. She took a deep breath. The air was crisp and fresh and smelled like horses and alfalfa. She sneezed suddenly. Bits of alfalfa from the front of her clothes blew into the air around her.

Katie looked at the strange horse in Cash's stall. "Did you just speak to me?" she asked it.

"Yes!" the horse answered without moving its mouth. *"Who did you think was talking to you?"*

Katie's eyes nearly popped out of her head. She heard that horse again, but he didn't move a muscle, including his face. How was it she could hear him speak to her? Maybe she really was losing her mind. She looked around. She still had a couple of horses to feed, and her clothes were covered in alfalfa from that horse's breakfast. She couldn't leave the other horses hungry. "If I put this back in your feeder, will you please not try to take my arm off again?" she asked.

Kashmir stood in the back of his stall and stared at the girl. He realized she also had a slight golden aura. Was this girl related to the woman he'd been watching with the horses in the arena? Was she just a younger version of that woman? After a few seconds, he nodded his head up and down in answer to the girl's question. He remained where he was while the girl got to her feet, brushed alfalfa off her clothes and put the flake and oats in his feeder, and returned to her job feeding the rest of the horses. He came to his feeder and began eating his breakfast after she left the barn and went back to the ranch house.

Maryann was in the kitchen, rustling through cupboards for cereal bowls and cereal when Katie stamped her feet and brushed off her clothes in the mudroom. She walked into the kitchen, and Maryann greeted her with a smile. "You were out feeding when I woke up, so I thought I would make us some breakfast," she told Katie.

Katie stood still for a second while she made up her mind. "Maryann, you are one of my closest friends. If I tell you something, will you promise me you'll never tell anyone else?"

Maryann's smile dropped off her face. She looked Katie in the eyes. She could see Katie was serious about something. She was almost afraid to hear about it, but that's what friends are for, right? "Of course, Katie. I'll keep whatever it is between you and me."

"I just did the morning feeding. I was putting a flake of hay in the feeder for a horse I've never seen before, and that horse tried to take my arm off. See where he bit my shirt? It surprised me, and I fell right on my butt in the barn aisle to get away from him. I looked at him and asked him who he was and what did he think he was doing."

Maryann nodded. She would probably have done the same thing if she'd been the one in the barn that morning. "Okay, what happened then?" she asked.

"This is the crazy part. I heard that horse ask me who the heck I was and where was the lady with the golden aura or something like that."

"What do you mean you heard it?"

"Maryann, as God is my witness, I heard that horse speak to me. I was looking directly at him, and he never moved a muscle, but I heard him ask me that," she explained. "I sat there for a minute, wondering if I was losing my mind, dreaming, or just thought I heard something. So I asked him if he'd just spoken to me."

"Well, what happened next?"

"He said yes and asked me who I thought was talking to me."

"Is there someone out in the barn trying to fool with you? You know, someone playing games with you or something?"

"Not that I know of. There are no strange trucks or cars on the property. There's no one here but you and me right now."

"Well, I know it isn't Brody because I just talked to him before you came in. He's still at home. I asked him if he could ride over here and bring La Duquesa so we can take a ride this morning."

"If it wasn't Brody, and it didn't sound like him anyway, I don't know who could be playing tricks on me this early in the morning," Katie said.

"I suggest we eat some breakfast, then," Maryann suggested. "When Brody does get here, we can go for a ride. Maybe that will clear your head. Maybe you just think you heard that horse talking to you. Maybe you weren't quite all the way awake."

"I don't have a horse to ride," Katie admitted sadly. "My parents sold my horse to one of mom's students a while ago."

"What?" Maryann questioned. "Why would they do that?"

"I haven't been to the barn since the accident. The horse was just standing around. I wasn't riding him. I couldn't bring myself to go into the barn."

"You have a whole barn full of horses out there. I'm sure we can find you one to ride. You need to get back to riding. It's something you love! Just because of one accident, you can't give up something you love like that!"

"You are probably right. I was not the least interested until I went to the barn this morning. The smell of fresh alfalfa and grain, the smell of horses, even the smell of horse poop was something I never realized how much I missed," Katie admitted as a tear formed in her eye.

"Brody and I will fix that. When he gets here, we're taking you for a long ride—no use arguing. But we better get our breakfast eaten, so we're ready when he gets here," Maryann said.

CHAPTER FOURTEEN

Brody rode up on Desert Rose, ponying La Duquesa, just as Maryann and Katie finished cleaning up the kitchen. Brody put both horses in the guest stalls and met them in the kitchen. "You guys ready to ride?" he asked.

"I just want to get a couple of water bottles to put in our saddlebags. Do you have one, Brody?" Katie asked as she turned to the refrigerator.

"Yeah, I have a couple. It's a beautiful morning out there. Perfect for a ride," he told the girls.

Katie walked in the barn and began searching for a horse to ride. She finally selected her mother's favorite mare, haltered her and put her in the cross-ties to tack her up. She finished quickly and walked the mare outside the barn to where Brody and Maryann sat waiting on their horses.

Katie mounted. "Which way this time?" she asked.

"Why don't we go South. We can find a few hills to climb. Maybe we can even find the place where my parents found La Duquesa," Brody suggested.

The three pointed their horses toward the mountains and trotted off. They found the run-off channel that brought snowmelt and rainwater down from the mountains into the desert. There was a bridge where the highway crossed it, so they didn't have to cross a major highway on horseback. Once they passed under the bridge, Brody took the lead to show them where they picked La Duquesa up in the small canyon only a couple of years ago. They found the cabin sitting there empty. The corral panels and shelter were gone, but the ground showed where they had been. It was scooped out a bit from La Duquesa walking and running around inside it. The last remaining scent of her former owner had long since faded from the property. The cabin looked lonely. Walking over the ground that held her old home brought La Duquesa several memories. She thought of the owner who loved her dearly until she died as Quesa watched through the window into the bedroom. Quesa also remembered her time of starvation and the beatings that came after losing her owner. She remembered how she thought about giving up, but the legs that touched her sides and the hands on her reins now, in the present, reminded her how lucky she was. She would be forever in debt to Aunt Ginny for getting her away from this place of death and despair. She thought it was funny that it just looked dusty and forgotten now. None of the bad stuff showed on the property.

But she was glad when Brody turned the horses away from that place. They walked and trotted several more miles along the base of the mountains before turning back toward Katie's family property. The kids chattered cheerfully as they rode. Tiny deep violet flowers peeked above the sandy soil for a few days in the early spring. Every once in a while, they spotted the brilliant orange of desert poppies, the tiny pale yellow flowers of the creosote bush, yellow of fiddleneck and wild mustard, and the purple sage. Clouds blew gently across the vast expanse of clear blue sky. The weather was perfect for a day of riding.

Katie wondered how she could ever think of giving this all up. Riding like this was like breathing to her. It's what she was born to do. She decided she should be grateful her two friends brought her out of her room and back into the one thing she loved more than anything.

"When we get back to the ranch, I'm fixing lunch," she told them. "We can sit on the patio and eat lunch there. It's too nice a day to sit in the kitchen."

"Hey, what's up with that Arabian gelding in your barn?" Brody asked. "I thought your parents were Quarter Horses only."

"Arabian?" Katie asked. "What Arabian?"

"Third stall down on the left," Brody answered. "I was surprised to see one in your barn."

Katie thought about it. That was the "talking" horse of this morning. She was surprised she hadn't even noticed he was not a Quarter Horse. "I don't know. I guess I'll have to ask my mom next time she calls home."

"Yeah, he's a bit lean," Brody said. "He looks like he's been through a war, too. Didn't you notice all the scrapes and bite marks on him?"

"No, I didn't. I guess I was in a rush to get the feeding done this morning. I will have to take a better look when we get back." Katie was quiet for the next mile. What in the world was her mother thinking with an Arabian? Why was he in their barn? It made no sense to Katie at all. She would remember to ask her mother when her parents called to check on her later. She hoped they had a good trip and that her grandmother was doing okay. She didn't have much to say for the balance of the ride. Her happy mood deflated a bit. She looked around as they walked down the trail. The flowers and the sunshine helped improve her spirit a lot before the three arrived back at the ranch. The three untacked their horses, rinsed them off, and brushed them down before putting them in stalls with a quarter of a flake of alfalfa to keep them busy.

Katie rushed into the kitchen to prepare lunch for three while Maryann and Brody sat on the patio talking. While she was making sandwiches, her mother called from the road. "Hey kiddo, how are you doing today?" she asked Katie.

"Good," Katie said as she nodded her head. "I went for a trail ride with Maryann and Brody this morning. I took your horse. I'm making some sandwiches, and we're going to eat on the back patio. Have you heard anything more about Grandma?"

Shanna was taken aback by Katie's news. She and Clint hadn't been able to get her out of her room or get her nose out of a book since the accident. They only left California yesterday.

"Honey, your dad called the hospital this morning to let them know we are on our way. They said your Grandmother was still in ICU, but we need to get there as soon as possible. I think we may be switching off with the driving and trying to get there straight through instead of stopping for the night tonight. Don't be concerned if you don't hear from one of us tonight. One will be sleeping while the other one drives."

"Okay, Mom. Please drive safely. By the way, where did that skinny Arabian in our barn come from? He tried to bite me when I fed this morning."

"Katie, I'm so sorry. I forgot to tell you about him. That's Kashmir. Do you remember my friend Betty that owns the boarding stable not far from our place? She had to take a client to court for non-payment of board and got stuck with him. She couldn't sell him, so she gave him to me. She thought I might be able to turn him around. I forgot to tell you he's not very people friendly."

"You could say that again," Katie laughed. "I thought I was going to lose my arm. But he seemed to settle down after I talked to him. I landed on my butt in the barn aisle, covered with alfalfa. He stayed in the back of the stall so I could feed him and get everyone else fed. Maryann stayed with me last night. I'm going to ask her if she wants to stay again tonight. I didn't think you'd mind."

"No, of course not," Shanna told her. "I think it would be nice if Maryann stays with you while we're gone. Would you like me to call her mother?"

"Nah, that's not necessary. Maryann and I can do that. You just get to Oklahoma as soon as you can and take care of Grandma. We'll take care of the ranch. I love you."

"I love you too, sweetheart. I'll give you a call in the morning."

Katie grabbed a tray and set the sandwiches on it, pulled three sodas out of the refrigerator and set them on the tray, picked up the tray, and headed out to the patio. "I heard from my mom," she told Maryann as she set the tray on the patio table. "That Arabian in the barn is Kashmir." She also told Maryann and Brody about her mother's comment that the horse wasn't people-friendly. Brody heard about the morning incident on the trail ride. He and Maryann both chuckled over the statement.

Maryann, not thinking, said, "Maybe you should ask him about that."

Brody laughed. "I'm sure he's going to fill you in while he chews off another limb."

All three of the young people had a good laugh over that, Katie a bit more uncomfortably than the others. She was still puzzled by the morning incident but didn't want to bring it up again.

Katie and Maryann talked about having Maryann stay with her until her folks returned from Oklahoma. Maryann talked to her mom about it and got permission. Her mom brought her extra clothes and school clothes. She told Katie she would be happy to take both girls to school. Katie declined. She said she would talk to her home school teacher and get assignments over the phone so she could keep up. Anything she couldn't get over the phone, the teacher would deliver to Maryann so she could bring them to Katie. She could do her studies while Maryann was in classes. She was very thankful Mrs. Wilcox was letting Maryann stay overnights with her.

CHAPTER FIFTEEN

Katie and Maryann fed the horses in the barn that evening. Katie stopped in front of Kashmir's stall and asked him not to hurt her. Kashmir stared at her from the back of his stall. He did nod his head one time, if that was a nod, Katie couldn't be sure. But Kashmir didn't charge toward the feeder with his mouth wide open. He stood quietly until she dropped his feed in his feeder and went on to the next horse before he came to the feeder to begin his dinner.

Katie was puzzled. He didn't "talk" to her. Was it all in her mind that he'd talked to her that morning? If so, that was okay. It was unusual that it seemed to happen in the first place. She would not be disappointed if it didn't happen again. She was also thankful he stayed to the back of the stall while she put his feed in for him. The open mouth charge of that morning was a little frightening.

The next morning, Katie got up to feed, and Maryann decided to make breakfast and have it waiting when she finished. Katie was the only one in the barn that morning as she walked from the back of the barn toward the front, adding alfalfa and grain in each feeder. When she got to Kashmir's stall, she stopped and stared at him. "I know your name is Kashmir. My mom told me where you came from. I'm sorry you are not very people friendly. You have a lot of scrapes that need to be cleaned. Would you allow me to do that after I finish feeding the others?"

Katie didn't expect an answer and dropped Kashmir's feed in his feeder and turned to the next horse.

"*I don't like most people,*" Kashmir told her.

Katie spun around and almost lost her balance. "Did you just say something to me again?"

"*You are the only one in here, aren't you?*"

"Did you hear what I asked you?"

"*There's nothing wrong with my ears.*"

"Okay, Kashmir, I know you don't like most people. Maybe you and I could talk about that sometime, and you could tell me why. But, you need some attention to those scrapes and cuts. I don't want them getting infected while my parents are not here, and I'm taking care of things. Will you let me look at them if I promise to be gentle?"

"*I'll think about it.*"

Katie finished feeding the rest of the horses and put the feed cart back in its place. She grabbed a bucket with some water and betadine solution in it and a couple of sponges and a towel. She walked back to Kashmir's stall. "Are you ready for me to look at you?"

"*Okay.*"

Katie stepped in and dropped one of the sponges in the bucket, wrung it out partway, and looked at several nasty bite marks on his neck and shoulder. "I'm going to wash those with this antiseptic solution. This will clean the wounds. I have a salve in my pocket that I need to put on after they dry. I will talk to you as I work so you will know what to expect. Okay?"

"*What are you waiting for?*"

Katie pressed the sponge onto the first scrape. Kashmir flinched. "*That hurts!*"

"I thought it might, but I promise to be as gentle as possible. If I don't get those cleaned up and get some salve on them, they could get worse and hurt a lot more," she told him as she worked.

"*Get it over with then. What are you waiting for?*"

Katie worked as quickly as she could, cleaning the wounds, drying them with the clean towel, then applying the salve to protect and heal them. She finished in 15 minutes. Katie dropped the last sponge in the bucket, screwed the cap back on the salve container, and tossed the towel over her shoulder. "That should do it for now," she told him. "I need to do that every morning until those heal."

"Okay. Do what you have to do. If you're finished, I'd like to eat my breakfast."

Katie picked up the bucket, tucked the salve back in her pocket, and left the stall. She latched the gate and hauled the gear back to the feed room so she could clean everything up and put it away. As she walked past Kashmir's stall on her way back to the house, she heard, *"Thank you."*

"You're welcome," she responded with a smile and walked to the house.

Katie walked in just as Maryann was sliding the last fried egg out of the skillet and onto a plate next to hashbrown and crisp bacon slices.

"You cook like my mom. Who taught you?" she said as she shoveled the first forkful in her mouth. She tasted it. It was wonderful. Perfectly cooked and seasoned eggs, perfect hashbrown potatoes, and bacon cooked just the way she liked it. Katie thought she should get together with Maryann while her parents were gone and learn how to do that herself. She could cook a few things, but not like this.

"Where did you learn how to do this?" she asked Maryann

"My aunt is a great cook. She's my mother's aunt, so she's my great-aunt. She grew up on a farm in Iowa. She learned from her mother. She told me about making big breakfasts during harvest time. Sometimes they had to feed the whole neighborhood. The wives got together in one kitchen and fried dozens of eggs, cooked pounds of bacon and pork chops and fried pounds and pounds of potatoes, just for breakfast. Then they cleaned up and started on lunch, cleaned that up, and made supper."

"Supper?" Katie asked.

"Well, we call it dinner, but it was the last meal of the day."

"So, what do you want to do today?" Katie asked Maryann. "Do you have enough clothes that we can take another ride and get dirty?" she laughed.

The two girls chatted happily as they finished breakfast and cleaned up the kitchen. Just as Katie put the last plate in the cupboard, her phone rang. "It's my mom," she said as she picked up and answered it. Katie listened. Tears began to well up in her eyes. "No, Mom, I'm okay. How about you and Dad?" she listened as her mother talked to her. "Okay, Mom. The only thing I would like is one of her aprons, one that smells like her." She listened some more, and the tears began to trickle down her cheeks. "Yeah, I'll be okay. Maryann is here with me. I'll see if she can stay until you get home. Her mom will come by and check on us. You and Dad do whatever you need to do, and I'll see you when you get home." She hung up the phone and grabbed the damp dish towel, pulled it over her face, and began to sob. "My grandmother didn't make it. She passed away a few minutes ago."

Maryann put her arms around her friend and let her cry for a few minutes. Katie wiped her face and stepped back. "I'm sorry, Maryann. I didn't mean to do that. I'm going to miss her."

Maryann poured a glass of water from the kitchen faucet and handed it to Katie. "Here, take a drink of this. We can sit down and talk about it if you want to."

Katie sniffed and sat at the kitchen table. "My parents need to make arrangements. Grandma wanted to be buried next to Grandpa. They have to close out the house and put it on the market for sale. My dad was an only child, and he doesn't want to move us all to Oklahoma. He says his home is right here with Mom and me now. It will probably take a couple of weeks before they can leave. Do you think your Mom will let you stay here with me until they get back home?"

"I'm sure she will. I'll give her a call in a while and explain what is going on. Are you going to be okay?"

"I missed Grandpa, but not like I'm going to miss Grandma. We got to visit their farm in Oklahoma several times. Grandma came here after Grandpa passed away and stayed with us several months a couple of times. She was a wonderful lady. She made the best oatmeal-raisin cookies in the whole world. She was a wonderful cook and a delightful teacher. She used to tell me about being a girl growing up on a farm in the mid-west. They used horses for farming back then. Her dad had a couple of mules he used for plowing and planting. She learned how to hitch up a wagon by the time she was eight years old. She learned to drive the mules too. She got to drive her mom in that wagon into town for feed and supplies. It must have been a different world. There were no cars, no tractors, no trucks, and they made all their own bread every week."

"I'm glad she had the time to tell you about it," Maryann said. "I didn't get to meet my mother's mom. She died before I was born. She and grandpa died in an accident on their way to the doctor after Grandpa got hurt on the farm. I wish I had a chance to know them. Grandpa's sister ran the farm after Grandpa died. Their farm was in Iowa, but it was land the Wilcox family owned for over 150 years and several generations. My mom now owns all that land. Mom tells me it is the largest privately-owned farm in Iowa. Several big commercial farms tried to buy the land many times. Mom refuses to sell it. Mom says I will inherit it someday."

"How does your mom run a farm and live here?" Katie asked.

"Mom went back to Iowa when her other aunt, my grandpa's sister, died a few years ago. She had been running the farm. Mom hired people who had worked the land for years for her aunt. They run things, and Mom keeps on top of it from here. She makes a trip to Iowa once or twice a year for business meetings with her employees there. She says I'm going to have to join her one of these days so I can learn."

"Don't you think it's a strange coincidence that we both came from farm families?" Katie asked. "My grandparents had a small farm. Grandpa did the work until he couldn't do it any longer. They sold off most of the land to their neighbor, a wheat farmer. They kept enough to live on and saved the money. That's what they lived on."

"There are probably a lot of kids our age who came from farm families if you go back in time a few years. Lots of people made their living growing things or ranching. You and I go to the supermarket to buy food. Our ancestors raised their own," Maryann laughed. "I think we got the easy way."

Katie sniffed again. "Yeah."

"What are you going to do about your plans to be the next Miss California Rodeo?"

"I don't know. I'm missing out a whole year. That is a setback. I'm not sure. I'm not even sure I want to anymore," Katie said. "I worked so hard to get to each step. When I knew I wasn't going to make this year, I sort of gave up on everything. I could try for the Young Queen for next year, but I'm just not sure I want it. The only thing about it is the tuition money I could win for my college. I don't want to give up on college too. I'm just not sure, and I can't seem to make up my mind if I really want to work that hard for it again."

"You were the best Little Miss, Young Miss, and Miss Rodeo Queen we've had. I'd hate to see you give that up. You were so good at it! You have earned some of the college tuition grants. You can earn a lot more if you look at it differently. Maybe you needed a year off. You've been doing this since you were five years old. That's ten years. Take the rest of this year off and get back into the program. You only have a couple more years before you can compete in the Miss California Rodeo competition. If I know you, you'll be competing in the Miss USA Rodeo competition right from there. You'd be great! You have the looks. You have the horsemanship skills. You have the personality. I would be proud to tell people Miss USA Rodeo is a good friend of mine."

Katie laughed. "If I needed a cheerleader, I shouldn't look any further than you."

"Come on, Katie. Think about it. You can do it! You just have to get back in the routine. If there's anything I can do to help you, I'll be there."

"With the home study program I've been on, I'm about halfway through the next year ahead of time. That would give me more time to start working again. My leg healed, but I've not ridden except for yesterday since the accident. I have to get myself in shape. Then, I'll need a horse to work with. I don't blame my parents for selling Cash. He sat in the barn for months. That was my fault entirely. But I will need a horse for competition."

Maryann grinned at her. She was pleased to hear Katie was even considering getting back in the saddle and riding in competition again. There wasn't one thing Maryann wouldn't do to help her if she could. She thought about talking to Brody and see if his Uncle Mike had a good prospect. All Katie needed was a good horse for barrels and pole bending; the two events she did so well. Maybe Uncle Mike could help find one if he didn't already have one.

CHAPTER SIXTEEN

Maryann and Katie decided to call Brody and see if he wanted to ride with them again. He was on his way over with Desert Rose when they went out to the barn to pull their horses out and tack up. As they walked down the barn aisle, Maryann was on the right side, closest to Kashmir's stall. In a flash, Kashmir charged the front of his stall with his teeth bared, reaching out for Maryann. Katie saw it and grabbed Maryann's arm and pulled her away from the stall front, stood in front of Kashmir, and yelled, "Stop! She's a friend of mine. You are not going to do that to her!"

Kashmir pulled his neck back inside his stall and looked directly at Katie. Katie stared into his eyes, with fire in her own. Kashmir contritely backed away from the front of his stall.

"Okay, okay. I'll leave your friend alone."

"You'd better if you know what's good for you," Katie said.

Maryann stood, astonished, on the far side of the barn. "What was that all about?" she asked Katie.

"He told me he doesn't like most people," Katie said without turning around.

"He told you that?" Maryann asked.

"Yes, this morning when I came out to feed. He and I will have to have a little talk about that. I can't have him attacking my friends." Katie said while staring down the horse.

"What do you mean, he told you that?" Maryann asked again. "Just how did he tell you that?"

"I don't know. I don't understand it myself," Katie answered, her eyes never leaving Kashmir's. "But he needs to learn some manners here while I'm in charge. I won't have him charging my friends."

The silence in the barn was palpable for a few minutes. Katie stared at Kashmir, and he stared back at her. Maryann stood shocked in the barn aisle, looking first at the horse, then at her friend.

"I'm sorry. I won't do that again," Kashmir told Katie. *"I don't know what comes over me, but I'm so tired of being cooped up in a stall with no time out to run in the sunshine, I get angry, and I just want to hurt someone. I didn't mean to scare your friend. I didn't mean to upset you. You are a healer. I need you now."*

"What are you talking about?" Katie asked. "What do you mean, I'm a healer, and you need me right now?"

Maryann stood in silence, but her mouth dropped open.

"I am a medicine horse. My mother told me when I was very young. I am a healer. I recognize other healers. You are a healer also, but you probably don't know that yet. Healers are unique. We can reach into the subconscious of others and help them heal. I don't have the training, and people abused me, so my healing powers have not been developed yet. I see that you need help in some areas where I can help you. But I also need some help in areas where you can help me if you will."

"How do you know this?" Katie asked him.

"Don't you recognize there is something special in the way you and I can communicate?"

"Yes, I thought I was out of my mind, going crazy, or something like that."

"No, I recognized you immediately. There is an aura about you. You are a healer even if you don't know it yet. Your aura is small but will get more powerful as you develop. You can talk to me, mind to mind and heart to heart. You don't have to speak as you know it. Give it a try."

"I don't know how to do that," Katie said.

"Close your eyes and think what you want to say. Don't speak it."

78

Katie closed her eyes. She stood close to the stall front. "I am trying. Is this working?"

"Yes, I can hear your thoughts. Can you see my heart?"

Katie opened her eyes and looked at Kashmir. She saw a glow in the area of his chest. It throbbed with the beat of his heart. It shocked her. She closed her eyes again. "I can see your heartbeat. Is that what I should be seeing?"

"Yes."

Katie looked down at her own chest. She saw a glow that pulsed in time with the pulsing of his heart. Fear rose in her. For an instant, she thought she would throw up.

"Do not be afraid. You and I are in sync. Our hearts are beating at the same rhythm. It is because we are healers, and now you recognize that. It is a good thing. You will see it again when you are in sync with another creature. Do not fear it."

"If I let you out today in the arena, will you promise me you will not harass the other horses? I can give you some time in the sun while we go for a ride. Will that help?"

"I will be grateful and give you my solemn word I will not harass the other horses. I would love to roll in the dirt and run in the sunshine. Healer to healer, I promise you."

"While you are out enjoying a good roll in the dirt, would you mind checking in with Samantha. She's in the third stall down from you. She's new here, and she's nervous. Will you talk to her?"

"I will try," Kashmir said. *"I will try my best."*

"Let's go get our horses ready to ride," Katie turned and said to Maryann. "Brody will be here soon."

Maryann stood with her mouth open. She shut it and walked down to pull La Duquesa from her stall. Neither of the two girls said a word as they tacked up their horses.

"Will you tell me what was going on between you and that crazy Arabian?" Maryann finally asked.

"I don't understand it myself. It is a little scary. Would you mind if we talk about it later, after our ride? I'd like to think about it first myself," Katie answered.

"Sure, as long as you are not going off the deep end, someplace," Maryann said quietly. "I'd like to get back here in one piece."

"Don't worry," Katie laughed. "I'm not going crazy just yet."

CHAPTER SEVENTEEN

Brody and Desert Rose arrived a few minutes later. The girls mounted up, and they walked out the driveway. "Which way today?" Brody asked when they stopped and the gate.

"You pick this time," Katie urged.

"Hey, let's go ride past those new homes that went in about the same time you tripped over the wire and got hurt. I bet they are done now. Maybe we can meet the new neighbors. Maybe they have horses."

Katie grimaced. "Don't remind me! That was a miserable experience."

"Isn't this the road?" Maryann said as they approached the corner of two dirt roads crossing.

"Yeah, that's the pole the electric company put up while we were riding that day."

The three horses turned down the road and walked their horses for a mile until they came to the first of five new homes. One of the houses had a large barn under construction at the rear of the property and a collection of pipe corrals and shelters adjacent to it. They could see a large riding arena in front of the barn from their vantage point on the road. The front gate was open. Two girls were sitting on the porch along the front of the house, drinking a soda.

The three stopped at the gate, "Howdy, neighbors!" Brody yelled at the girls. The girls got up and walked toward the gate.

"Hi, guys. Where do you come from around here?" one of them asked

"I'm from Hartley Ranch, about two miles south of here," Brody told them.

"Oh, I know Hartley Ranch. My older sister used to take lessons from Ginny Hartley a few years ago. She's off at college now."

"I'm from C-BAR-S Ranch, just a mile east of here," Katie said. "I'm Katie, and this is Brody and Maryann. She keeps her horse at Hartley Ranch too."

"I know that place," one of the girls said. "My friend has her quarter horse there for barrel training."

"Which horse, do you know?" Katie asked.

"Not for sure," the blonde girl said. "Hey, are you Katie, the Young Queen?"

"I used to be," Katie admitted. "I didn't compete this year."

"I'm delighted to meet you. I'm Trish. This is my friend Doreen. I've heard a lot about you from Karen, the one who has her horse at your ranch. She is the Young Queen this year. She told me she hoped to get on the Court this time, but didn't think she'd ever beat you for the Young Queen spot. She told me you had some kind of accident and couldn't compete this year. She thinks you were the most wonderful Young Queen. She hopes she can be as good as you were."

"Maybe I'll see Karen at the ranch sometime. My parents are in Oklahoma right now. My grandmother just passed away. They are taking care of her business. They should be back at the end of next week."

"Ahh, I'm so sorry to hear about that. I'll let Karen know your mom is out of town. She will probably still want to come see her horse. Will that be okay with you?"

"Yeah, sure. If I'm not in the barn when she comes, ask her to knock on the back door."

Desert Rose was getting antsy and was ready to get moving again. The riders said goodbye and headed on down the trail. "You okay, Katie?" Maryann asked about a half-mile down the road.

"Sure, why wouldn't I be. I didn't make Young Queen this year, and her horse is standing in my barn, waiting for my mom to get her ready for barrels. What could be wrong with that?"

"Katie, from what Trish said, the new Young Queen is a fan of yours. Maybe you could help her out a little. 'Remember, when you help someone else, you also help yourself.' That is one of my Aunt's favorite expressions."

"Well, I have to find out the new Young Queen's horse is in my barn from some stranger I just met. Wouldn't you think I'd have known about that before now?"

"Wait a minute, Katie. How much time have you spent talking to your mother in the past month or three? According to her, you refused to have dinner or breakfast with your parents and kept yourself shut up in your room all the time. When did you expect your mom to tell you about that?"

Katie rode on in complete silence for another mile. "You are right, Maryann. I've been a complete dope. I've treated you like garbage. I've treated my parents like garbage. I've even treated myself like garbage. Thank you for sticking by me. "You can never have too many friends." That is my grandmother's favorite expression. Now it makes sense. I need to get back on track if I'm going to take that crown from Karen next year so I can wear it myself. Maybe I shouldn't get to know her too well. It might make me feel bad if I do that."

"There's a couple of ways to look at it," Maryann suggested. "If you take the Crown from Karen next year and you help her, she'll be fully trained for doing the job the next year when you are wearing the Queen's crown. And, maybe when you go off to college, she'll earn the Queen's crown from you."

"I like the sound of that. Maybe I'll find a new friend in Karen."

"It is time for you to step back into your life, you know," Maryann suggested. "You've been holed up in your room for how long now? You've ignored all your friends until this weekend. You left your beautiful horse standing and ignored him so long your mom sold him to someone who would care for him. I'll be there to help you, but I don't know much about the Rodeo circuit or the Queen's role in that. Maybe you could teach me."

Katie laughed out loud. "You are right, Maryann. I need to get back and do the stuff I love. It will be hilarious, though."

Maryann looked at her with a question mark on her face. "What do you mean by that?"

"It will be fun watching you and La Duquesa run the barrels with me," Katie laughed. "I can't wait to see her bend poles." Katie dissolved into spasms of laughter.

Maryann, feigning insult, snapped back, "I'd love to see you on one of your big butted Quarter horses trotting down the rail in a flat saddle with a double bridle too! They jog so slow they look like they're going to fall on their noses or trip."

"Will you listen to yourselves," Brody interjected. "I promise you that Rosie here will round those barrels in a good 14 seconds. All I have to do to turn her is shift my butt in the saddle. She'll make mincemeat out of both of you."

The balance of the ride included each one of the three poking fun at the other two until the three were laughing so hard they had to stop their horses so they wouldn't fall off.

As they walked into the drive at C-BAR-S ranch, Katie took a deep breath. "This was just what I needed to get my head back on straight and get my heart working again. Thank you both. I'm ready to get back to work again."

"Is that barrel pattern in your arena set up for high school rodeo or the real deal?" Brody asked.

"I think Mom has it set up for the regular rodeo events. It spaces out the barrels farther, and it also changes the times. You want to give it a go with Rosie and see how she does?"

"Sure, we have time to do that. Why don't you run the pattern on your mom's horse so these Arabians can watch what you're doing before we ask them to do it?" Brody suggested.

"Mom has it all set up on a trip timer. I just need to switch it on," Katie said as she jumped off her horse and handed the reins to Brody.

"Hang on to her while I turn the timer on, will ya?" She dashed off to the switch on the inside of the barn, flipped it up, and dashed back out to mount her horse. She walked her horse into the arena and stopped between the two points across the arena that tripped the timer. "When you cross this point, the timer starts counting. When you finish your turn around the last barrel, you dash back this way, and you trip it when you cross this spot. There is a small panel on the outside of the barn," she pointed to it, "and it will show you the time between your start and your finish.

"How does that work?" Brody asked.

"Mom is a barrel trainer, so she has to either have one of these laser timers or someone out here with a stopwatch all the time. She said the laser timer was cheaper and more accurate. In competition, they count times in thousandths of a second. A stopwatch wouldn't work for times that close. But that tiny difference either gets you the win with the money or out with no money."

"Wow, I didn't know that," Maryann said. "How much money can you win doing barrels at the rodeo?"

"My mom won three brand-new horse trailers, a new pick-up truck to haul one with, a year's supply of feed for the horses, and cash money besides. She was scary good at this event."

"Whoever came up with the idea for barrel racing in the first place," Maryann asked.

"According to my mom, women attended rodeos all the time with their cowboy husbands and boyfriends. Some of them were very good horsewomen. They wanted an event just for the cowgirls, as they called themselves. They came up with the idea back in the 1930s. At first, they just did a pattern of some sort, and judging was on their outfits and their horsemanship skills. By the late 1940s it became a speed event that changed the sport. It became challenging, required a lot more skill and training, and depends on a rider having a close relationship with their horse. At the professional level, the time it takes to hit the start, complete the cloverleaf pattern around three barrels and stop the clock is a shade over 15 seconds these days.

In High School rodeo, the pattern is shorter so you can get 14s. But if you knock over a barrel, they add five seconds onto your time, so that drops you out of the money."

"Wow, I didn't know any of that," Maryann remarked. "It sure makes me look at it with more respect."

"Yeah, I know. My mom started running barrels when she was seven years old. She's been doing it now for almost 25 years. She got me started when I was about five. It takes a long time to get good at it, and you have to practice a lot. You bang your knees into the barrel or the fences, you fall off your horse, you get stepped on by your horse, and if you don't get your boot out of the stirrup, you can get dragged by your horse. It's not a sport for everyone."

"How does your mom train barrel horses, then?" Brody asked.

"She starts the horses off first and teaches them the pattern and the speed. Then she works with the horse and rider together and coaches the rider so they can get it all together and get the speed they need. It's really not much different from showing horses. A trainer does the saddle training for the horse first, then teaches the student and the horse together."

"Why does your mom train instead of competing?" Maryann asked.

"Me," Katie said. "My parents talked about it after I was born. If mom were competing, she'd have to be on the road a lot. My parents decided it would be better for me if one parent were home all the time. She decided to switch it up and start training, so she's always home with me. My dad is the one who competes these days. He's gone quite a lot. He also figured out how to make extra money with hauling horses and cattle between rodeos. That's how they could afford to buy and set up this place as our home ranch."

"Well, why don't you show us how it's done then?" Brody suggested.

The three walked their horses a few feet back from the arena gate. Katie pushed her horse into a full out gallop in an instant. She broke the timer light, and the clock on the barn began counting. She raced toward her first barrel and spun around it, then charged toward the second barrel, circling it and flew toward the last barrel. As she completed the turn, she urged her horse faster and streaked back to the end of the arena at top speed. When she passed through the laser beam, the clock stopped at 18.2531 seconds.

Katie looked at her time. "Not bad for no practice lately. It wouldn't get me in the money, but I can improve on that." She stroked the mare's neck in appreciation of her effort. "It takes a good horse and a lot of practice, but I'll take 18 and a quarter seconds for now. Who wants to take a spin now?"

Brody got Desert Rose in position and gave the barrel run a try. He knocked one barrel over, and the last barrel nearly fell but righted itself. His time was 24.5681 seconds.

"When you add in the five-second penalty for knocking that barrel over, your time goes up to a bit over 29 and a half seconds. You couldn't touch the money with a ten-foot pole with that time," Katie laughed. "But, your run wasn't all that bad. With some work, we could get you going. Your horse is agile, and she's speedy. Rosie looks good running with her tail in the air."

Maryann got set to try a run at it with La Duquesa. When Katie gave the signal, Maryann pushed her into the gallop and rushed toward the first barrel. At the back of the spin, Quesa's shoulder knocked the barrel over. Maryann didn't notice as she encouraged her toward the next barrel. Maryann's knee hit that one and sent it flying as she and Quesa tried to complete the circle around the final barrel and sprint for the wire. When she stopped Quesa, Maryann rubbed her knee. "That barrel was harder than I thought," she grimaced. Her time was 26.6110 but came up to a bit over 36 seconds with the two-barrel penalty added on.

"Maryann, the problem you had was your horse wanted to canter like in the show ring. You can't canter around the barrels; you have to go flat out as fast as you can. She can learn the difference, and you can improve your balance. That's what helped you upset the barrels. But, overall, that was a good try for the first time," Katie told her. "Your horse also looks good running with her tail up. I don't think I've ever seen an Arabian running barrels and now I've seen two of them," she laughed.

Each of the three did a couple more runs around the barrels and improved their times. Maryann's last run didn't knock over any of the barrels, so her time improved the most without the dreaded penalty points.

It was time to stop and feed the horses their dinners. Brody needed to get on the road so he could get home before dark. Maryann decided to keep her horse at Katie's ranch for the time being, as long as she was staying there with Katie. Maryann and Katie had just enough time to rinse their horses off before putting them away and getting the feeding started.

CHAPTER EIGHTEEN

Both Katie and Maryann were starving after their ride. They went to the feed room to prepare feed for the horses. Katie suggested Maryann go back to the kitchen and start making their dinner while she fed. Maryann was in complete agreement. The sooner they ate, the better. She dashed off to the kitchen while Katie began feeding.

When she put the grain in Kashmir's feeder and turned to get his hay, he said, *"I talked to Samantha like you asked."*

Katie hadn't expected to hear him, spun around nearly dropping his hay, and asked, "What did you say?"

"I said I talked to Samantha like you asked me to."

"Oh, okay, I'd forgotten about that. How is she doing? Is she okay being here?"

"She misses her person. She's very bonded with the girl. She's not happy being here and not seeing her every day. Now that the blonde lady is gone, she's not getting worked, AND she is missing her person. Is there anything you can do?"

Katie thought about it for a few seconds. "Yes, there are a couple of things I can do. I can call her person and suggest she come over to see Samantha, and I can work with Samantha myself until my mother gets back home. Why don't you ask Samantha if that will help her? I would be grateful if you will do that for me."

Kashmir stood and stared down the barn aisle at Samantha. She stopped eating and stared back at Kashmir for a minute. Kashmir looked at Katie. *"She would be grateful if you can call her person and ask her to stop by to see her as soon as she can. She misses her very much. Samantha also watched you in the arena today and would be very happy if you will work with her. She thinks you have the same love and talent as the blonde lady does. She was impressed with you."*

"The blonde lady is my mother. Her name is Shanna. She is very good with horses. She inherited her ability from her father, who was an excellent horseman. He taught her so much. She grew up loving horses more than she does people."

"That explains much," Kashmir said. *"I am the product of my mother. She was also a Medicine horse, as was her mother and her grandmother. When I was very young, my mother told me I had special abilities. I had no idea what she was talking about. I grew up and forgot a lot of her teachings. I was angry with humans because of how I was isolated and kept from those of my kind; I forgot those lessons. I am trying hard to remember them now."*

Katie walked over to Kashmir and put her hand on his cheek. He stood and looked at her despite the shock of electricity that flowed through his body from her gentle touch. "Kashmir, you will never be isolated from your kind here. You need to stop attacking people, though. There will never be a human in this barn who would harm you. You have to believe me. Never! I promise you."

"I see the sincerity in you. I believe you, and I thank you." Kashmir murmured. He turned his head away to begin eating his dinner.

"Oh, I forgot to ask you, but who is the person that owns Samantha? I need her name if I'm going to call her about coming over to see her horse. "Katie told him.

"I forgot to mention it to you. Her name is Karen," Kashmir said clearly with a mouthful of hay.

"Karen Bledsoe? Oh, my goodness! She's the one who earned my crown this year. I promised Maryanne I would call her and offer her my help. Now she really does need my help. Her horse needs some help. Wow! This is going to be interesting," Katie sighed. "I will call her tonight and see if she can come home with Maryann tomorrow after school. Samantha needs to see her. I will work with Samantha tomorrow, so I can let her know how she's doing."

"I knew you would," Kashmir said. *"You are a medicine woman. That's what you do."*

Katie finished up the feeding and hauled the buckets and hay cart back to the feed room before dashing back to the house for dinner with Maryann. After dinner, she dug around in her mother's paperwork and got the phone number for the Bledsoe's and called Karen.

Katie told Karen about her grandmother's passing and told her she was filling in for her mom with the training. She told her Samantha needed to see Karen because she missed her. She suggested she might be able to come to the ranch with Maryann after school because Maryann's mother would be bringing her there. Karen promised to make the arrangements and would be there after school the next day. Katie told Maryann about the plan, and she called her mom to set things up. Maryann and Karen would be at the ranch the following afternoon.

All Katie had to do was worry about how Samantha would do for her tomorrow. She'd never so much as haltered the mare and led her around. Now she was committed to working under saddle with her and hoped she could live up to her mother's standards. She wasn't worried about getting along with Samantha. She'd never encountered a horse she didn't get along with until she met Kashmir, and that felt mended for the moment. She decided she might tack him up and see what he knew tomorrow as well.

Katie went to sleep that night with hope in her heart for the first time in months. She had some projects to take care of, and they were all about horses again. Despite the circumstances of her life at the moment, Katie fell into a peaceful sleep that night. She dreamed of riding a fast horse around the barrels. This time the horse she rode held its tail high in the air.

CHAPTER NINETEEN

The morning was a mad scramble. Horses needed feeding, and Maryann had to be ready for her mother to pick her up and get her off to school. Both girls needed breakfast as well. "You can't run an engine on an empty tank." That was a favorite expression of Katie's dad, Clint. The two were just chugging down the last of their glasses of milk when Maryann's mother arrived in the driveway. Maryann dashed off. Katie sat down for a minute to collect her thoughts.

Katie went to her bedroom and made her bed, grabbed a load of laundry, and started the washing machine. She finished doing up the dishes in the kitchen before heading out to the barn.

She walked down the barn aisle as the horses finished their breakfast. She stopped at Kashmir's stall. "Samantha's person is coming over after school today. I hope that makes her feel better," she told Kashmir.

"I will let her know right away. I know she will be happy to hear that." Kashmir said as he finished up the last scrap of hay in his feeder.

"I will work with her today as well. She and I will get to know each other a little better, and we'll work on the barrel pattern to see where she is. That way, I can help Karen with her."

"I'm sure she will be happy to hear that," Kashmir said.

"Why can't I just talk to Samantha?" Katie asked. "Wouldn't it be easier if I could just tell Samantha myself what my plans are?"

"It would be easier, but I don't know if it works that way. You are a Medicine Woman. I am a Medicine Horse. We can communicate directly. But I'm not sure you can communicate in the same way with other horses. We don't speak the same language you do. I think you may be able to let them know what you feel and how you think by body language and how you approach them. Still, I'm not sure you can talk to them the same way you and I can talk to each other. We'll have to see. This is all new to me as well." Kashmir admitted. *"Maybe it would depend on Samantha. If she wants to talk to you, maybe you can tell her what you plan. If she doesn't want to talk to you, I will be a go-between for you."*

"It is important to me that I help Karen, her human, and Samantha. I want them to be the best they can be. Karen took a role I wanted because I couldn't do it this time. I want to help her do the best job she can. Helping her with the competition is an important part of that."

"You can rest assured Samantha knows that. She has heard you, and she understands. She's ready to work with you when you are ready," Kashmir told her. *"She's heard our conversation."*

"Well, alrighty then," Katie said as she marched down the barn aisle to Samantha's stall. She pulled the halter and lead rope down, unlatched the gate, and walked in. Katie walked up to Samantha and stroked her shoulder. She spoke in a soft voice. "Sammy, you and I are going to do some work together. My mom would be doing this, but she has to be away for a couple of weeks. I will step in and help out. You and I are going to be great friends. I hope you know that. Your special friend, Karen, will be here to see you this afternoon. Let's show her what you can do."

Katie put Samantha in the cross-ties in the barn aisle and brushed her down, then tacked her up to work. She walked her out of the barn and mounted. Samantha was relaxed and ready to work. Katie walked her to the arena and trotted her around the barrels a couple of times. She didn't ask for speed, only that she stay close to the barrels and complete the pattern. She talked to the mare the entire time she was riding her, getting her used to her voice, and hoping to gain her confidence at the same time. After a couple of trips, she told Samantha they needed to speed things up. Katie checked that the clock was working and began. She asked Samantha to run as hard as she could. Samantha did. She ran a nearly perfect barrel pattern with only a slight bobble on the backside of the second barrel. She swung a bit too wide. But the time was good for a first run. Katie was pleased and praised the mare for her effort. She gave Samantha a minute to relax and asked her to run the pattern again.

They ran the cloverleaf pattern four more times at top speed. Samantha did better with each run. Her times improved, but she was starting to sweat. Katie decided Samantha worked enough for this session. She walked her around outside the arena for ten minutes before taking her to the wash-rack. Katie pulled out the shampoo and coat conditioner. She gave her the complete spa treatment while congratulating her on the great times she'd done. Katie braided her tail up and put it in a tail bag and braided her mane as well, fastened with tiny rubber bands. She found the supply of carrots and made sure Samantha had several before putting her back in her stall.

Katie sat on a tack box in the barn aisle for a few minutes, eating an apple she brought from the kitchen. She thought about her work with Samantha. The mare was almost as good as Cash had been. She'd let Cash go because she neglected him. She vowed she would never let that happen again. When she finished up half the apple, she walked over to Kashmir's stall and offered him the other half.

"Are you ready to try a barrel pattern?" she asked him.

"I've been ready my whole life," Kashmir said between bites. "Let's go see if I'm as good as one of your quarter horses."

Katie pulled him out of his stall and put him in cross-ties while she located tack that would fit him properly. She put a double pad on his back and the smallest full-sized western saddle in the tack room on him. She found a small girth and adjusted it. She adjusted one of the smaller bridles to fit his face properly with two wrinkles in each corner of his lip. She used a D-ring snaffle bit with no shanks. Nothing she put on Kashmir was harsh or excessively controlling. It was the gear one used on a well-trained horse. She crossed her fingers. She unsnapped him from the cross ties and walked him out of the barn. "How does that feel on you?" she asked him.

"Adequate. Shall we go to work?"

Katie mounted and rechecked the girth for proper tightness and walked Kashmir around the property to get used to his movements and so he could get used to her weight. They walked all the way to the rear fence line before Katie turned him around and headed toward the arena.

Katie approached the arena gate and squeezed Kashmir's sides with both legs while leaning a bit forward to encourage him to go. He didn't hesitate a nano-second. He put on a burst of speed that surprised Katie. He headed directly for the barrel on the right side of the arena. He passed the barrel with his right shoulder. He slowed just enough to spin around the barrel before putting the speed back on and heading for the barrel across the arena. He did precisely the same thing and slowed enough to rotate around the barrel and remain close to it until he passed it with his shoulder. He put on another burst of speed heading for the last barrel and completed that turn perfectly as well. Once clear of the final barrel, Kashmir put an even greater effort to get to the finish line and slowed as he passed through the arena gate. He stopped, breathing hard.

Katie needed to catch her breath too. She was shocked at what they'd just done. It was a nearly perfect run. She couldn't believe the time. She forgot to set the timer clock up before they ran it, so she didn't know exactly how much time the run was, but she knew it was good. She'd ridden enough winning times to know that much. She stroked Kashmir's neck while her shakiness calmed down. She'd never imagined running barrels on an "untrained" horse and doing that well. Kashmir responded to every cue she gave him instantly. That was the first time she felt like she and the horse were one being rather than two separate ones. She was confused and not sure how she felt about the experience. It was thrilling and scary at the same time.

Katie dismounted and walked Kashmir back to the barn. "You are a little out of shape right now. We need to build you up some and get your muscles tightened up. You did a super job with that run. I'm proud of you. I've never seen a first-run like it before. With practice, you will be even better. You are going to smoke some people at the rodeo. I guarantee it. But how did you know what you were doing?"

"I've been watching and waiting for a chance. I watched the blonde lady, your mother, for several weeks. I watched you and your friends yesterday. They showed me what not to do. And I found it exhilarating. I can't wait to do that again. When do you think we can do that?"

"Kashmir, you and I need to put some miles on trails to get your body in shape. I don't want you to run the barrels again until we get your muscles, ligaments, and tendons used to working. We need to be sure you are up to full weight too. You look a little thin to me right now. If we rush it, you could end up injured and not able to do it at all. One bad turn could leave you permanently broken, and we could take a terrible fall together. I want to do it the smart way."

"What you say makes sense. I would enjoy riding with you. I would like to strengthen my body so I can do better. I can't think of anyone I'd rather spend my time doing that with than you. Thank you for today. Can we ride in the mornings? I love the mornings. I love the feel of the sun rising."

"Kashmir, that brings up another subject for me. I've always talked to my horses and the other horses in the barn. I talked to my pony, my POA, my first horse, and my last horse, BUT they have never talked to me! Never! It never happens to anyone I know. It's weird. When I think about it later, it creeps me out a little. I'm not afraid of you. It feels weird that you can convey your thoughts to me in words I understand. Seeing your heart light and seeing mine too was something else that felt weird. I've never seen that with anyone or any animal before. I don't understand this. I'm not asking you to stop. I just need to figure out why it is happening to me. My mom has a friend who is an Animal Communicator. I will call her and see if she can come over and see us. Maybe she has some insights for me so I can understand this better. Would you mind?"

"Not at all," Kashmir said softly. "Maybe she can tell me what my role in life is supposed to be. I've forgotten so many lessons my mother tried to share with me, and now she's gone, and I'll never see her again. I could use the help."

CHAPTER TWENTY

Katie spent the afternoon straightening up the house, preparing the dinner menu, doing some laundry, and finishing up the final chapter of her school work. She thought about her "conversations" with Kashmir. Was she going crazy? She didn't think so, but it creeped her out that she could actually talk to a horse and have him talk back to her. She decided to call her mom's friend, the Animal Communicator. She would do that tomorrow when Maryann was at school. She needed the time to think of how she would present the problem to her mother's friend first.

Katie was waiting in the kitchen when Maryann and Karen arrived from school. She showed Karen to the bathroom so she could change out of her school clothes. Maryann used Katie's bedroom. The two girls met Katie in the kitchen, and the trio headed for the barn.

Karen went straight down the barn aisle to Samantha's stall. The mare had her head over the stall gate, waiting impatiently for her "human." She nearly squealed with joy when she saw Karen entering the barn. Maryann and Katie stood back and let Karen stroke her mare and hug her neck. Karen pulled back and tried to feed Samantha bits of carrot, but the mare wanted no part of them. She wanted Karen. Karen pulled the halter and lead rope off the stall front and opened the stall door. Samantha stood anxiously while Karen put the halter on her and led her outside the stall, into the barn aisle. Samantha tried to pull Karen into an embrace with her neck.

"Katie, you were right. I think she missed me!" Karen laughed. "She doesn't even want her carrots. She wants me to hug her."

"I worked her this morning. She did really well on the barrel pattern, so I thought I'd put you up and see how you two do together. She had the complete spa treatment after her workout. She should be feeling good right now." Katie told her. "She's got a lot of speed, and her turns are pretty tight. I think you can win some money this year."

Katie helped Karen tack the mare up. "You need to get on and work her a couple of times around the arena to stretch her legs first," Katie told Karen. "We don't want to push the speed on a cold horse." Karen mounted and asked Samantha for a slow jog around the arena. After two complete passes, Katie stopped her.

"I think we're ready to see how you two do a run together." Karen brought her mare outside the arena to the waiting area, outside of the clock trip zone. She took a deep breath and cued Samantha to a gallop. The two sailed through the arena gate, tripped the clock, and rushed to the first barrel. They made it around the first barrel. Karen cued Samantha to a fast gallop, and they crossed the arena toward the second barrel. Karen and Samantha hugged close to the barrel as they made the complete turn and charged off toward the last barrel. Samantha put her shoulder down and close to the barrel as they spun around the last barrel. Karen urged her mare into the fastest gallop she could manage while Karen leaned over her neck and stood in the stirrups, and headed toward the finish line. They tripped the clock while Katie watched.

"That was great time, Karen! You've got speed going for you. There are a couple of things I want you to work on and try a second round. I want you to watch your horse's shoulder. When your horse's shoulder passes the barrel, that's when you need to cue her to gallop. It only means a couple of ticks on the clock, but those ticks add up quickly. It can shave a quarter-second off your time. But you two are going to be the horse/rider combination to beat this year, especially in High School Rodeo, where the course is a bit shorter. Great job!"

Karen leaned over and hugged Samantha. She sat up and stroked her neck and smoothed her mane as the two of them caught their breaths. Karen walked Samantha back a few paces from the arena gate and urged Samantha into the gallop again. Their second run was better than the first one by a quarter of a second. They took a few minutes to catch their breath and ran the pattern a third time. The third time they came in a full half-second faster than the first time.

Karen was on top of the world. She understood what the times meant. She couldn't have been happier with her horse. She could already see wins in their future. She took Samantha for a long jog around the ranch to cool her down before heading to the wash rack to rinse her off.

When she walked Samantha back into the barn, Katie and Maryann were sitting on a tack box in the barn aisle. "When should I come over and practice again?" Karen asked Katie.

"How often can you come over?" Katie asked her.

"I can come every day if you want me to," Karen replied.

"That's what I wanted to hear," Katie grinned at her. "If you want to win, you need to ride every day. You don't have to do too many runs each time, but you get better with each one like you did today. If you really want this, it takes a lot of practice, and you have to be willing to do the work."

Karen looked down, and her face reddened. "Would you be willing to help me with the Young Queen duties as well? You were the best there is. I know why you didn't compete this year, and I feel so bad about that, but I feel like I'm floundering, and I have no one else to ask but you."

"I would be happy to help you," Katie said. She choked on the emotion of the moment. "I didn't get to do it this year, but I would be happy to help you in any way I can. I've decided to compete for next year, so you and I will go head-to-head on that later on. I want you to know I have no hard feelings about you winning the crown this year. If I win next year, I only have one year before I can compete in the Queen competition, which will leave you to compete one more year as the Young Queen. I only get one year as Queen. If I win that, I can serve only once before I go off to college. I'd love to have you take over as Queen when I do. Are you okay with that?"

"Katie, I knew I didn't stand a chance at the Young Queen spot this year until you had to drop out. I feel lucky to have that spot this year. I want to do as good a job as you've done. I always looked up to you. You were perfect, representing Rodeo girls and women. I am not sure I can live up to the standards you set."

"Karen, it's a hard job sometimes. You don't want to do anything or say anything that will disgrace our community. You are the Young Queen, so you represent all of us. That's the hardest part. I've heard talk at school and at rodeos on occasion where I wanted to rip into someone for the words coming out of their mouth, but I couldn't. You have to maintain the dignity of the role you play, just like a Queen or Princess would. They can't lay into someone for smarting off. It is our job to lift people up, not put them down. We need to draw a circle to include others, not draw a circle to exclude anyone. We have to maintain a sort of dignity at all times. It's not just a pretty face or nice clothes that make a queen or a princess. You are a representative of a lot of people. It's an extraordinary burden sometimes, but a complete delight at others."

Karen took that in and thought about it for a minute. "You're right. I've never thought about it in that way before. I appreciate you sharing that with me. I understand the role a little better now."

"My mom told me a long time ago that being a Rodeo Queen was a great honor, but it has a price. You become the young woman every little girl wants to become. You are their role model. What kind of role model do you want to be?" Katie told Karen. "That's a decision you should make before you decide to try out for the position. You've done a great job so far. I'm proud to know you."

"Katie, I've looked up to you for years. Thank you for sharing that with me. My mom tried to tell me some of it, but she didn't understand it the way you do. What time is good for me to come over tomorrow? I would love your opinion on some new clothes I bought too?"

"Why don't you hook up with Maryann again and come over with her mom after school? You can bring some extra riding clothes with you, and we can put them in the mudroom for you to wear when you get here."

"My mom won't have a problem dropping you off with me," Maryann said. "I'll talk to her tonight."

"If I can suggest a few more tips," Katie said, "Don't goop yourself up with makeup. I've seen girls compete with pounds of makeup on their faces. You are naturally pretty. Don't put pounds of makeup on. Don't goop your eyes up with eye shadow and tons of mascara and false eyelashes. Let your natural beauty shine through. You are a pretty girl. You don't need all that, and it detracts from your appearance. You are representing "cowgirls," not Hollywood stars. Don't get into the trap where you think you have to put makeup on with a putty knife."

All three girls laughed at that. None of them wore generous amounts of makeup. It tended to streak funny when they sweat. Girls with horses tend to sweat a lot more than girls without horses. That comment came up as well.

The three girls got the feed cart ready and fed the horses their dinners before heading back to the patio for a cold drink while they waited for Karen's mom to pick her up.

"I'm so glad I met you," Karen said. "You've given me some things to think about. And I'm happy with how Samantha is doing too. The next competition is in two weeks. Will you be there to coach me?"

"You bet!" Katie said. "I want you to win!"

Karen nearly choked on her soda. "Well, we're in it to win it!" she said gleefully.

CHAPTER TWENTY-ONE

Katie woke early the next morning. She was a bundle of energy. She went to the kitchen to fix breakfast for her and Maryann while she thought about calling her mom's friend that day. She was nervous about it, wondering what her mom's friend would say about her "talking" with Kashmir. The more she thought about it, the more she wanted to put off the call. But she also wanted to make that call to help solve her dilemma. By the time Maryann got to the breakfast table, she was a nervous wreck. She didn't want to tell Maryann what she had in mind to do that day, so she tried to cover it up with humor. It wasn't working. Maryann could see she was nervous about something

"What's going on with you? You are acting like a crazy person this morning?" Maryann asked her.

"Oh, I guess I have a lot of things on my mind. I heard from Mom last night. The funeral for Grandma is today. I won't be there. I am sad about that. I will miss my Grandma a lot. She was a wonderful lady. I will have to tell you more about her later today when you get back from school. I wish I have more time with her. I asked Mom to bring home her recipe for oatmeal-raisin cookies and one of her aprons that smells like her. She always wore a special perfume. That smell will remind me of her forever. They are going to bury her next to my Grandfather. I will never see them again. Mom says generations go and leave the next generation behind. My children will know my Mom and Dad as their Grandparents. They won't remember them as young and healthy the way I do. It makes me sad in a way."

"You could always start your family early, you know. You just have to find the right guy, get married, and have kids right away," Maryann laughed. "You could do that in a couple of years if you want to."

Katie almost snorted her orange juice across the kitchen table. "Yes. I suppose you are going to help me pick the guy, right?"

"Not so fast, girl!" Maryann laughed at her and tossed a crust of her toast across the table at her. "You think I'm going to help you pick the poor guy? I can't find one I like for me! There are a couple of guys in my history class that are cute, but they play football and ride dirt bikes on the weekends. I need a young, good-looking cowboy. Where are we going to find one of those?"

"Oh, you silly girl!" Katie giggled. "Why do you think I enjoy the rodeo circuit so much? There is nothing there but cowboys who know which end of the horse eats and which end poops. They know how to ride and stay on."

The girls continued their banter about cowboys and rodeos as they finished up breakfast and piled the dishes in the kitchen sink. Maryann dashed out the door with her book bag when her mother showed up to take her to school. The house got very quiet after she left. Katie sat down at the kitchen table with another glass of orange juice and stared into space for a few minutes. She thought about all the things she needed to get done that day and made a mental list of them as she listened to the peace and quiet in the sunny kitchen. She chugged down the last of her orange juice and took the glass to the sink and began washing up the breakfast dishes.

Katie took her mother's address book out of her desk. She flipped pages until she found the name and number for her friend, the Animal Communicator. Katie dialed the phone and squeezed her eyes closed. She almost didn't want the woman to answer the phone. But, she did.

"Hello, Shanna," the voice on the line said. "I haven't heard from you in a couple of weeks. Is everything okay?"

"Miss Valerie, this is Katie, Shanna's daughter. My mother and dad are in Oklahoma. My Dad's mother passed away, so they are taking care of her final business. The funeral is today. I wanted to talk to you about something here at home."

"Oh, Katie, I'm so sorry to hear. Will you let your mom know that my thoughts and prayers are with them? Is there something going on at the ranch I can help you with?"

"I don't know. Oh, I guess. I, um, am having a, I'm having sort of a problem I thought you could help me with," Katie stuttered out finally.

"Okay, why don't you tell me about it. Just start at the beginning."

Katie began by telling Miss Valerie about her accident, her depression, how she felt her dreams were shattered. She told her about the incident in the barn with Kashmir. "I thought I was going crazy, Miss Valerie. I've talked to my horses all my life, but I've never had a conversation with them where they spoke to me."

"You said he told you he is a Medicine Horse?"

"Yes, he did. He also told me that I am a healer too. I saw his heart glow through his chest, and I looked down and saw that my heart was glowing too. At the time, I thought it was strange and sort of beautiful, but when I thought about it later, it creeped me out. I don't know if I'm losing my mind, going crazy, or something really weird is happening. I hoped I could talk you into coming over and seeing it for yourself. Maybe you can tell me what it all means."

"Your mother has some special talents, you know. She takes in horses other people have messed with and created problems for. She figures out what the problem is and calls me over; I think to confirm what she already knows. She's generally right. I get information from the horse and tell her so she can fix the issues other people have created with that horse. She's very intuitive, but I think this sounds like you've taken it to a whole new level. Yes, I will be over in a few minutes. I'd like to talk with the horse, then you, and maybe the two of you together. I am excited about this. No, you are not crazy. You have special talents. You just need to learn what they are and how to use them. I'll see you in a few minutes."

Valerie drove up and parked her car in the driveway a half-hour later, walked to the back door, and knocked. Katie answered the door, offered her coffee, which she refused, and pointed her toward the barn, the third stall down on the left side.

"I'll be back in a while. I want to get to know Kashmir a bit and get his story from him. I'll have that coffee then. We can sit and talk about it, okay?"

Katie went in and made her bed and cleaned up the bathroom. Two girls getting ready for the day tended to leave it in a mess. She straightened up towels, put away makeup and hair products, cleaned the counter and sink, and mopped the floor. She needed to keep busy while she waited for Miss Valerie to come back from the barn. Once she finished the bathroom, she vacuumed the hallway and the living room. Then she dusted the furniture, straightened the chairs around the kitchen table, wiped it down, and was wiping down the kitchen counters when Miss Valerie returned from the barn.

"I'll take that coffee now," Valerie said as she stepped into the kitchen. "Do you have cream for the coffee?"

Katie pulled a cup out of the cupboard and poured a cup from the fresh pot she'd made when Valerie went to the barn. She grabbed the creamer from the refrigerator and set it on the counter next to the cup and laid a spoon down beside it. Valerie fixed her coffee and put the spoon in the sink. "Let's sit down, and I'll tell you what I know," she told Katie.

The girl and the young woman sat down across from each other at the kitchen table. Katie was too nervous to drink anything. She folded her hands together and laid her forearms on the table. She looked directly at Valerie and listened as the woman talked.

"Kashmir was subjected to neglect and abuse for many years. His owner was afraid of him, so she left him in his stall, by himself, most of his life. He told me when you turned him out in the arena just a couple of days ago, that was the first time someone has done that for him since he was a baby. Before he came here, the property owner turned him out with eight other horses, mares and gelding, for the first time since he was a nursing baby. He didn't know how to act. He made the other

106

horses angry with him. His mother was the boss mare. She didn't seem to remember he was her son, so she bit and kicked him away. His mother did not remember him. He knew that, and it broke his heart. He also knew she was ill and would not live much longer. That also broke his heart. She died a month and a half later. He knows he will see her again when his time to cross over the Great Rainbow Bridge comes."

"Oh, that is so sad. I don't understand why people have horses if they can't treat them right. I'm sorry to hear about his mother."

"He told me her health problem was a minor one that their owner neglected. She could have lived with proper treatment. He was especially upset by that. She suffered neglect from her owner, and it eventually killed her."

"He told me he doesn't like people. The people who were around him were not very likable in the first place. I hope we can show him things are different here and give him a reason to like people." Katie said as tears stung her eyes.

"Kashmir told me he could see an aura around your mother when she picked him up and brought him here. He started to remember some of the things his mother told him when he was a baby. He'd forgotten much of her teachings. He feels encouraged here because of your mother and because of you."

"Kashmir is a Medicine Horse. His job is healing. Can you help him?" Katie asked

"First, he needs to heal. That will take some time. He is making progress. You are already helping him with that. He told me you asked him to talk to one of the other horses in the barn. He did. He found out what caused her anxiety and assured her he would do what he could to help. He told me he talked to you about her, and you did something that helped the mare. She is thrilled you did what you did. She was glad to spend time with her human, and she told him you will coach them. Did you know that lifted the spirits of all the horses in the barn?"

"I was never aware the horses communicate with each other that way," Katie said. "Can I learn to talk to them too?"

"Katie, you may develop that skill. It takes time, and you need to heal yourself before you can be an effective healer. You told me about the accident and how you gave up on your dream. One roadblock shouldn't make you change directions if you really want something. You may have to find the detour, but you can still get what you are willing to work for. As I understand it, you will take a year off from your Rodeo Young Queen duties this year. That one year will mean very little to you in a few years. But you can take that one year and improve yourself to become an even better Young Queen for next year. I see the route to that opening before you. You have a chance to coach the current Young Queen this year. You have a chance to develop your communication skills with Kashmir this year, and you can develop some of your healing skills too. You have so much opportunity this year will fly by before you know it. This is not a time to spend huddled in your bed, feeling sorry for yourself. Get up, get out, get going, and learning and doing. I see a very bright future for you. The interesting part is I see Kashmir being a large part of your future. I hope you can get excited about that." Valerie sipped her coffee and looked across the table at Katie.

Katie stared back at Valerie. "But he's an Arabian! Arabians don't do Rodeo! That's what I will be coaching Karen and Samantha for, Rodeo. That's what I know. That's what I do. How does Kashmir fit it with that?"

Valerie smiled at Katie. "You will just have to figure that out for yourself. Kashmir told me he is excited about working with you. He told me about your practice run. He said he felt a little out of breath, but he felt like the King of the Mountain when you ran a barrel pattern with him. He's excited about working with you to build up his muscles and get in shape. Just think of it this way, he's a horse. You don't have a horse right now. He's willing. Give it a try and see how it goes. Look, you both need a little healing. He's a healer, and you're a healer. Maybe this is exactly what is supposed to happen."

"Okay, Miss Valerie," Katie said. "I'll give it some thought. So, I'm not going crazy? So I really can have a conversation with Kashmir and not be nuts?"

"No, Katie, you have a special talent. Who knows? Maybe that knock on the head brought it out. I know you are going to be just fine. Do you know when your parents are coming home?"

"I talked to Mom last night. The funeral was today. My Dad was an only child, so there's no one else to close up their house. Mom and Dad are going through things, selling what they can, packing up what they want to bring home, and giving a lot of stuff to charity. She's trying to keep me posted as they do everything. Mom first thought it might only take two weeks. Now she's not sure. They found so much more stuff in the attic and the barn, plus they are putting the house on the market, and Dad needs to get some repairs done first. They might be three weeks or a few days more. A good friend of mine is staying here with me. Her mom takes her to school and drops her off here and checks in on me. I'm doing fine and have company. I'm going to see if I can keep my Mom's training horses worked while they are gone, plus keep the house up. I'll be busy."

"Look, if anything comes up and you need me, I'm just a few minutes away. Give me a call anytime. I'm serious. I'm a friend of your mother's. She would do that for me. I will be checking in with you too. Are you girls okay being here at night alone?"

"Miss Valerie, I'm my Dad's daughter too. I know where he keeps the Mossberg and shells, and he's made sure I know how to use it. I think a burglar should be afraid of me!" Katie laughed.

They stood up from the table, and Katie walked Miss Valerie to her car. Valerie hugged Katie and reminded her to call anytime for any reason and told her she would give her a call sometime the next day. Katie watched as her car disappeared down the driveway and turned onto the highway. She decided what she needed right then was the company of horses, so she walked into the barn, stopped just inside, closed her eyes, and took a deep breath. The smell of hay, shavings, horse, grain, leather, and dust comforted her. It was the smell of home.

CHAPTER TWENTY-TWO

Katie walked to Kashmir's stall. "Are you ready to ride?" she asked him. "I'm sorry I'm late this morning, but I wanted Miss Valerie to talk to you. I hope you don't mind. She is a good friend of my mother's. This talking you and I are doing is strange, and I wanted another opinion."

"Miss Valerie is nice. I enjoyed talking with her, although she wanted to know some pretty personal stuff about me. I get the feeling she is trustworthy?"

"I believe she is. Thank you for talking with her. It also helped me. Do you still want to go for a ride with me?"

"I was hoping you'd ask."

Katie opened the stall door latch and grabbed Kashmir's halter on her way in the stall. "Let me look at your booboos first. I will treat them after our ride if that's okay with you. We'll take a nice ride, and I'll bath you. Sound good?"

Kashmir nodded his head and followed Katie out of the stall to the cross tie area. Katie put the cross ties on and pulled the tack out of the tack room, put the gear on him, and wrapped his legs in polo wraps last. "We're ready if you are," she told him as they walked out of the barn. Katie mounted and guided Kashmir along the outside of the barn toward the open desert space to the back fence line. They walked at first to give Kashmir time to stretch his legs. Once they reached the back fence, Katie turned him alongside the fence and cued him to a trot. The dirt was reasonably smooth in that area because so many horses had traveled over it, the desert brush was trampled down and failed to regrow after so many years. They reached another corner of the property and turned alongside the fence line to the road in front of the ranch property. Katie turned Kashmir north along the road for two miles before turning him back toward the ranch and the waiting bath. Kashmir was beginning to sweat from the exertion, so Katie slowed him to a slow jog until they reached the driveway to the barn. She walked him to the washrack and began pulling his tack.

She tied him into the wash rack and gave him the full spa treatment. She used a good shampoo and coat conditioner and let him stand in the wash rack for a few minutes after she used the sweat scraper to wipe off the excess water from his body. She grabbed the mane and tail comb and went to work on his forelock, mane, and tail. Katie braided up his tail and attached it in a brand new tail bag to keep it clean. She braided his mane in long tight braids to keep the wind tangles out if it and did a single braid in his forelock. When she finished, his body was nearly dry; his dark brown coat shined in the morning sunlight.

"You sure look better than the first time I saw you," Katie giggled.

"I have not had a bath like that one in longer than I can remember," Kashmir chortled "It sure makes you feel good. Thank you. Thank you for the ride too. I was getting tired at the end, but I already feel stronger. I hope we get to keep taking these rides. I want to run the barrels with you again – soon!"

"Oh, we will!" Katie laughed. "We will kick some butt doing it too. You have agility I didn't expect. Once you're in better shape, we will tear up that timer."

Katie dashed back into the vet area in the barn for the salve she put on Kashmir's wounds. She touched them up, one at a time, and noticed several were nearly gone already. "Hey, these are looking much better, Kashmir. We won't be needing this salve too much longer. You are healing up well."

"I know. The wounds started healing the first time you treated them. I could feel the difference right away. The soreness was gone almost imme-diately. I'm feeling better and stronger every day. You are a healer, Katie. All they needed was your touch. Thank you."

"Kashmir, you are also helping me. A few months ago, I had an accident that took me out of competition for the Young Rodeo Queen position this year. I felt like my life was over. I hid in my room for months and gave up everything that had been important in my life. Since that day, when you tried to bite my arm off, I've had a chance to re-evaluate my situation. I will have this year off from my Young Queen duties, but I have an opportunity to learn and grow. I'm going to help Karen, who took my spot, as she fills that position this year. I will coach her and Samantha so they can do well in the competition. That would have made me hide under my covers a month ago. Today, it makes me feel good and content. I feel needed, and like I can contribute to another horse and rider team. Thank you for trying to rip my arm off and getting my attention."

"I'm sorry I did that, you know. I wouldn't have if I'd taken the time to look at you. I also feel content here. Look at me. I'm gaining weight. My wounds have nearly healed. I'm having a conversation with someone I love and respect. I've gotten out, been ridden, given a fresh bath that makes me feel good all over, and I feel like we are becoming good friends. What could be better?"

"I'm going to coach Karen and Samantha for the next two weeks, then go with them to a High School Rodeo for competition. Would you like to go along and watch with me?" Katie asked. "I'd love you to see what the Rodeo is all about, so you know why we run barrel patterns and pole bending patterns here for training."

"I would love that," Kashmir told her. *"I would like to see the events you love to participate in. I would love to learn more about your life."*

"Okay, it's a date. I will make plans to haul you with Samantha. You and I can watch from the rail."

"Are Brody and Maryann going to participate?"

"No, they don't do much Rodeo stuff. Brody has done some with Rosie in Cutting and Reining work, but he's not a dedicated Rodeo Cowboy."

"Why not?"

"Arabians are not generally used in Rodeo. They usually use American Quarter Horses for those events. Rosie is special. Her father was an American Quarter Horse, but her mother was an Arabian. She looks more like her mother." Katie explained

"Why don't Arabians do Rodeo?" Kashmir asked.

"I don't know. Rodeo came about to show off the talents of horses that worked cows on the range. They were cattle horses. They were compact, light horses that had to be able to move with a herd of cows over long distances. The cows pastured in the high ground during the summers and had to move to lower areas during the wintertime when snow covered the high ranges. The horses also had to move cattle from their pastures to railheads where they sold them. They didn't want to work the cows hard, so they didn't lose weight over long journeys. The working horses had unique talents. They had to cut a single cow from a herd so it could be vaccinated, castrated, and branded for ownership. It took skill to do that and not injure the cow. Many of those unique talents are what Rodeo is all about. Roping has to do with holding the cow in one position so all that could take place. Cutting had to do with separating that cow from his herd and his mamma, which was not easy. Pole bending had to do with moving your horse through obstacles to get those jobs done. Barrel Racing came about so women had an event of their own where they could prove their equestrian skills too."

"So why don't Arabians do Rodeo?" Kashmir asked again.

"I don't know. I guess it is because Arabian horses were not here in the United States when all this cattle work started a couple of hundred years ago. They didn't show up until much later. Arabians are fine-boned horses of extreme beauty. The average cow horse was a small, compact horse appreciated for function only. No one ever appreciated them for their beauty. Things are different today. Cattle horses are much bigger, heavier, and prettier than they used to be. People value Arabian horses for their talents. Some ranches use Arabian horses exclusively for moving their cows. But it is not the general practice yet. Rodeo goes back to old beliefs, and they usually exclude Arabian horses. So do Rodeo competitions at the moment. They don't prevent them, but they don't use them much."

"I have one more question for you," Kashmir said. *"Why don't you think of Brody as a possible mate?"*

"What?" Katie sputtered.

"I know you and Maryann talked about finding a cowboy, so I assumed you meant you were looking for a cowboy as a mate."

"You heard our conversation over breakfast?" Katie sputtered again.

"Yes, I'm uniquely connected to you. I hear your thoughts sometimes. I just thought I should mention him. He is what you would call an attractive young man, is he not? He's a good horseman. Desert Rose told me that. I think you should consider him as a possible mate."

"Are you giving me dating advice now?" Katie asked with difficulty. She began laughing and couldn't stop herself. 'Now, I've heard it all. A horse is giving me dating advice. What is this world coming to?" Katie doubled over laughing.

It took Katie a few minutes to stop laughing. "I'm sorry. I don't mean to offend you, but we humans generally like to pick out our own boyfriends. We don't rely on our horses to do that for us." The suggestion was pulling at her sub-conscience, though. She decided to store it for a while.

"I didn't mean to offend you. I just thought you were looking, and Brody seems to be a good candidate." Kashmire said quietly.

"I appreciate your concern, Kashmir. I've never heard of someone taking dating advice from their horse before. You could be right, but now is not the time. We humans don't usually mate for several more years. It will be a while before I'm ready to mate with anyone, even Brody. But thank you for the suggestion. I'll keep it in mind." Katie struggled to keep a straight face as she walked Kashmir back to his stall. She hugged him and told him she appreciated him thinking of her before she walked out of the stall and closed the latch. Katie walked back to the house, struggling to maintain her composure until she got inside. She nearly fell on the floor laughing until tears fell from her eyes. Brody Hartley? Who would have thought? Of all people? But then, maybe Kashmir was right. He was an attractive young man, and he was nice, and he was a great horseman. Perhaps she should think about that for the future. She wasn't ready for a boyfriend right now. But she didn't mind having Brody as a good friend.

CHAPTER TWENTY-THREE

For the next two weeks, Katie worked Samantha on her barrel patterns in the morning for a couple of runs then coached Karen and Samantha every afternoon after school. Their times were better and more consistent as the days progressed. Saturday morning, Karen's mother brought their trailer over and picked up Samantha and Kashmir. Karen had all her Rodeo Young Queen clothes and her hat with her crown on it. Karen took part in the opening ceremonies, then changed into regular jeans and boots for the competition. Katie took her aside before her first run. She gave her a "pep talk" about how good they had been doing, and there was no reason she couldn't do as good or better in the competition where it counted.

Karen had the best runs of her life. She won. She won money. She was ecstatic. She couldn't believe she and Samantha did so well. She couldn't thank Katie enough.

Kashmir stood at the rail and watched every event. He asked a few questions. But he learned a lot that day. The energy in the arena affected everyone outside the arena and in the stands. It infected Kashmir as well. He wanted to participate himself. He knew he could beat the times for barrel racing, and he wanted to practice pole bending with Katie as well. He was hooked.

He also noticed what Katie had prepared him for. There was not a single Arabian horse in the arena, and he was the only one on the grounds. He heard whispers from competitors directed at Katie. Why did she bring an Arabian horse to a Quarter horse event? Was she crazy? Didn't she know Arabians didn't compete in Rodeo?

The "was she crazy" part bothered him. Kashmir knew she was not crazy at all. Why the other competitors would suggest that was beyond his comprehension. By the afternoon, it began to upset him. He was not "chopped liver." Why were they so biased against him? It made him all the more determined to show them up someday. He knew he and Katie would do that. They would pull times that would shatter the norm for most of the High School competitors that day. He knew it in his heart and his mind. He couldn't wait for that opportunity.

The day ended with a final parade around the arena with the Young Queen and the Rodeo Queen before Samantha and Kashmir loaded in the trailer for the trip home. Karen was excited about how they finished the day, the money they'd won, and the prestige they'd gained. She talked nonstop with Katie about the next competition and wanted her to be there to coach again.

"You know my mom should be back in a few days," Katie reminded her.

"Yes, I know that, but we've had so much fun, I'd rather work with you." Karen laughed. "And look at what we got accomplished! I won prize money this weekend. That's the first time I'm going to take home more money than it cost to participate. My parents are happy about that too. I paid them what they gave me for entry fees and still have money I can put in the bank for my college fund. I want to keep this up and get myself one of those new horse trailers and saddles like you have."

Katie laughed. "That year-end high-point awards meeting can be a lot of fun, especially when you do well and get to haul it all home with you."

"What's is going to take to get you to agree to coach me so I can haul the good stuff home at this year's high-point awards?" Karen pleaded

"I guess you could help me get Kashmir back in shape, so I have a horse to compete with. I've been riding with Maryann and sometimes Brody. You come to the ranch almost every day. Why don't you start riding with me too? We're trail riding, but we put in some hills to build up his rear end and shoulders. It's not hard work. We do it every day."

Karen stopped and stared at Katie for a few seconds. "Are you serious?"

"Yeah, I'm serious. We can work with Samantha in the arena and take the horses out on trails to help get Kashmir in shape."

"No, Katie," Karen said. "Are you seriously going to try competing on an Arabian on the Rodeo circuit?"

"Why not? Remember, my parents sold my horse. That was my fault, of course. But I can't compete without one, and he's the only one around right now."

"Katie, he's an Arabian!" Karen looked shocked. "You've been on the circuit for what, ten years now? You know they don't use Arabian horses in Rodeo."

"I looked it up in the rule book. No rule says you can't ride an Arabian horse in Rodeo. No rule says you can't ride a donkey in rodeo either, or a Tennessee Walker, or a Saddlebred, or any other breed. There is no rule that you can't ride a buffalo either. What difference does it make? I wouldn't mind seeing someone try to ride a buffalo in a barrel pattern sometime, but not sure I'd ever try it myself," she giggled. "So, I may be going outside the box a little, but there's nothing in the rules that say I can't."

"Katie, you are going to get so much grief!" Karen said. "I like Kashmir too, but I don't think I would ever try him against the other girls on their Quarter horses."

"I might not do so well, but, then again, he and I might do very well. We'll have to see." Katie said to end the conversation. She finished packing the gear in the trailer tack room for the drive back to the ranch.

Katie thought about what Karen said. She never saw an Arabian horse at the competitions she'd been to, even as a spectator. She didn't know what her dad and mom would think of the idea, either. But this time, she was determined. She and Kashmir would compete, and they were going to blow the other competitors away. She could feel it in her bones. She knew Kashmir was just as determined as she was. He wanted to do well. He told her that several times. She would keep her practice runs with Kashmir a secret and only do them when no one else was at the ranch. That way, when Kashmir was ready, they could spring it on people and show them what he could do. She also knew Karen was right. She and Kashir were going to take some flack for competing in American Quarter horse events. But, she didn't care.

Once the horses were back in their stalls and the equipment was put away, Karen and her parents left for home. Katie and Maryann fed the horses, grabbed a cold drink, and sat on the back patio to relax.

"What's with the snobbery of those girls today?" Maryann asked.

"What do you mean?"

"Did you hear the comments they were making about Kashmir?"

"Yup, sure did."

"What are you going to do about it?"

"Beat the pants off every one of them. That's what!" Katie said quietly. "Sometimes, doing well is the best revenge."

"Oh my goodness," Maryann laughed. "I can't believe you said that. Do you really think you can?"

"Oh, yes," Katie told her. "I let him run a barrel pattern after you and Brody left here after your first time. Remember that day? He asked if he could try. I didn't expect much from him, so I let him give it a go. Holy Cow! I couldn't believe how tight his turns were and how fast his time was. I'd already turned the timer off by then, but I've been doing this for years. I know a good time when I ride it. He was also very out of shape. That's why I'm riding him every day. I need to get him back in good condition. He wanted to run the pattern a second time that day, but I wouldn't let him. I told him, as out of shape as he was, he could get hurt permanently and maybe get me injured too. So I promised him we'd give it another try as soon as he's in better physical shape. He agreed to that. He's literally chomping at the bit to run that pattern again. I know he's capable of beating the pants off every one of those girls that looked down their noses at him today. They are going to be shocked! I guarantee it."

"What are your parents going to say about that?" Maryann asked her.

119

"I don't know. I'm hoping they are not as one-sided as those girls today were. My dad and mom have been Quarter Horse only people. I don't even know why Mom brought an Arabian home in the first place. I think it was to help a friend of hers. I have no idea what she planned to do with him. I think the only way I can pull this off is to get him in shape, which he almost is now, and begin running the patterns late at night after everyone else is in bed. My folks' bedroom is on the other side of the house. I might be able to get away with it. Please keep this to yourself, the same as the "talking" part. For the moment, I'd like to keep this between us until I figure it all out."

"Hey, I have to admit I talked to my friend Becky about it. She's my friend from San Juan Capistrano I've told you about. She will keep it to herself, but she'd love to come up and see you and Kashmir sometime. If she brings Prince Ali, we can ride together. That would be so much fun. You'll love Becky. She's smart, and she's funny. Prince Ali is a gorgeous horse! Maybe that's what we should do. Maybe we should try to get Todd and Desperado to come here from Colorado for a couple of weeks. If we got Becky up here from San Juan Capistrano, maybe we could show your parents something about Arabians. Desperado and Desert Rose both do reining very well. That's cowboy work. Rosie is a superb cutting horse as well. That's cowboy work too. Maybe if your parents saw Arabians doing that kind of thing, it might change their minds about Arabian horses. What do you think?"

"Let's work on that once school is out for the year. I'd love it," Katie said. "Now, that's what I'd call an action plan! Having Brody show off Rosie's cutting skills will impress my dad for sure. I bet he'd like the reining work too. They both do the slide stops and spins, don't they?"

"Oh, yes!" Maryann said. "Desperado slides without a single hop and spins like a top. All you see is that black mane and tail whipping around Todd. Rosie is no slouch at that either."

The girls adjourned to the kitchen to get dinner ready. Maryann took a few minutes to make some phone calls before they ate. They set the plan in motion. Katie crossed her fingers it would work.

CHAPTER TWENTY-FOUR

Katie's mother called Sunday night and let Katie know she and Katie's dad would likely be home by Friday or Saturday that week. She and Katie talked about some of the items they were bringing home with them. It made Katie sad. It was a reminder that she would never see her grandparents again.

Katie filled her in on Karen's day at the rodeo competition and let her know Karen asked her to coach her. Shanna was surprised and pleased. If Karen asked for Katie to coach her, and Karen did so well at her recent competition, Katie was doing a great job. She was proud of her daughter. She noticed how much Katie had changed during the weeks they were in Oklahoma and was pleased about that as well. Her daughter sounded like herself again. She almost couldn't wait to get home and hug her.

Katie, Karen, and Maryann met Brody on the road, and the four of them rode back toward the mountains to get in a little hill climbing for Kashmir. He put on weight, and his muscles began to show where they should. Kashmir was becoming a handsome horse. Maryann told her he was showring material. Kashmir had a natural arching neck and headset that went with his graceful jog down the trail. His coat shined. His cuts and scrapes disappeared. Kashmir's attitude was warm and friendly, especially with Katie. He was not the same horse who tried to remove Katie's arm in the barn aisle not so long ago.

Katie gave Maryann and Brody a few more tips for barrel racing, and they tried it several times, improving their times. Karen showed off her skills too. Katie decided to give Kashmir one run at the pattern before her parents returned. She set the timer this time.

Kashmir was like an uncoiling spring when Katie urged him to gallop. He clung to the barrel, even on the backside, to shorten the distance, and dashed toward the second barrel in excellent time. Kashmir rounded that one and turned for the last barrel, rotated around it, and flew headlong for the finish line. When he tripped the timer, Katie glanced at it and began to yell. "Yes! That's how you do it!" Their time was almost a quarter of a second faster than the horses in competition the day before. Karen, Maryann, and Brody clapped and cheered

"Wow! That was a great run!" Brody shouted.

Katie pulled Kashmir to a slow stop outside the arena and hugged his neck. "You did great, Kashmir!" she told him. She walked him around for a while while he caught his breath. Katie continued stroking his neck and praising him. He thought about it. It was just like what Katie's mother did with the horse he watched her work a few weeks ago. He liked the praising part. It made him feel good, even though he was tired. His world was changing fast. He wasn't watching someone else get the pets and praises. He received them now. His heart glowed with happiness. As Katie walked him to the wash rack, his neck arched a bit more, and he carried his tail a little higher. He felt pride for the first time in his life.

Kashmir knew he felt another change in his life. His feelings for Katie had gone from considering her "an enemy at arm's length" to a friend. The more time he spent with her, the deeper his feelings for her became. He walked beside her and saw her happy expression. He noticed her dark ponytail swishing with every step she took. He noticed how she carried herself with her chin up and her shoulders back. He began to notice her. He noticed little details he'd never seen before. He embraced those things. He wanted to remember them for the times they were not together. He realized the feeling he had for her was no longer friendship. She was his partner, and he loved her.

It was a new feeling for him. He hadn't loved any creature since Crazy Trainer forcibly separated him from his mother at five months of age. Crazy Trainer called it "weaning." It was torture for him. He could see his mother part of the time, but he could not touch her. He called out to her for days. She responded to his cries for the first day or two and did not respond to him after that. He felt abandoned. He missed her. He wished he remembered the details of her the way he was storing the details of Katie.

He suddenly shook his head. He knew he should enjoy this time with Katie. He would not know when the last time came. He didn't want to miss anything in the here and now.

CHAPTER TWENTY-FIVE

Katie's parents drove into the driveway the next day while Katie was in the arena coaching Karen and Samantha. She saw her dad's truck pulling in and shouted to Karen, "My parents are back. Why don't you just jog around the arena a few times? I need about 10 minutes with them. I'll be right back."

Katie dashed straight to the passenger door of the truck as her dad pulled to a stop.

"Mom, Dad, I'm so glad to see you! I missed you!"

Shanna and Clint were a little surprised by their reception but delighted by it. It looked like their pretty, active daughter was back!

"How have things been here at the ranch?" Shanna asked.

"Great. The horses are all doing well. Karen asked me to coach her while you were gone, and we get along so well, she wants me to continue. She won money over the weekend. Her parents were happy about that too." The words tumbled and jumbled out of Katie's mouth in such a stream, Shanna finally said, "Hold it. You're going too fast. Let us get out of this truck and onto solid ground again. I feel like we've been driving for days. Actually, we have. But I'm so glad to get home. You look wonderful. We missed you too."

"I need to get back to the arena with Karen and Samantha. Why don't you and Dad go inside? Find something cold to drink and sit down for a few minutes. We can talk all about stuff over dinner if that's okay with you. I have dinner plans. You don't have to cook, Mom. I'll do it this time."

Shanna looked over at Clint with her eyebrows raised. He nodded and smiled back at her. He also smiled at Katie. "You go ahead. I'll get your mom inside. We'll wait for you until you finish up."

Katie dashed back to the arena and picked up with Karen where they left off. Once their workout finished, Katie suggested Karen take Samantha to the washrack and give her a good rinse off. "Put her back in her stall. I'll be out to feed the horses in a little while. I need to catch up with my parents. Is your mom on her way over to get you?"

"Yeah. Mom should be here in about 15 minutes. That will give me time to rinse Sammy and put her away. I had a great time today. That little trick you gave me worked. I shaved a little off my best time. I need to practice that, but it will help. Thank you so much!"

"Karen, you are going to be the ones to beat this year. You and Samantha are a great team. She gives it everything. You'll have your new horse trailer in no time, and you'll probably get one of those new saddles at the Awards Banquet this year. You've earned it!"

Katie walked to the back door of the ranch house beaming. Her only student was doing well. That would also help Katie. She thought she might want to become a trainer herself after college and the year of representing Rodeo as Miss USA Rodeo Queen. Her face lit up at that thought.

Katie found her parents sitting at the kitchen table, enjoying tall glasses of sun tea she made earlier that day for them. It was something else Maryann showed her how to make. Katie poured herself a drink and joined them at the kitchen table. In their family, this location is where significant decisions took place, meals enjoyed, and family discussions happened.

Shanna beamed at Katie. "You look like you're doing much better. Tell us what you've been up to."

"Mom, first, I need to apologize to you and Dad about my behavior before you left. I was acting like a spoiled brat that didn't get her way. I was so depressed about missing the Young Queen Competition; I felt like my life was over. It's just one year. I know that now. I talked about stuff with Maryann. One good thing is I have half of next year's schoolwork completed right now. I don't know if I want to go back to school in August and throw all that work away. How would you feel about me staying on homeschooling through the end of next year? I would like to go back to regular school for my last year in high school. That way, I can be with more of my friends. This year, I would like to work with you. I want to learn how to train barrel horses. I can't think of a better teacher. I think I want to be a trainer like you after I finish college."

"Wow," Shanna said. "You've already thought this out. I hope you can find yourself a cowboy who makes as much money as mine does." Shanna grinned at Clint over her iced tea glass. "If you want to be a trainer, I'd be delighted to share my secrets with you. I think having you at home this year would be fun. I have no problem with that as long as you complete your schoolwork."

Clint cleared his throat. "I'm all for that, on one condition. I get to agree with your selection of cowboy down the road in a few years."

"Dad," Katie grinned at him. "I'll be looking for someone like you. I won't be dragging in someone you don't like. I promise to be selective."

"Okay," Clint said. "As long as I get to approve, you can marry a cowboy of your choosing, years from now. Many years from now."

"Dad, I don't have a boyfriend. I don't want a boyfriend. I don't have time for a boyfriend."

"I hear Brody Hartley has been over while we were away. What about him?"

"Dad, Brody is a friend, that's all. He's nice. He's funny. Maryann and I enjoy having him along on our trail rides. Neither of us has plans to marry him." Katie chuckled. "As I said before, I don't have time for a boyfriend."

"Then, he didn't stay over here with you two girls while we were gone?" Clint turned serious.

"No, Dad. Brody rode home by himself. I don't think his Aunt Ginny would let him stay here with two girls unsupervised anyway. Aunt Ginny was always checking in with Maryann and me."

"I like Mike and Ginny Hartley. I didn't think they'd allow it, but I did have to ask."

"Dad, I know you did, but you need to learn to trust me, too," Katie said. "You and Mom are my parents. You are my examples. I have to live up to the standards you set. You set them pretty high, you know," she chuckled again.

"Well, enough about you, Katie. We need to fill you in on what happened with your Grandmother," Shanna said with a tear in her eye.

"I meant no disrespect," Katie said. "I guess I was putting off the bad news. Tell me what happened."

"My mother had a heart attack alone," Clint said. "She had enough strength to call the neighbors. They came and found her unconscious on the kitchen floor and called the paramedics. They said her heart was still beating, but irregularly so they took her by ambulance to the hospital in Tulsa. The doctors there were able to get a regular beat going for a while. But they were concerned she would fall back into the irregular beat, and her heart would eventually stop."

"Which neighbors found her, Dad?" Katie asked.

"The same people who bought most of the land from your Grandfather's farm when he couldn't do the work any longer. They became close friends with your grandparents. They checked in with your Grandmother every day after your Grandfather passed away last year. They are good people and cared about your grandparents," Clint told her. "I couldn't have been more pleased about who bought that land. I knew I didn't want it. I'm no farmer. Your Mom is no farmer. That's not the life we wanted for ourselves or you. At first, they hesitated about buying the remaining land and your grandparent's house. I did some repairs to make it more livable, and they finally agreed to buy it. They now own the entire property. They will care for the land and the house I grew up in. I think they are giving that house to their son and daughter-in-law so they will help farm the land again.

That land is prime wheat-growing land, and it will stay that way. I am happy about how it turned out."

"Who are these people?" Katie asked.

"George and Isabelle Kamatsu. Their daughter and son-in-law live with them. Now their son and daughter-in-law will live next door. George and Isabelle are not young. Their son and son-in-law will do most of the work. They have plenty of room for the grand-children and great-grandchildren as well. Ask your mom. They are a wonderful family."

"Kamatsu?" Katie asked. "That sounds Japanese or Chinese."

"They are Japanese. George and Isabelle met in one of the internment camps for Japanese people during World War II. They were quite young then. George's father owned a strawberry farm in Washington State. Isabella's parents owned a dry cleaner business in San Francisco. They lost their home, their land, their business, and almost everything they owned when the government forced them into the internment camp right here in California. George and Isabella grew up right outside of Lone Pine. We've been past that place on several trips with you."

"Are you talking about Manzanar?" Katie asked?

"Yes, Katie. That's the place. Now, it's not much to look at, except for one building turned into a museum and the cemetery. I think we took you there once," Shanna answered.

"I sort of remember. But I never knew any people who were stuck in there. Why did they get stuck in there in the first place?"

"The Japanese bombed Pearl Harbor in Hawaii. That set off the war against Japan at the same time the Americans were at war with the Germans. It was a terrible time. People were afraid of people who looked different than themselves. The Japanese people who immi-grated to the United States were rounded up and put in internment camps to prevent them from causing problems. George and Isabelle were both first-generation Americans. They were born here. But they looked Japanese, so they and their entire families were rounded up and put in the camps until the war was over."

"Oh, my gosh, Mom, they were Americans. They shouldn't be rounded up and put in camps like that. I hope that never happens again here in America."

"So do I," Clint said. "Selling them the land and the house for the price we got was one small way to make amends for what happened to them. And I know they will care for it."

"I have a history paper to do. This gives me a great idea for what to use for the subject. Do you think Mr. or Mrs. Kamatsu would talk to me about their experiences? I'd love to hear from someone who was in the camp at Manzanar. And it is very close to where we live. So my paper would be relevant to us today since people can go visit the camp and the museum."

"They are delightful people. I'm sure they would talk to the granddaughter of the man whose land they own now," Shanna said. "I encourage you to tell their story in your paper. Bet you get an "A" on that one."

"Mom, I have some things I need to talk to you about tomorrow, but I need to get dinner started right now. Why don't you and dad check out the barn while I get busy," Katie suggested.

"You are going to cook dinner for the three of us tonight?" Shanna asked

"Yes. Maryann taught me some things she learned from her Aunt. We messed around in the kitchen every morning and every evening while you were gone. I learned quite a lot from her. Wait until you taste it," Katie said proudly.

"We have a truck and trailer to unload. Why don't we get started on that while she cooks us up a gourmet meal," Clint said to his wife with a grin.

CHAPTER TWENTY-SIX

S hanna and Clint were pleasantly surprised by the meal Katie cooked up for them. They ate until their sides were bursting and enjoyed every bite. The family chatted over dinner that night, as they always had in the past. The parents learned what their daughter had been up to while they were gone. Katie learned more about her grandparents than she knew before. They discussed what they would do with the furniture brought home from the family farmhouse. Katie got her apron that smelled like her grandmother, and a copy of her grandmother's oatmeal raisin cookie recipe. Shanna brought Katie her grandmother's recipe box with all her favorite recipes in it. Katie vowed to keep it and use the recipes in it.

Katie held back on discussing Kashmir with her parents. She wanted to talk to her mother privately in the morning. She set things up so Shanna and Katie would do the morning feeding. Katie thought the barn was the best place for that discussion.

Katie was up, dressed, and in the barn, loading the feed cart when her mother showed up in the barn the following morning.

"Your dad's pretty tired. He did most of the driving on the last leg of the trip home. I'm letting him sleep in," she told Katie.

"I wanted to talk to you about the Arabian," Katie told her mother.

"Oh, I forgot to mention him and his situation before we left. He ended up here in our barn because my friend that owns the boarding stable didn't know what to do with him. He's not very people friendly, as I told you on the phone. Did you have problems with him?"

"Yes, I did. Only the first day, though. He and I talked it out. He's doing quite well now," Katie told her mother.

"Oh-kay," Shanna said. "Maybe you can explain that "talked it out" part."

"Mom, this is going to sound crazy, but please give me time to explain it all," Katie pleaded.

"I'm listening," Shanna said.

"I think I might have told you already. The first day you were gone, I came out to feed, and when I tossed his flake into his feeder, he tried to take my arm off. I ended up on my butt in the middle of the barn aisle covered in hay. I looked at him and asked him who the heck he was and what the heck he thought he was doing."

"Okay, so what happened?"

"He asked me who the heck I was."

"He did? How do you know that?"

"I heard him."

"What do you mean, you heard him?" Shanna was getting agitated.

"Mom, I heard him as clear as a bell. He asked me who the heck I was. I'm not kidding you. It spooked me. I've talked to horses all my life. I've never had one talk back to me. I looked around to see if someone else was in the barn playing games with me, but I was the only human in here."

"What happened next?"

" He told me the same thing, kind of in a smart-mouth way."

"Okay, then what did you do?"

"I asked him not to bite me so I could finish feeding the horses. He agreed. Then he asked me what happened to you. He called you the pretty woman with the golden aura."

"The golden aura? What does that mean?"

"I asked him the same thing. He told me you are a healer. He also told me he is a medicine horse, so he sees healers, and he told me I am a healer too."

"He told you all that in a conversation?" Shanna asked with some skepticism.

"Yes, Mom. He said all that. I heard it. I knew I shouldn't have told you, that you'd never believe it," Katie turned away to finish the feeding and put the cart away.

Shanna stood in the middle of the barn aisle with her mouth open. She had a look of disbelief on her face. Shanna didn't know what to say or do. Was her daughter going "around the bend" or did she think this really happened? Could it happen? She knew her friend Valerie talked to animals all the time. Valerie was a skilled Animal Communicator. The things she relayed the animals told her were often verified. Valerie had no way of gaining that knowledge except through the animals. Was it possible her daughter developed that same skill?

"Katie, come back here, please," Shanna pleaded. "We need to talk about this a little more. I think I will call my friend Valerie and discuss it with her too."

Katie walked back to Shanna. Shanna enveloped her in a hug, then pulled back, holding her shoulders in her hands, and looked her in the eyes. "We'll figure this out together, okay?"

"Mom, I've already talked to Miss Valerie. I called her. She came over that day. She talked to me first. Then she went to the barn and talked to Kashmir. He confirmed what he said to her. I'm getting used to it, so it doesn't spook me the way it did at first. I've learned a lot about Kashmir from him. He let me work on his wounds. I know that stung. If I hadn't been able to talk to him first, I don't think he would let me treat them. You can't see where they were now. He's gaining weight. I've been riding him every day. His condition is coming along too. He doesn't look like the same horse that tried to bite me. Take a look."

Shanna and Katie walked to the front of Kashmir's stall. He had his head in the feeder, eating his grain. He pulled his head back, stepped back, and looked expectantly at the mother/daughter duo in front of him. Shanna opened the stall door and stepped inside.

Katie followed her in. Shanna walked around both sides of Kashmir looking him over from top to bottom, from head to tail.

"Wow! You've done a job with him! He's looking so much better. He's a handsome horse. I had no idea this much gorgeous was hiding under all that dead hair and all those scrapes and cuts. He's a bit taller than I remember. His weight is almost perfect. His chest filled out nicely, and so did those hips of his. He's short backed, but that is typical for Arabians. From what I see in front of me, I'd say he's a nice representative of his breed." Shanna reached out and stroked his silky neck. It felt nice to him, so Kashmir leaned into her hand.

That surprised Shanna. She kept it up and let her hand trail down to his withers so she could scratch those itchy places horses can't scratch themselves. Kashmir enjoyed it so much he stretched his neck out further and adjusted his position to get her fingers on just the right spots. He let out a long, low sigh. Shanna continued running her hands over his body, feeling his muscle tone and how much coverage he had over his ribs now. His coat felt silky. This was not the horse she'd left in the barn a few weeks ago. He was a completely different animal.

Shanna gave him one last look over and walked out of the stall, closing the door behind Katie when she joined her in the barn aisle. "You've done a great job with that horse. I think we should be able to find him a new home easily and very soon."

"What do you mean, a new home?" Katie burst out.

"Well, now that you have him going under saddle well and you've cleaned him up, I don't see why we couldn't find him a new home very soon. I never intended to keep him. All I planned to do with him was clean him up, get him going, then find him a perfect home," Shanna explained. "We don't use Arabians. We use Quarter Horses, Paints, and sometimes Appaloosas. They are bigger horses designed for the kind of work we do with them."

"Mom! No! You can't sell Kashmir. He's my friend. Please, please let me keep him. I don't have a horse now, so can I please keep Kashmir?"

"I thought you wanted to get back into competition, and you want to continue with the Rodeo Queen process? You can't do that with an Arabian." Shanna said. She was taken aback by the very idea. Her daughter competing on the Rodeo Circuit with an Arabian? She couldn't imagine that.

Katie walked to the blackboard on the front of the tack room, picked up a piece of chalk, and wrote in large characters a two-digit number followed by a decimal point and four additional numbers. She underlined it twice. "That's the clocking speed for his second ever barrel run. You can verify that with Karen, Maryann, and Brody. They were all there to see it. Kashmir and I are going to kick some butt!" Katie walked back to the house.

Shanna walked to the end of the barn and stared at the number her daughter wrote on the blackboard. She was shocked. She couldn't believe it. That score would put the two in first place at most events where her barrel horses competed. That put a new wrinkle in things. She thought about it as she finished up in the barn and walked back to the house.

Katie was in the kitchen, making breakfast. The bacon was sizzling in the pan as she broke eggs in a bowl. She looked up when her mother entered the kitchen. "What did you think?" she asked.

"If that number is correct, that's amazing," Shanna told her. "Are you sure he tripped the start on that run?"

"Yes, Mom, I'm sure."

"How did it feel to you?"

"It felt amazing!"

"Can you explain your statement that it was his second barrel run ever?"

"Sure," Katie smiled at her mother. "He told me he watched you working with horses for the time between you bringing him here and the night you and dad left. He watched and learned. The day I got to know him, I saddled him up and asked if he'd like to take a ride with me. He said yes, so I got him ready. When we got outside the barn, he asked to make a barrel run, and he told me about watching you and your training horses. He also told me his original owner kept him cooped up in his stall for 14 years. He wanted to run. He wanted to have some fun. So I let him try it. I didn't set the timer because I wasn't expecting much but having to set the barrels back up when he finished. I was not expecting the speed or agility he has. It was amazing. He wanted to do it again after he caught his breath. I told him I needed to get him in shape first."

"How was that first run?" Shanna asked Katie.

"Mom, you wouldn't believe it. I didn't believe it. His turns were so sharp he rubbed my leg on the barrel, not enough to push it over, and his speed at the end blew my mind. I knew it was a great time. I am sorry I didn't set the timer for it. He had the technique down. He is as agile as a snake going around each barrel. His finish speed was even better. I told him we needed to get him in shape before trying it again, so we don't break him down and get him hurt. He was okay with that, so we've been riding once or twice a day since."

"When did you do the run you showed me that time for?"

"Yesterday. Karen, Maryann, and Brody were here for a trail ride, and they wanted to try it again for fun. He was anxious to try too, so I let him have one pass at it. That number I wrote in the barn was his time yesterday." Katie seasoned the eggs and grated some cheese to add to them and poured them in a skillet to cook.

"I didn't teach him the pattern. He learned it watching you. He's only done it twice. That's why I've been riding him every day. I want to get him in good physical condition so we can practice the way I've always done with my horses. I can't wait to see what he'll do after practicing the runs, can you?" Katie carefully stirred the eggs in the skillet, turning them over, so the runny parts filled the bottom of the pan.

"Well, what do you have in mind for him?"

"Mom, you and Dad sold my horse. That was my fault, and I accept that. I don't have a horse to compete with now, so I'd like to keep him and do it with Kashmir. Please."

Clint walked into the kitchen, rubbing his eyes. "Man, all that driving takes the starch right out of me. I smell coffee. I need a cup."

Shanna poured a cup of coffee and handed it to her husband. He sat down at the kitchen table. "What have you two been up to this morning. Something smells wonderful!"

"Katie is fixing breakfast today," Shanna said. "I agree with you. It smells wonderful. Katie, where did you learn to cook like this?"

"Maryann taught me. She learned from her Aunt. I got spoiled the first couple of days; then I asked her to show me how to fix it. I have a few surprises for you coming up. Her breakfasts were great."

Katie brought a plate each of crisp bacon, buttered toast, and scrambled eggs to the table and set them down in front of her parents. "Dig in," she said as she rounded the table to her chair.

The conversation at the table lagged for a few minutes as the three dug into their breakfasts. "Wow, Katie, this is delicious. You should take more lessons from Maryann," Shanna said. "I've never eaten scrambled eggs done this way."

"Wait until you try the French Toast recipe she taught me," Katie said after swallowing a sip of orange juice. "I'd love to have dinner over there and watch her Aunt in the kitchen. I could learn a few things from her."

"This hits the spot," Clint said. "By the way, besides fixing up this delicious breakfast, what have you ladies been up to this morning. Sorry I slept in so late."

"Katie wants to keep Kashmir," Shanna said between bites.

"Who is Kashmir?" Clint asked.

"He's the one I picked up from the boarding stable that nobody wanted," Shanna told him.

"Didn't you also tell me he is an Arabian?" Clint asked.

"Uh, yes, and not a people-friendly one at that," Shanna told him.

"Why in the heck would you want an unfriendly Arabian horse, young lady?" Clint asked Katie.

"Dad, he's not unfriendly anymore, for one thing, and he's fast as greased lightning, for another. I want to get back to my dream. I want the Young Queen crown next year, and I want the Queen's crown the next year. I want to go to college, and I want the Miss Rodeo California crown then. I think Kashmir will get me there."

"Katie, honey, he's an Arabian. Arabians don't do Rodeo events. Do you know what kind of flack you are going up against if you try that?" Clint asked her.

"Dad, I've checked. There is no rule against riding an Arabian in Rodeo events. None. I went on the website, I've made a few phone calls, I've done the research. Nothing says I can't ride an Arabian in barrels, pole bending, or goat roping. Nothing! I do have some idea what I'm going up against. The prejudice against Arabians was obvious when I took him to the grounds with Karen and Samantha to compete last weekend. I heard the whispers. I saw the stares of disbelief. I saw those angry looks. I don't care. I think sometimes you just have to show people. If he's as good as I know he is, we'll be bringing home all the cash when we compete, and those fools who looked down their noses at him will be very sorry they did that."

"Katie, I can see you have your mind made up, but I am not sure. I don't want to get in any fights with my brother competitors over my daughter riding an Arabian horse. It doesn't feel right to me."

"Dad, give me one competition before you make up your mind. If we get skunked and have to come home dragging our tails, I will give up on the idea. I promise. I am confident that won't be the case, but I will make you that promise and never bring it up again." Katie smiled at him.

"Katie, I'm so glad to see you back, I'll agree to that. I was worried about you when we left for Oklahoma. You were not yourself. Now you are the same cheerful, confident daughter you were before your little accident. I know you will get some grief over this decision, but I'll give you that competition. I'll be standing there rooting you on too. I love you, honey. I want the best for you. And now, I find out you are a chef in the kitchen. What could be better?"

Katie jumped up from her seat, ran around the table, and threw her arms around her dad's neck. "I love you, Daddy. You won't regret it. I won't let you down. I promise you."

Clint hugged his daughter back and kissed the top of her head. "I know you won't. I will always be proud of you."

Katie began clearing up the dishes when her mother stopped her. "You did the cooking, so let me do the cleanup, okay? Don't you have some riding to do?"

Katie grinned at her mother and dashed to the barn.

CHAPTER TWENTY-SEVEN

Katie dashed straight to Kashmir's stall. "I have some great news!" she told him. "My mother never intended to keep you because you are an Arabian. I talked her into letting me have you as my horse. I'm so happy; I could almost burst."

"Please don't do that," Kashmir told her. *"You would make a complete mess out of my stall, and you wouldn't be around to clean it up."*

"Oh, you silly horse. I didn't mean that literally." She chuffed at him.

"I know. Other horses tell me my sense of humor is a little dry. I heard part of your conversation earlier with your mom. I was afraid she was going to send me away. I'm relieved to hear I get to stay with you. Why don't we go for a ride?"

Katie pulled Kashmir out of his stall and cross-tied him in the barn aisle while she pulled out the tack she needed for a ride. She brushed his coat, fly-sprayed his legs, shoulders, and hips, wrapped his front legs, and tacked him up. Katie walked Kashmir out of the barn, mounted him, and walked down the driveway. "Which way do you want to go today?" she asked him.

Kashmir struck out in an easy trot to the South. He knew the routes around the ranch, so he picked one he enjoyed. They crossed several roads and made their way to the highway under crossing and headed uphill toward the mountains. Once they turned out of the riverbed, the footing was better, although rockier. The riverbed was composed of soft, silty sand. Kashmir's feet tended to sink into that, so it was more challenging to traverse. They rode for several miles without seeing another human being or habitation. In that time, they climbed several hills and dropped into canyons between them. The exercise brought a light coating of sweat to Kashmir's neck and shoulders. His body was healthier than it had ever been. He was enjoying the morning workout and hesitant to turn back.

Katie knew she needed to work Samantha that morning, so she reluctantly turned Kashmir toward home. They took it easy on the ride back to the ranch, walking part of the way and trotting part of the way. The sweat dried on Kashmir before they reached the barn. Katie untacked him and walked him to the washrack for a good rinse and coat conditioning before she put him back in his stall with a half flake of alfalfa to nibble on. Before she walked out of the stall, she grabbed his face and held it in both hands while she stared into his eyes. "I'm starting to love you, you know. I've always loved my horses, but you are special. Thank you for being my friend."

He looked back into her soft eyes. He had an emotional moment of his own. *"I've never loved anyone or anything since I was a baby who loved his mama. I don't know what I would do without you now. I promise you I will never disappoint you. I love you too."* A tear formed in his left eye while a tear formed in her right one. His heart light shined brightly through his chest, as did hers. Katie threw her arms around his neck and hugged him, holding on for a minute or two. Then duty called her. She scratched his withers and backed out of the stall, latching the gate and walked down the aisle to Samantha's stall to prepare her for a workout.

Katie was putting Samantha through her paces when her mother came out to the barn. "Hey, are you doing my work for me now?" Shanna asked her.

"Didn't I tell you I was working your horses for you while you were gone? If not, I'm sorry. I've been doing this for three weeks now. Karen is the Young Queen this year. She took my crown when I couldn't compete for it. She was a little reluctant, but she and I worked together with me coaching her right after you left. We had a great time. I went to the competition as her coach, and she came home with money. She asked me if I wouldn't mind being her coach this year. She wants to be the best Young Queen she can and asked for my help. I didn't think you'd mind."

"Poaching my clients, are you?" Shanna laughed. "Do you want to be a trainer after college? If that's what you want, there's no time like the present to start. I did when I was younger. I coached some of the younger girls. That's when I decided to go into training full-time, so I could be home with you. It all worked out. No, I don't mind in the least. Let me know if I can help you."

"Will you watch our runs and give me your opinion?" Katie asked.

"Of course!" Shanna said. "What are moms for, if not good advice?"

"Thanks, Mom," Katie shouted as she cued Samantha into her next run at the barrel pattern.

Shanna watched with a critical eye as Katie and Samantha ran the pattern without knocking over a single barrel. They flew through the timer and stopped the clock with an excellent time.

"That was a great run. On the next one, you might pull your left leg slightly back as you round the barrel. It will give you a bit more clearance and maybe another thousandth of a second off your time. If that helps, you could shave three thousandths off your total, and that could win more money. You can ask Karen to try that too and see how it helps her time."

"Thanks, Mom. Let me give her a second to catch her breath, and we'll run that again. I really appreciate your help."

"One more little thing," Shanna told Katie, "Sammy knows when she's gone around the last barrel. She knows her way home from there. Throw the reins away! Give her head. Let her go! If you try to guide her with the reins, it will cost you one or two-thousandths of a second. That could be the difference between money or no money. Get off her back, lean forward, and let her race for the finish line."

"Mom, did anyone ever tell you what a wonderful coach you are?" Katie grinned down at her.

"Oh, I may have heard that once or twice," Shanna grinned back. "Trouble is, I've been doing this so long, I sometimes forget I had a coach myself once upon a time. I hope I showed her as much appreciation as you show me."

"Who was your coach, Mom?" Katie asked.

"Unfortunately, you never met her. She was the Number One Barrel Racer in the country when I first met her. She saw something in me, what I don't know, but she decided to coach me. She was funny, demanding, endearing, and pushy all at the same time. She would drive me crazy with tiny little things, but my times improved after every session. We went over and over the same stuff until she knew I had it locked. She was a little disappointed when I dropped out of the Miss USA Rodeo Queen competition. She wanted credit for helping the queen get her crown, but she understood our feelings and wished us well. I was sad to hear she died just before your first birthday. I still miss her and wish you had a chance to meet her. Her name was Barbara. She was a skinny little thing. She spent so much time on horseback; her skin looked like tanned leather. Her brown hair bleached by the sun, not a bottle. She wore faded jeans, worn boots, and plaid shirts. Her hat was crumpled, dusty, and stained with sweat. She didn't look like much until you watched her ride. She was poetry in motion! She was the most elegant rider I've ever seen, or will ever see again. I miss her terribly. I wish she were here to coach my daughter."

"Mom, what was special in how she coached you?" Katie asked.

"Her attitude, I guess," Shanna said. "She seemed to know when a rider had more to give and pressed them to give it even when they wanted to stop trying. Her favorite saying was 'Never Give Up!' I used to have that printed on a card taped to the bathroom mirror, so I saw it every day as I washed my face and brushed my teeth. Maybe we should do that for you."

"Now that I have my head on straight, that's not a bad idea," Katie giggled. "I gave up once. I didn't feel good about that. I don't want to do that again."

"I'm so glad to hear that," Shanna said. "I want to be the mother of the next Miss California Rodeo Queen and maybe more."

CHAPTER TWENTY-EIGHT

Katie continued working Samantha and riding Kashmir in the mornings. She coached Karen and Samantha in the afternoons until school let out for the year. Karen asked Katie lots of questions about her duties as the Young Rodeo Queen. Katie answered them as best she could. Karen finally asked her about a situation that went on during school. "You know Ann, and you also know Ann was dating Bill, the football captain, didn't you?"

"Ann was on the Cheer Squad and went to all the football games. Who would she go for except one of the players?"

"You're right about that," Karen admitted. "But she set her cap for the Captain of the team and flirted with no one else but him for months until he finally noticed her. Just before school let out, they broke up. You should have heard the other girls talking about her then. A couple of them tried to drag me into the conversation. Fortunately, I was able to walk away and get out of that situation, but some are relentless. They keep bringing it up. How would you handle that?"

"I'll tell you what my mother told me. If you were a real Queen, everyone else would be subjects of yours. They would look up to you. They would look to you for advice. A Queen must lead, not follow.

You don't want to wallow in the gutter with pigs when you are the Queen. Ann and Bill's problem, whatever it is, is between them. It may be temporary. They could get back together next week. The last thing you should do is offer advice, unless he or she asks you, or give your opinion about a personal situation. You shouldn't get involved in gossip about them or anyone else. Be the Leader."

"I think I figured that out, but I needed to talk to you about it to be sure. Thanks. The other person I'd like your help with is Brittany Wills. Do you remember her? The girls pick on her constantly. It makes me sad. Poor Brittany isn't a beautiful girl, and she doesn't dress as nice as some of the girls, but she doesn't deserve them picking on her all the time. What would you do?"

"I talked to Brittany. Her father is disabled and unemployed. Her mother works at the Skillet in town as a waitress. She is the only wage-earner in the family. They have three kids. Brittany is the oldest one. Brittany looks after her brother and sister, helps them with their homework, does the cooking, most of the laundry, and most of the housework. She has a burden right there. She also helps take care of her dad. But, Brittany is brilliant in Geometry, Math, and World History classes. I've gone to her for help myself. The next time you hear one of them bad talking her in the hallway, ask them how they are doing in Math. Point them to Brittany for help because she always gives it. You can make a point that Brittany has math skills and history skills besides her straight-A report cards, and she's always willing to help a fellow student. That usually shuts them up," Katie giggled. "You don't have to be mean about it. Sometimes you need to talk to others and see what their burdens are before making judgments. You can also tell the bad-talkers that."

"How did you get so smart, Katie?" Karen asked after thinking about what she said.

"My mother is a genius," Katie laughed. "She should have been Miss USA Rodeo Queen. She was perfect for that job. She's taught me a lot."

"I like her as a coach too, but I have more fun with you," Karen told her. "When are you going to get a new horse so you can get out and compete again?"

"You know Mom coached Miss California, Miss Utah, Miss New Mexico, Miss Arizona, Miss Oregon, and Miss Idaho over the years, didn't you? One of them, I can't remember which, was crowned Miss USA Rodeo Queen. Mom wants to be the mother of Miss USA Rodeo Queen someday. I already have my horse. We're going to start practicing this week so we can compete against you and Sammy at the Leona Valley Rodeo in three weeks."

"When did you get a horse?" Karen asked, puzzled.

"He's been here all along," Katie told her.

"I knew your parents sold the buckskin because I know the girl who got him. That is such a nice horse. I wish she would get serious about competing with him. She's just doodling along when she feels like it. She's not doing well with him at all. So, which one is your horse?"

"Kashmir," Katie said.

"Kashmir?" Karen repeated with a wide-eyed look of astonishment on her face. "Are you talking about the bay Arabian?"

"That's the one," Katie answered with a smile.

"Katie, are you sure you know what you're doing?" Karen asked. "He's an Arabian. They don't do Arabians in Rodeo, at least, not that I've ever seen."

"Karen, I checked the rule book. There's no rule against using an Arabian horse in Rodeo. It seems to be a tradition. They use the bigger Quarter Horses, Paint Horses, and Appaloosas that they used in ranching 100 years ago. I know I'm going to buck a tide of judgment over it, but I want you to look at the numbers on the blackboard in the barn. Look for the numbers underlined twice. That was his time in his second-ever barrel run. I'm starting him in practice this week so that we can compete in the Leona Valley Rodeo. My dad is against it too. I told him if we don't do well, I'll never bring it up again, but I know we're going to shock some people. I'd love to get the last run for the day. I'm going to get heat from the other girls, so I'd like to take our turn last and beat their pants off. Please keep that to yourself for right now. I'll let you know how he's doing in practice as we go. Wouldn't it be nice if we can finish first and second together? Sammy is doing well. Maybe we'll make some money in Leona Valley."

Katie began working with Kashmir on the barrel runs the next morning after a short two-mile trot. Kashmir surprised Shanna with his speed and agility. She gave Katie a few pointers to help her speed, and neither of them had to set a single barrel upright that morning.

Over a glass of wine after dinner, Shanna told Clint, "I've never seen a horse enjoy his work like that one does. He gives 100% on everything she asks of him. His times are winning times right now, and they are only going to get better. It is just different to see a barrel horse with his tail in the air on the run for home. As a matter of fact, he's got his tail in the air for the entire cloverleaf pattern. I wonder if that long neck of his will give him an advantage in stopping the clock. The funny thing is, if a horse could smile, he does when he's working with Katie."

"Do you think the horse is going to hold up to the strain?" Clint asked her.

"No doubt," Shanna answered. "He's fit, healthy, and getting better with each pass. Now she wants to teach him pole bending as well. If he's as agile with that as he is with barrels, he's going to blow some minds. Clint, that horse has his front feet on one side of the barrel, his hind feet on the other side, and he bends in the middle. I've never seen anything like it."

Katie began writing Kashmir's best time down on the blackboard in the barn every day. Karen caught on and did the same thing with different colored chalk. It was almost as if they were competing without competing. They compared notes after Samantha's workout and discussed ways to improve her times each day. Sammy was getting closer to Kashmir's times, but Kashmir was improving his daily. The spirit of competition had both girls fired up for the Leona Valley Rodeo.

Shanna set up six 6-foot-tall poles in a straight line, 21 feet apart. Clint made them for her out of PVC pipe set in cement in a one-gallon can with a flange at the bottom to stabilize them. He painted the top foot of each pole red to increase their visibility. When she had everything set up with a start line 21 feet from the first pole, Katie brought Kashmir over to walk the pattern the first time. He crossed the start line and passed the first pole on his right. Katie turned him between pole one and two, so he could pass pole two on his left side. He passed pole two and turned between pole two and three and passed pole three on his right. He continued the twisting pattern through the poles until he passed the sixth pole. He completed a circle around the sixth pole. He began making the serpentine pattern back the other direction until he passed the first pole and sped to the start line to trip his timer.

Katie walked him twice more through the pattern before she asked him to speed it up a bit. After the first walk-through, Kashmir understood what she wanted him to do, so their walk was quick and efficient. When Katie asked him to speed up, he bolted through the pattern as if he'd been doing it all his life. Shanna was astonished at the time on the clock. Kashmir stuck close to the poles but left just enough room that he didn't knock a single one over.

Katie went back to the start line and asked Kashmir to do it again. His time was faster the second time, and he still left all the poles standing. Katie gave him a couple of minutes rest and asked for the third run. Kashmir went all in that time and dashed through the entire pattern at speed, tripping the clock at the best time of the day, leaving all the poles right where they were at the start of the day. When they crossed the start line, Katie looked at the clock and yelled, "That's how you do it!" Shanna was clapping her hands for them. Katie jumped off her horse and hugged him around the neck as she jumped up and down. "Mom, we're going to kill it in Leona Valley!"

146

CHAPTER TWENTY-NINE

atie had Karen walk Samantha through the poles the next day when she came over to work her horse. Karen led Samantha the first time and rode her at a walk the second and third time. Sammy seemed like she had the idea when Karen asked her for more speed. Sammy did well but knocked over the third pole when she cut the corner a bit too close. Katie set the pole back up and had Karen do it again several more times. Samantha got better with each turn. They recorded her best time that day in colored chalk on the blackboard before they went out for a few runs around the barrels.

A week later, after their workouts, Karen and Katie met at the chalkboard to record their scores again. "I see what you mean about Kashmir," Karen told Katie as they printed the numbers on the board at the end of the day. "I can't beat him in either event, but I'm getting close. This little competition we are having is helping me do better and better. I like it. The other girls are not going to believe it. I know Kashmir now. I like him. I see what you see in him too. He's adorable, and he gives you everything every time you ask him. The others will give you no end of grief for bringing him to Leona Valley. They will be shocked! Don't you worry. I'll hang with you."

"Thanks, Karen. I was afraid I would be on my own out there. I know I'm going to take some heat so it will be nice to have one friendly face on the grounds. I'll be there cheering you and Sammy on too, you know."

"This little competition between Sammy and Kashmir is helping us both. I think Sammy wants to win almost as bad as I do, so she's pushing hard. It's making us better competitors. I'm sure you are going to beat us anyway. I will not feel bad about that. I'm happy for you. Sammy and I are so much better than we were before.

"Karen, this is a competition on horseback. Anything can happen and usually does. Don't count yourself out just yet. I hope you beat the pants off the other girls. Show them what good competition is!" Katie laughed. "Haven't you been to events where you forgot some important piece of equipment and had to scratch a run? If it hasn't happened to you, you've probably seen it happen to someone else. I know I'm going to triple check my stuff because no one there would dare loan me something. I've seen horses get hurt in one event and not compete in others. It happens all the time. Let's hope it doesn't happen to us."

The time flew by. Karen and Samantha practiced every day. Katie also helped her practice her run around the arena with the flag so she would make the best impression at the Opening Ceremony. The two girls helped each other, made fun of each other, and enjoyed the build-up to the competition. They decided to do the packing for the trip on Friday and give their horses that day off. "Let's take our trailer," Katie offered. "We have that four-horse with a huge tack room. We can get everything in there for the Young Queen and a regular competitor. You have a lot more stuff to bring that I do this time," she laughed.

Karen's mother drove her to the ranch that afternoon with the trunk and back seat of the car filled with gear. The two girls unloaded it and set it in the barn while they piled up Katie's things as well, sorted everything out, and began to pack the trailer. All the leather gleamed from saddle soap and neatsfoot oil. Karen brought the saddle she won as the Young Queen in addition to her working saddle for the competitive events. Katie only had one saddle to haul to the trailer. Karen had her Young Queen outfit in zipped clothing bags to keep the dust off her white shirt and the white fringed chaps with red roses appliquéd up the sides. "Do you think you have enough sparkle on that?" Katie giggled, looking at the Swarovski crystals on the chaps, yokes, collar, and sleeves of the shirt.

"Oh, no. I also got these to go with the outfit," Karen said as she opened a small jewelry box to show off sparkling earrings and choker style necklace. "I also had crystals put on the white gloves for the Opening Ceremony," she said.

"I love those!" Katie said. "I'm going to get you to tell me where you got them if I get the crown next year. Those will light up the place with bling."

"Don't think I'm silly, but I also had crystals put on Sammy's special saddle pad for the Opening Ceremony. I thought she should have more bling than just the browband on her bridle. If I'd had my way, I'd get reins with them too. My mom thought I was crazy. I don't think a girl can have too much bling," Karen laughed.

"I'm with you!" Katie said. "Bring on the bling!"

The two struggled to get everything in the tack room before dark. It was a large tack room, but with boot bags, hat boxes, clothes bags, saddle pad bags, three saddles, bridles, and all the other equipment they would need for two horses, it filled up quickly. They filled the water tank, added buckets for feed and water, then piled the hay for the horses in last.

"What time do you plan to haul out tomorrow?" Karen asked.

"I think we should plan to leave at 5:00 a.m. The Opening Ceremony begins at 8:00 a.m. The events begin at 8:30 a.m. and probably don't end until close to 9:00 p.m. with the Closing Ceremony. It depends on how many competitors show up," Katie said. "I've been to the Leona Valley Rodeo lots of times. It begins early and ends late every time. We'll all be dog-tired by the time we get home. If you'd like to stay overnight here with me when we get back, that would be okay. We could get an early start on unpacking the trailer. Check with your mom on that. My mom won't have a problem."

"Are Brody and Maryann going to come and watch?" Karen asked.

"They wouldn't miss it. They are so excited I'm taking Kashmir. I hope he does well. I have something to prove, and I need to convince my dad and mom too. Having a couple of other "friendly" faces there will help," Katie admitted. She was beginning to get knots in her stomach about the whole thing.

Karen's mom came to pick her up, leaving Katie in the barn by herself. She walked down to Kashmir's stall and opened the door. "Do you want some company?" she asked him.

Kashmir nodded his head. Katie entered the stall and closed the door behind her. "You and I are going into our first competition tomorrow. I hope you are comfortable with that," she told him.

"Are they going to turn the bulls loose on us?" he asked her.

"I would never let them do that!" Katie told him. "How do you feel about this?"

"I don't know. I've seen horses coming home from competitions most of my life, but I've never competed in one. What's it like?"

"There's lots of excitement, for one thing. The competition is all the stuff we practice here at home, but there is a crowd of people watching. They make noises when they like what they see, and they make awful noises when they see something they don't like. Other than that, it's about the same as what we do here. You went with me when Karen competed the last time. Don't you remember? You were standing right next to me while we watched her run. You and I are going to show them how it's done with barrel racing and pole bending. You do those things well here at home. I think you and I will do them better there. If we do, I will bring home prizes and ribbons that I can hang on your stall so everyone who walks in here can see how talented you are."

"I've heard the comments about Arabian horses being not right in Rodeo events. Is that true? Am I going to stick out like a sore hoof? Will people make fun of me?"

"Kashmir, there may be some comments before we get our turn in the arena. I don't care what breed you are, you are my best friend,

150

and you are talented. We are going to show some people that Arabian horses have as much talent as the horses they usually see at these events. I'm sticking with you. I wouldn't care if you were a Zebra or a Mule. You and I are going to be the team to beat."

"Katie, I love you and will do my best with you, you know that. I've seen a lot of different breeds. I've seen Quarter horses, Paints, Warmbloods, Friesians, Percherons, and mixed breed horses. But I don't think I've ever seen a Zebra horse or a Mule horse. Can you describe them to me so I will know one when I see it?"

Katie laughed. "Zebras are technically equines like you are, but they were born in a different part of the world. They live in Africa. Africa is clear around the world from us. They are similar to a horse, but they're stripped from nose to tail. I learned in school that every Zebra's stripes are different, but they are all black and white. I'm not sure if they are white with black stripes or black with white stripes. I've only seen them on TV and at the Zoo. A Zoo is a place where different animals from around the world are displayed so people can learn about them. Mules are the product of cross-breeding a donkey with a horse. They have some horse parts and some donkey parts. Donkeys are usually smaller than a horse like you but similar. They have different hooves than you do. Their hooves are smaller. They don't have much mane. They also have long ears. Wild donkeys are mostly grey-brown with a black stripe down their backs and one black stripe across their shoulders. Their tails are short-haired except for the tip like a cow, and they don't neigh or nicker, they bray. You would have to hear one. If you did, you would remember it."

"So, what does a mule look like?"

"Oh, yes. Mules look a lot like horses except they sometimes have feet more like donkeys, they bray, and they have long, long ears. You wouldn't forget if you ever saw one."

"What would be the purpose of long ears?" Kashmir asked.

"If you can hear for five miles, a mule can hear for fifty miles, I guess," she laughed. "I don't really know. Mules are nice. I've been around a few. They are more like a horse than donkeys. I've heard donkeys can be obstinate. I've never been around one, so I can't say for sure on that either. Some people are put off by their long ears and their braying. They can be noisy."

"I hope I'm not going to be compared with a Zebra or a donkey tomorrow. I'm a proud Arabian. Do you think that will make a difference?"

Katie hugged Kashmir around his neck. She whispered, "I don't think what you are is going to matter after we show them what you can do. We'll show your breed in the best way. I'm proud of you."

Kashmir pressed Katie's body close to his chest with his neck and held her there for a few minutes. *"You are special to me too. Thank you for teaching me. I'll do my best tomorrow. Thank you for being my friend."*

CHAPTER THIRTY

First light came 45 minutes after Katie fed the horses in the barn. She wanted Kashmir and Samantha to eat as much as they could of their breakfast before Karen's parents brought her over to ride to Leona Valley with the horses. Karen's mom would drop her off, and the family would follow later.

Stage fright struck Katie the minute she woke up that morning. She was nervous and jittery as she fed the horses and came back into the kitchen to set up the coffee for her parents. She was packed and ready. The trailer was packed and ready. All they needed to do was load two horses and get on their way. The drive to Leona Valley would take about an hour and a half.

All of a sudden, Katie wanted it to be over and done with. She was sick of worrying about what other people were going to say about her riding an Arabian horse. Tears began to flow. She didn't know if she could do this, after all.

Katie rushed out to the barn and unlocked the door to Kashmir's stall. "Can I talk to you?" she asked him.

Kashmir felt her emotions. He looked up from his feeder and saw tears running down her cheeks. *"Please come here,"* he asked her and pulled her into a hug with his neck. *"I see you are leaking water from your eyes. That is usually a sign of something wrong with your eyes, or your emotions. Talk to me. Tell me what's bothering you."*

"Kashmir, I don't know if I can do this. I don't know if I can show my face at the Rodeo without my Quarter horse. I've never done anything this crazy before. I'm afraid of what the others will say about me," she sobbed into his neck as he held her tight to his body.

"Katie, I thought you and I were a team. You are not alone here. I am with you. We, together, can do what one of us cannot do alone. Please dry your eyes and think of us together. We will do it together, or we will not. But we will be together either way. That's what is important to me."

"Kashmir, you have no idea what you've done for me. I was in the depths of a black depression. I thought my life was over. I'm a silly girl, I guess. I missed an important item on my list of things to do. I'd been working on that list since I was four or five years old. That first bump in the road knocked me senseless. Then you came along and tried to rip my arm off. You knocked some sense into me and helped me discover life continues after failure. But I'm afraid of failure again."

"Maybe you just need some perspective. For me, getting breakfast in the morning is a triumph. I've had mornings and evenings where I didn't get fed at all. I can't exactly go forage for my feed in a locked stall. So every morning with feed in the feeder is a happy day. You have many more opportunities than I do. You can spend your day learning new things, spend time with your family, spend time with your horses, you have unlimited possibilities. You should celebrate that, not worry about what some silly girl might say because of the horse you bring to a competition. Their words can not cut your skin. Their thoughts can not bruise you or break your bones. Only you can do that if you let them. Why don't we decide not to let them?"

"Kashmir, how did you get so smart?" Katie asked. "You're right, of course. I'm sitting here worrying about what some girl might say when I know I have the best horse on the planet working with me, loving me, and helping me be the best I can be."

Kashmir took another bite of hay. He chewed it slowly. *"You are a silly girl. We are going to, as you say, kick some butt today, and show the others what an Arabian horse can do. We are going to be the team to beat. You can dry your eyes, stop worrying; we're going to take on all challengers and beat the pants off them. It's time for you to eat your breakfast and get ready to roll."*

Katie wiped her face on Kashmir's neck, hugged him again, and dashed off to the kitchen to get breakfast ready for her parents. She had a new attitude. Victory was within her grasp. She needed to reach out and take it.

Shanna and Clint finished their breakfast while Katie picked at her's. They didn't say anything. They knew Katie was under pressure going to an event with a new horse. Any new horse could bring a problem. They knew Kashmir would be entirely different. Clint worried about his brother ropers making fun of him over his daughter's choice of horse. Shanna hoped Katie's choice wouldn't depress her business either. It took income from both Clint and Shanna to keep the barn afloat. They had plans for the future too. The breakfast table was unusually quiet this day.

Karen's mom dropped her off just as Katie walked back outside the house to start getting the horses ready for the trip. Karen's hair and makeup looked beautiful. She helped Katie wrap polo wraps on Samantha and Kashmir and get them loaded in the horse trailer. She and Katie sat in the back seat during the drive. Karen had her own case of nerves. She hadn't been a participant in the Opening Ceremonies for many Rodeos. She wanted to make no mistakes this time. She would be competing later. She had a part to play in the Closing Ceremonies as well. It was going to be a long day.

The drive to the Fairgrounds in Leona Valley took an hour and a half, hauling the trailer with two horses. Clint stopped the truck long enough at the office area to let Katie and Karen off so they could check-in for their events. He pulled the trailer around to the trailer parking area. He found a good spot with plenty of room for the families who were supporting their daughters and parked. Shanna and Clint pulled both horses out of the trailer and tied them to the side. They set up fresh buckets of water and feed pans for the horses to keep them busy.

Karen and Katie dashed to the trailer parking area as soon as they finished checking in. It was all about getting Karen ready for the Opening Ceremonies at that point. Shanna tacked Samantha up in her fancy saddle pad, saddle, and bridle. Katie helped Karen get into her Young Queen clothes. The chaps gave them a bit of a problem with the long zipper up the inside of Karen's leg. Once Katie got that fixed, she looked Karen over, flipping a collar, adjusting a cuff, adding the earrings and necklace, and setting the hat just right on Karen's head. She brushed Karen's curls in place. Karen used a mirror to apply a coat of lipstick that matched the color of the roses on her costume. She stepped out of the tack room, ready to go. Shanna helped boost her up on Samantha and handed her the American Flag with the pole in the holder attached to her stirrup. Karen rode off to the meeting place at the entrance to the arena. The show was about to begin.

The Queen Coordinator for the Leona Valley Rodeo Association began putting the girls in line for their entrance into the arena. All of them carried the American flag on a pole. She put the Leona Valley Rodeo Queen up first, followed by the Leona Valley Young Queen. The Queen from Karen's area was next, followed by Karen. There was an assortment of Princesses and Little Misses from both regions who followed the older girls. The flags became smaller with the size of the riders. As soon as the Queen Coordinator got everyone in place, she asked for the arena gate to open and cued the National Anthem on the loudspeakers. The stands erupted with cheers as the girls galloped their horses inside. The Queens and their Courts looked beautiful, holding their reins in one hand while they steadied the flag poles with the other. Every one of them had a smile on their pretty faces. Their outfits sparkled, their hair shined in the sunlight, and the gold medallions on their white cowgirl hats gleamed like the coats of their horses. They stayed close to the rails, making two complete passes in the arena before turning out the in-gate as the Anthem finished playing. The games were on, and competition began.

Katie met Karen and Samantha as they left the arena and walked back to the trailer beside them. Karen was a little out of breath from the exertion and the excitement of the moment. Opening Ceremonies did that to most of the girls participating. Shanna and Karen's mom met them at the trailer so they could undo what they'd just finished doing. Shanna and Karen's mom removed all the fancy tack and saddle from Samantha. They brushed her down, retied her to the trailer, and offered her water and carrots. Katie went inside the trailer with Karen to help get her out of the fancy clothes and put them away for later. Karen pulled on a regular pair of jeans, a plaid shirt, and riding boots for the competition. She pulled her hair back into a ponytail to keep it out of her face while she competed. Then they sat and waited for their turn.

Maryann and Brody arrived with Aunt Ginny and Uncle Mike. They found seats in the grandstand and enjoyed the Opening Ceremonies. The next event on the calendar was team roping. Mike and Brody watched it with interest.

"Now, that's something you could do with your horse, Rosie," Uncle Mike said. "Bet she'd be pretty good at it too. She's not afraid of the cows, and she's quick."

"I'd have to practice my roping, though. I'm not sure I could lasso a moving calf the way those guys do."

"You could with a lot of practice," Uncle Mike said. "If it's something you want to do, you can always find time for the practice."

Maryann and Brody were both excited by the next couple of events that came up on the schedule. Maryann left to find Katie and Karen before their Pole Bending event came up. She wandered the parking lot until she saw them sitting behind their trailer and joined them.

Several events came before the pole bending, which was the first event Karen and Katie would compete in. Katie specifically asked to be last in the line-up for the two events she selected. The women in the office had no problem with that, especially after seeing the breed of the horse Katie planned to ride. When the girls left the office, Katie could hear whispering among the office staff. She shrugged. It was already starting. She threw her shoulders back, pulled her chin up, and walked with as much grace as possible until they were out of sight of the office. Karen started to giggle. She heard it too. She poked Katie. "Wait until they see your times! That will change their attitudes!"

The two families set up their camp area beside the horse trailer. Karen's dad brought a pop-up shelter and a stack of folding chairs for their group. His wife fixed sandwiches and snacks packed in a cooler for the day, along with another cooler full of cold drinks. Family members came and went between their camp and the arena as the day progressed. The whispers from the front office spread slowly through the crowd. People began walking through the trailer parking area, looking for their camp out of curiosity. When they spotted the Arabian horse tied to the trailer next to Samantha, the whispers got louder. Several of the young girls who would be competing later in the day saw the horse and make rude comments. Most of the competitors knew Clint, Shanna, or Katie well, having watched them for years at the Rodeos. Katie had been absent for months. Most of them knew Samantha was Karen's horse or had seen her ride the mare during the Opening Ceremonies. That left Katie with the beautiful bay Arabian. It didn't take much to add two and two and come up with a "Holy Cow! She's riding an Arab!"

Everyone in the camp area did their best to ignore the comments. If people waved or spoke to anyone, members of the two families were cordial and happy to see them. But the dark looks and snide remarks got under Katie's skin. She finally got up and took a walk around the grounds by herself. She stood up straight, put her shoulders back, and held her chin up. She wasn't going to be intimidated by anyone.

Shanna caught up with Katie and put her arm around Katie's shoulder. "We knew this would happen. It shouldn't be a surprise. All I can say is I've seen his numbers, and they are all in for a big surprise. Sometimes the way to deal with this is to say nothing but do well. I know you can do it."

"Thanks, Mom. Kashmir and I will do our best. I'm surprised so many of my friends are like that. They didn't do that when I was the Young Queen, Princess, or Little Miss. Nobody cared when I rode a pony. I don't get this. Kashmir is a horse. He has four feet and a tail, just like every other horse on this property."

"My guess is most of them know nothing about Arabian horses. You will get an opportunity to teach them something. Maybe they've never seen an Arabian horse up close. Maybe they have the wrong ideas about what Arabian horses are like. Kashmir is a wonderful horse. You get to show them that. Be patient. Your turn is coming. We need to get you tacked up for the Pole Bending event. Let's get back to the trailer and make sure Kashmir looks his best."

Shanna and Katie walked back to the trailer. Karen and her mom were working with Samantha to get her ready for the event. Maryann jumped in to help Katie and Shanna get Kashmir ready.

Karen rushed over to Katie and extended her pinky finger. "I pinky promise we are going to show those girls up. You and I will whip their tails. They won't be trash-talking you after your run!"

Katie giggled and linked her pinky finger to Karen's. "Pinky swear. We're going to kick some booty here today. Sammy is only a tiny bit slower than Kashmir now. I think we're going to take first and second place!" The two girls and Maryann got busy and finished tacking up their horses. They checked their clothes, pulled on their gloves, and mounted up. They walked to the waiting area outside the arena for their turn. Maryann went back to the stands and sat with Aunt Ginny and Brody to watch. Samantha asked for the second to last position, so her run would be just before Katie and Kashmir made theirs.

The first to run through the poles was a Rodeo Queen from San Diego County. She got a respectable time. Several of the competitors gave her a high-five hand-slap as she passed them coming out of the arena. She stayed on top through two more runs. The Leona Valley Queen bested her time by a little and took over the lead. Twenty-three girls signed up to compete in this event, one at a time. Katie and Karen were the last two on the list. They watched each of the others make their run with interest. The Leona Valley Queen held the top spot.

Finally, it was Karen's turn. She hooked pinky fingers with Katie again before heading into the arena. She and Sammy hit the starting line at full speed and rushed through the series of twisting turns and hit full speed back to the finish line. Katie watched the clock. When Karen's time popped up on the screen, Katie screamed! Karen took the lead away from the Leona Valley Queen. Katie knew Samantha was not as fast as Kashmir. She was close, but Kashmir was always faster. She took a deep breath, slapped Karen's palm with a high-five as they passed each other at the in-gate.

Katie stroked Kashmir's neck. "Now's the time, my friend. We need to do this perfectly, and we need to do this fast. I know you can do it." Kashmir nickered, so she knew he heard her. When the starter gave her the signal, she told Kashmir, "Go, Go, Go!" He hit the start line at top speed and flew between the poles with his tail in the air. He dashed around the final pole and repeated the twisting route back to the start line like a rocket on rails.

The audience in the stands knew they'd seen something extraordinary in that run and collectively held their breath waiting for the official time to post. When the numbers flashed, the gasp left about five seconds of dead quiet on the grounds and in the stands before the cheering erupted. People were stomping their feet on the aluminum grandstand flooring and screaming and yelling so loud, Katie couldn't hear her own heartbeat. Kashmir's official time was better than anything he'd done in practice. He had the best time overall. The announcer interrupted the cheering for a second. "Ladies and Gentlemen! I have an announcement to make. The Pole Bending run you just witnessed broke the official Leona Valley Horseman's Association record for that event. That record was set 35 years ago by a young lady, Terri Hammer, and her horse King Kong, directly off the King Ranch in Texas, USA, set that record. Let's congratulate Katie and Kashmir for a fabulous, record-breaking run!" The crowd in the stands and on the ground around the arena clapped, whistled, cheered, and stomped their feet. The sound was deafening.

Katie and Kashmir won the event, leaving Karen and Samantha in second place. Katie jumped off Kashmir and rushed around to hug his neck while she jumped up and down for joy. "We did it! Kashmir, you were brilliant! We won!" Tears ran down her cheeks, but she ignored them and hugged her horse until her mom and dad came to help her. Katie laughed and cried all the way back to the trailer. She was shaking so badly; Clint took the reins to lead Kashmir. He stroked the horse as they walked. "You are one fast son-of-a-gun," he told Kashmir with a new admiration in his voice.

Shanna still dazed at the numbers that flashed on the screen, said, "His finish time shaved a full a second off the best time I've ever seen in National competition. I can't believe it. I saw it, but I still can't believe it. What did you put in his Wheaties this morning? And his times keep getting better with practice."

When they arrived at the trailer, Karen rushed over to hug Katie. "Didn't you say we were going to take first and second? We did! My time was the best we've ever done, but your time was spectacular! Congratulations! Wait until they see you run the barrel pattern. He's even better at that!" The two girls held each other and jumped up and down for a few seconds. People began swarming the trailer parking area looking for the fabulous bay Arabian horse. Everyone wanted to pet him and talk about him. Suddenly, Kashmir was the star of the day in this small Rodeo World.

The Leona Valley Queen was one of those who stopped by to see him. "Where did you get this amazing horse?" she asked Katie.

"A friend of my mom's gave him to her. Nobody wanted him, and she couldn't afford to keep feeding him. She told Mom he wasn't people-friendly."

"That's quite a story. How is he doing in barrel racing? I see you've entered that too."

"He loves barrel racing more than pole bending. He should do okay today." Katie grinned at her. Katie knew this girl was one of the ones who looked down her nose at Kashmir when they first arrived at the show grounds. She seemed to be taking a different look at him now. It was satisfying. But she knew they would all be watching the barrel races with a new interest. She hoped they could keep up their winning times. She didn't want them to fall on their faces now.

Two events ran before the barrel racing. That gave them an hour and a half to catch their breaths and prepare mentally for the new challenge. Katie and Karen tried to relax under the pop-up with soft drinks but were too excited from the Pole Bending to do that. People kept stopping by to see them, see the horses, especially the Arabian, and talk to them about their winning times. Karen's time was better than most of these people had seen before, so she and Samantha were heroes among the quarter horse people. Samantha was a beautiful mare beside her extreme talent, so she attracted a fair amount of attention anyway. People also showed surprise when Karen told them Katie Barclay was her trainer and coach. Several mothers jotted that information down and collected a business card from Shanna or Clint Barclay. It looked like Samantha's, and Kashmir's performance was going to improve the Barclay Ranch business too.

CHAPTER THIRTY-ONE

Twenty minutes before the start of the barrel racing event, Karen and Katie got ready. They tacked up their horses, had their numbers pinned to the back of their shirts, pushed their hats down on their heads, and wandered over to the show arena to wait.

The two sat on their horses and watched the event in the arena until it finished, and the announcer called the winners. They walked the horses over to the waiting area and sat quietly on their horses while the men set up the barrel pattern in the arena. The starter called the first competitor's number. She rode to the open spot between the in-gates and watched for his signal. At his sign, she charged forward into the arena, tripped the start clock, and began her run. When she rounded the final barrel, the crowd in the stands started cheering for her as she streaked to the start line. The display went dark for a few seconds, while the number was verified and posted. Cheering broke out in the stands again as the second competitor made her way to the open in-gate. This went on through twenty-four girls and horses before Karen's turn at the gate came up. Katie crossed her pinky finger with Karen's before she went to the starting line. "You go show 'em how it's done!" Katie grinned at her.

Karen got ready to rocket into the arena at the starter's signal and proceeded to run a perfect pattern. Rounding the final barrel, Karen urged Sammy on as fast as she could run. Katie watched the clock ticking off time. She knew Karen took over first place with her run. She was excited for her, but she was getting her head and heart ready for the race ahead. Katie crossed her fingers and prayed silently. She prayed for speed and surefootedness on the part of her horse. She prayed for a clean run.

When the starter gave the signal, she urged Kashmir on with "Go, Go, Go!" Katie paid no attention to the numbers climbing on the arena signboard. She heard no sound from the crowd in the stands. Katie ran their race in complete silence. She focused everything on her horse and where they were going.

Katie heard the sound of her breathing and the sound of Kashmir's. She listened to the sound of his hoofbeats in the dirt of the arena and the sound of dirt hitting the empty metal barrels as they rushed past them. She also heard the sound of one heartbeat. Kashmir's heartbeat and hers were synchronized. It was as if one heart beat for both of them.

Kashmir stayed close to the barrels, but not touching, as he rounded each one of the three. When he passed around the last barrel, he put on a burst of speed like he'd never done before. He crossed the finish line almost before she realized it. The waves of sound from the arena crashed in on her ears painfully. She didn't even know she blocked out all sound during the run until that moment. She heard the boots stomping the grandstand flooring and the screaming of the crowd. She stroked Kashmir's neck and turned him around so she could see their numbers on the sign. When the numbers flashed up, she nearly fell off Kashmir. If the arena had been noisy before, it was two or three times noisier now. It was almost more than she could handle.

Shanna and Clint rushed to her. Clint took the reins while Shanna helped Katie dismount. Katie's knees began to buckle, so Shanna held her up and held her close. "I'm so proud of my little girl. I can't tell you how much I love you." Shanna whispered in her ear. Katie began crying again. She cried from pure joy at doing something she loved with an animal she loved and doing it better than anyone else there. She cried because it was over. She cried because she loved Kashmir. She cried because her parents were right there with her. She cried for the victory. She cried because she didn't know what else to do. Then she remembered Kashmir. She hugged his neck and cried wet tears into his mane and the silky hair on his neck. It took her a minute to calm down. The strength came back into her knees. She stood as tall as possible, threw her shoulders back and lifted her chin. If she could do this, she could do anything. She knew it.

Katie heard the announcer call for quiet again. He said, "I have another announcement to make, Ladies and Gentlemen. The last run of the Barrel Races showed the best time of today. But I never dreamed I'd have to do this again. That run broke another Leona Valley Horsemen's Association Record. That record was set 41 years ago by Miss Annie Gordon and her horse Kings Leo, another marvelous horse directly off King Ranch. Please, let's all congratulate Katie and Kashmir on two spectacular runs!"

Katie walked to the center of the in-gate, pulled her hat off her head, and bowed once to acknowledge the people cheering for them. She turned around, put her hat back on, and walked back to the trailer with Kashmir in stunned silence. Clint and Shanna followed behind them. Katie tied Kashmir to the side of the trailer just as Karen and Samantha rushed up. Karen tied Samantha to the trailer, and the girls made sure they had food, water, and some carrots for treats. The girls left their cowgirl hats in the tack room, grabbed a soft drink, and sat in the shade of the pop-up. It didn't take long for swarms of people to stop by to see Kashmir. He had a new moniker, "The Wonder Horse," which was how people referred to him. Everyone wanted to pet him, talk about him, and ask questions about Arabian horses.

Karen didn't know much of anything about Arabian horses. She deferred to Katie. Katie knew a little about Arabians through her friendship with Maryann and Brody. Aunt Ginny, Brody, and Maryann dashed back to the camp area after the announcement on the Barrel Race. Katie deferred questions about Arabian horses to them.

With all the strangers coming up, Katie was relieved to see her two friends and Ginny. Karen also knew them. Brody looked like every other young cowboy at the event. He wore jeans, boots and a shirt tucked in. He wore a well-used cowboy hat on his head. People were astonished when he told them he owned a prize-winning Arabian Cutting horse. He told them she was also a winning Reining horse, and he was working her as a Ranch Riding horse for competition as well. He gave several people who seemed genuinely interested one of Aunt Ginny's business cards and invited them to see for themselves.

It took several hours for things to die down. Peace and quiet settled over the little campsite in the parking lot as they waited for the Closing Ceremonies. Karen still had to perform two last passes around the arena with her American Flag before the event would be closed for the year.

Many of the competitors followed the Rodeo events around Southern California. Katie and Karen planned to compete next month in San Diego County. The following month, there was an event in Santa Barbara County. There was usually one every month through November. Next year opened with a Rodeo in February. Occasionally, some of the Queens and their Courts attended events across state lines in Arizona, Nevada, or Oregon. One of the Queens Katie knew well traveled over 70,000 miles in one year attending Rodeos in the Western United States. Katie would have to win herself a truck and trailer first and be old enough to get a driver's license before that was a possibility. She would also have to earn enough money to pay for all that gas and truck maintenance. She wasn't sure she would be ready for that until maybe as Miss California Rodeo Queen. That was still a few years down the road.

Before everyone walked back to the arena for the Closing Ceremonies, everything but Karen's clothes and fancy tack was put away in the tack room. The pop-up and chairs came down and stowed in Karen's parent's rig along with the coolers and extra things they brought for the day. Katie helped Karen into her costume once again while Karen's mom and Shanna got Samantha ready. Katie put

Kashmir in the trailer with the back door open before the group headed to the arena for Karen's last performance.

Under the arena lights that night, Karen and Samantha sparkled even more than they did that morning. All of the girls in the Queen's Court sparkled. With the flags flying and the National Anthem playing, it brought many in the stands to tears. It certainly brought them to their feet.

The troop headed back to the trailer so Katie could help Karen out of her fancy clothes. They had to go to the dry cleaners for cleaning, so they didn't have to be so careful this time. Everyone was tired and wanted to get home. Last-minute items were picked up and stashed. The trailer door closed, and the trucks headed out on their journey for home. Karen rode with her parents. They decided to go straight home. Shanna and Katie promised to put the horses up that night. Shanna's hired help cleaned and re-bedded the stalls for Kashmir and Samantha. They also left feed in the feeders for them. All Shanna and Katie needed to do was put the horses away and close up the barn for the night. Everything in the trailer could wait until morning.

Once Shanna and Katie got back to the house, Clint had special hot chocolate in mugs waiting for them. They sat at the kitchen table to enjoy them. "I guess I have an apology for you, Little Miss," Clint said to Katie. "Arabian horses can do Rodeo. They can do it very well, indeed. I will never question your judgment on that again. You are welcome to compete with your horse anywhere you want to."

"Thanks, Dad. You just referred to Kashmir as my horse. Mom, does that mean I get to keep him?"

"No question. Kashmir is your horse. He loves you, and you love him. I don't think I've ever seen a horse and person better suited for each other. He's helped bring you back and get you on the path you wanted to travel. I know you must be good for him too. He's a normal horse now instead of a "problem" horse. I'll be happy to feed him for a few more years," she laughed. "Seeing him today was special. I remember the horse I brought home from the boarding stable. He was not the same horse. You two are good for each other."

"Thank you, Mom, and thank you, Dad. I'm so tired, I don't think I can finish this delicious hot cocoa you made. I need to say good-night to my horse and crawl into bed. I'll see you in the morning." Katie yawned as she stood up. She put her cup on the counter by the sink and wandered out the back door to the barn. She opened the door enough to let herself inside. She walked to Kashmir's stall and opened the door. Kashmir looked sleepy too.

"I wanted to give you one more hug and tell you goodnight. My parents decided you are my horse. You get to stay, and I get to keep you. That's the best gift they could give me."

"That is good news. I'm pleased. It is what I prefer, but that generally doesn't make much difference with horses. You can let them know I am pleased to be part of the family too. You look as tired as I am. It was a long, exciting day today. I think we did well. Is that how you think? I did see some people look at me strangely when we got there. They seemed to make up their minds and accept me, though. I could see the difference. Could you see that?"

"Of course! Even my Dad questioned why I wanted to take an Arabian horse to a Rodeo. He told me he would give me one chance. If we fell on our faces, I was to give up on the idea with no second chance and no arguments. We did well. We showed them all how well Arabian horses do Rodeo. My dad was impressed. He's now a believer."

"I'm glad. Your Dad seems nice. I like your Mom too. I did the first time I saw her when she picked me up and brought me here. I'm still curious about her. I don't understand why you and I can communicate as we do, but she's not done it with me. Her aura is stronger than yours. She must have the ability. Maybe it frightens her?"

"I will talk to her privately about that. Maybe I can get Miss Valerie back over here with her and you and see how that goes."

"Not a bad idea. I liked Miss Valerie. She has a golden heart."

"How do you know these things?"

"Because I can see them. I'm guessing it is because I am a Medicine Horse. Maybe she can tell us."

168

"By the way, did you know you set records in the two events we did today?"

"You should explain "record" to me. I have no idea what you are talking about."

"The last team with the best time in Pole Bending at the Leona Valley Rodeo did it 35 years ago. Their record for the best time in that event stood for 35 years until you did a better time today. Congratulations! You also broke the record for the best time ever in Barrel Racing at Leona Valley. The previous record for that event happened 41 years ago. You beat two records today. You are amazing! I love you. Let's keep breaking records together! But let's keep having fun together."

"That sounds good to me. You better get some sleep. We have practice again tomorrow."

Katie hugged Kashmir around his neck and pressed her face into the silky hair under his mane. She breathed deeply, taking in his scent. It was perfume to her. She couldn't get enough of it. Sleep was calling her. She let go, backed out of his stall, and latched the gate. She let herself out of the barn and crept into the darkened house. Her parents were already in their bedroom. She went into her's, pulled off her clothes, pulled on her pj's, and crawled beneath the covers. She was asleep before her head hit the pillow. She slept the satisfied sleep of someone who set out to do something monumental and succeeded beyond her expectations. It was a peaceful, restful sleep.

CHAPTER THIRTY-TWO

Maryann was on the phone with Becky the day after the Rodeo in Leona Valley. The girls talked for two hours about the Rodeo and how much fun it was to be there and see everything. Maryann and Brody spent time in the grandstands watching other events that day. Brody had been to Rodeos before, but it was a first for Maryann. She loved it. It was something new they could do with horses.

Becky was never interested in Rodeo before. She'd seen Rodeo cowboys and the Rodeo clowns during the Swallows Day Parade but never thought Rodeo would interest her. She listened to Maryann and began to get excited about it.

"Why don't you talk your mom into bringing you and Prince Ali up here for a few days. We can ride over to Katie's place and see her Arabian. You'll love it. Brody and I watched her at the last Rodeo. We got to see her record-smashing run in Barrel Racing that day. Wow. You wouldn't have believed it. She let us try the barrel race pattern at her house. Her mom is a famous barrel race trainer and a former Rodeo Queen. Her dad is a Quarter Horse only kind of guy. He does Rodeo too. I think he does team roping. Katie told me he's on the national charts for what he does. He travels to Rodeos all over the country to compete. Between what he wins doing that and what

Katie's mom earns with training, they've bought and built a 20-acre ranch from scratch. I told Katie we should set something up with Brody so he can show her dad an Arabian Cutting horse. We really should get Todd out here with Desperado too. He's a champion in Arabian Reining. That might impress the man. It might make him feel better about his daughter bucking the tide and taking an Arabian horse to Rodeos."

"Let me see what I can cook up," Becky told her. "It all sounds like a lot of fun. It is definitely something we've never done with our horses before."

Maryann sparked a fire. After all the endurance riding they did the previous summer, this summer was boring everyone to death. They needed some excitement. Becky mentioned it to Nathan. She suggested he and Freedom might want to come to see a Rodeo ranch and what goes on there. He agreed it sounded like fun. He and Freedom were in training for the next Tevis Cup race at the end of July/first of August. The organizers hadn't set the date because of the amount of snow that fell in the Sierra Nevada Mountains over the previous winter. Two weekends were under consideration, but the decision was not final.

Parents, Aunts and Uncles, and Grandparents all talked about it, stirred up by the young people. The adults decided it would be fun to get together at Hartley Ranch for a tri-tip barbeque and a sleepover for the kids. They included Karen's and Katie's parents as well as Todd O'Neal's parents in Colorado.

Sharon O'Neal checked the show calendar. Chris had a few days between travel to shows for other clients. Sharon called Aunt Ginny about bringing Todd to California on those dates. It worked for Aunt Ginny and Uncle Mike.

Aunt Ginny called Shanna and told her about the plot the kids were hatching. She and Ginny laughed over it. "Sounds like us as teenagers. If it had a horse involved, we wanted to be involved too." Ginny asked her how her husband would feel about a load of teenagers hanging around. "I think he will find it interesting. Since we have a daughter, our customers and visitors are usually female. Having some boys around might be fun for him."

Aunt Ginny mentioned Nathan McCall planned to come for a few days. She explained how they became connected and about his horse, Freedom. "I rode Maryann's horse, La Duquesa, last year in the Tevis Cup as Nathan's sponsor. We made 94 miles of the 100-mile trip before I accidentally came off Quesa and sprained my ankle. We were riding with one of the Legacy Riders, Gretchen Rodgers. She took over as sponsor for me so Nathan could complete the 100 miles. It was quite an experience and one I'm very proud of. Nathan is a good kid."

"I don't know much about endurance riding and even less about autism," Shanna told her. "But now that my daughter is stuck on Arabians, I'd better catch up," she laughed.

"I heard the boys want to do a demonstration for your husband," Ginny said. "I heard them talking to my husband, Mike, about it. They want to show him Arabian Reining and Cutting."

"Clint was not very convinced about Arabian horses in Rodeo until he watched his daughter on her horse in Leona Valley. Those two smoked the competition. If the boys want to show him some more, I think he will enjoy it."

"I'll give you a call when we finalize the dates for the visits. It looks like I'm going to get the boys here at my ranch. Maryann will have Becky stay with her. The horses will all be here too so the kids can ride all they want."

"Katie is going to love it!" Shanna said. "She's an only child. But she loves sleep-overs and getting together with her friends to ride. This will be good for her. She doesn't have another competition until next month. She is so driven before an event; that's all she thinks about. It will be a welcome break for her to enjoy the company of kids her age for a while. I'm looking forward to it myself! Clint and I will host a barbecue one night. That will be fun."

Plans moved forward. The school closed for the year. Chris and Sharon O'Neal hauled Desperado to California once again and stayed for a few days with Ginny and Mike Hartley. Todd was happy to be back with his friends staying at Aunt Ginny's. Walter and Caroline Howard loaded up Freedom and Prince Ali. They hauled them to the Hartley's High Desert Ranch, bringing Becky and Nathan along to stay for a few days. Nathan's parents followed and brought the extra luggage for the two teenagers.

The minute the dust settled at the ranch, Maryann suggested the young people mount up and ride over to C-BAR-S Ranch and meet Katie and Karen. Since it was still early in the day, they would have time for a trail ride before dinner that night. Aunt Ginny suggested the horses might need a rest after their haul and thought they might want to invite Katie and Karen to ride to her ranch instead. Uncle Mike announced it qualified as a good reason for Barbequed Tri Tips, so the bustle began. Rose Wilcox and her aunt went to the market for last-minute items, ice, and drinks. Grandpa and Grandma Carnegie set up the patio with the help of Chris and Sharon O'Neal, Walter and Caroline Howard, and Megan and Peter McCall. Todd and Nathan took their bags into Brody's room, and the three boys drew straws for who got the folding bed. Becky put her luggage in Rose Wilcox's car for later.

The kitchen was bustling from end to end as the women got together all the fixings for the barbecue. Uncle Mike and Grandpa Carnegie got the barbecue pits lit and ready, then started smoking the tri-tips. Walter and Caroline found the big coolers and loaded them with ice and soft drinks. Celeste Carnegie found the table covers and set up the tables for a large group. Within two hours, things were all done, and the adults sat on the patio, waiting for the tri-tips to finish cooking.

The new people in the group were Katie's and Karen's parents, who drove over while their daughters rode their horses. It was a comfortable group of adults, so Shanna and Clint fit right in. They introduced Barbara and Dan, Karen's parents, to the group. Everyone grabbed a soft drink and sat on the patio, chatting about horses, the beautiful weather in the high desert, what the kids were up to, and such.

The young people didn't stick around once the set-up was completed. They headed for the barn. Karen had never seen Uncle Mike's horses, so Brody took her on a tour. She was surprised to see the young steers. "How do you think Uncle Mike can teach a cutting horse without the cows?" Karen agreed it was a silly question. She and Katie wanted to meet Prince Ali and Freedom, so they headed off to the other side of the ranch. Becky brought Prince Ali out into the barn aisle so the new girls could get a close up look at him.

"He's a stallion?" Karen asked in astonishment. "He's so sweet! I thought stallions were hard to handle."

"Not so much when you look at Arabian stallions. A lot of them are more like Prince Ali. He's been my best friend since the night he was born. He and I grew up together," Becky explained.

"Do you think that's why he's so sweet or is it an Arabian trait in general?" Karen asked.

"It's more a trait with Arabian horses, I think. You have to look at the history of the breed. The horses were brought right into the tents of their owners. They lived there with the owner's wives and children. They couldn't bring a nasty stallion inside. They bred them to be like this for thousands of years. People have mishandled the only ones I've seen that are hard to handle. It's not in their genetic makeup," Becky explained.

"He's the most beautiful horse I've ever seen," Katie said. " Look at those pretty ears, those liquid eyes, and his silvery coat." She reached out and stroked his neck. "He's so soft!"

Prince Ali looked at Katie and nickered softly. For a second, Katie thought she heard something in that nicker, and it sounded like a "*Thank you.*" Her eyes popped open for just a second. She stepped back and looked at the horse. She closed her eyes and tried to connect her mind with his. "Did I just hear you say thank you?" she asked him.

"*Yes. I appreciate your praise.*"

"Oh, my goodness. I can hear you. Are you a Medicine Horse too?"

"I may be, but did you know that not all Medicine Horses want to be Medicine Horses? I think I can connect with you because you have the heart of a Healer. You are a Medicine Woman."

"I'm still trying to figure that out. Thanks for talking with me." Katie said from her mind, then turned around to see Freedom. Nathan brought him into the aisle to show Karen.

Becky pulled Katie and Karen aside to explain Nathan's quirks to them. "Nathan is autistic. When he talks to you, he never looks directly at you. It's just something he feels weird about. He's not stupid at all. He's one of the smartest boys I've met. He has a few quirks. But we like being around him, and I think he is getting better and better about being around young people his age. I like to thank Freedom for that. Freedom is quite a horse."

"Ahh, that's what it is," Katie said. "I thought he was a little different. But he seems nice, and he sure loves his horse."

"We all got together last spring and summer and helped him. Nathan wanted to ride the Tevis Cup Race. Maryann, Brody, Todd, and I helped him. Aunt Ginny coached him. We rode short endurance rides together. We did training rides every day. We did 25-milers and 50-milers to get him ready for the big 100-miler. Aunt Ginny rode La Duquesa in the race. We met one of the Legacy Riders that Aunt Ginny used to ride with when she did endurance riding before Brody came along. Gretchen Rodgers planned to ride with Aunt Ginny and Nathan during the race. Gretchen's horse had an accident two days before the race. We all offered her the use of our horses so she could still compete. She took Prince Ali. He and Freedom finished the Tevis Cup Race together. It was a huge deal!"

"Tell me about the Tevis Cup Race. I don't think I've heard of it," Katie asked Becky.

Becky spent the next ten or fifteen minutes describing the Tevis Cup Race for Katie while she looked more and more astonished. "That's amazing," Katie said. "I've never heard of doing that with a horse. What an accomplishment it would be to complete that ride."

"Nathan plans to tackle it again this year. He's waiting for them to confirm the dates. They had a lot of snow in the High Sierras over the winter. That affects the trail. Sometimes they have to postpone the race a week or a month, depending on trail conditions." Becky explained. "He's riding with Gretchen Rogers again this year. I think she wants to get closer to the front of the pack if they can. Last year they finished with minutes to spare. She's used to coming in somewhere in the top ten finishers. They might not make it this year, but I bet they do better than last year."

"Are you planning to crew for him again this year?" Katie asked.

"Heck, yeah. I wouldn't miss it. Maybe you should join us. We can show you what to do. You will miss sleep in spots and be bored to death in others, but overall, it is very exciting."

"I'd love to try that. I ride an Arabian now. Maybe I should check out the other things people do with Arabian horses."

"You should!" Becky told her. "You have a fast Arabian. Maybe someday you will want to ride Tevis yourself!"

"How do you get ready for Tevis?" Katie asked.

"You ride! And you ride a lot!" Maryann told her as she walked up on the conversation. "We rode the Pacific Coast Trail from here to get the altitude training. We did the 25 and 50-mile rides from here and in Arizona, plus we did the Tevis Educational Rides in the area up north where that ride begins. It was a lot of fun, but a lot of hard work. But it was sure a pretty place to ride your horse."

"I don't think I've ever been to that area. What's it like?" Katie asked.

"There are places where you go downhill on switchback trails for two or three thousand feet to the river, then you switch and go up the same things on the other side of the mountain," Nathan told her. "There are fun places like the Pucker Point where you have a sheer cliff up on one side of the trail and the sheer drop of several thousand feet on the other with only space for one horse on the trail around a point before you head back into the woods. You don't get to the "Black Hole of Calcutta" until it's pitch dark out, and you can't see

176

your hand in front of your face. You can only make it if you listen for other horses on the trail in front of you or behind you."

"That sounds scary!" Katie said. "How did you do that?"

"I had a great coach and Gretchen Rogers along. They got me to the finish line. That was the greatest accomplishment of my life." Nathan admitted. "I want to do it again. I'd like to be a Legacy Rider someday and earn a Thousand Mile Buckle."

CHAPTER THIRTY-THREE

Just before Karen left with her parents for the gathering at Hartley Ranch, she got a phone call. She was surprised to see the caller-ID on her phone. It was from Heather, the Rodeo Queen. She'd never called her before. She was curious when she answered the phone.

"Hi, Heather. What's up?" Karen asked.

"I just wanted to know how you felt about being beaten out by Katie and that Arabian horse of hers," Heather responded. She emphasized the "RAY" in the middle like it was a dirty word.

"What? Kashmir?" Karen was taken aback.

"Yeah. That's the one," Heather said in a sulky tone. "How did you feel getting beaten by one of THOSE horses?"

"I have no idea what you mean. I've been working with Katie and Kashmir for weeks now. Thanks to them, we've gotten better and better," Karen said. "What's the problem anyway? I seem to remember we beat you!"

"You are not supposed to beat the Queen!" Heather snapped.

"Heather, we work seven days a week. I heard you only ride three days a week. What am I supposed to do? Let you beat us? Why? Because you're the Queen? Maybe if you'd work a little harder, we wouldn't beat your times so much," Karen suggested.

"I have other things I have to do because I'm the Queen," snapped Heather. "Don't you smart-mouth me about how much time I spend. You are the Young Queen. You should be supporting me, not some bimbo riding an Arabian horse. Rodeo is for Quarter Horses, Paint Horses, and Appaloosas only, don't you know?"

"Heather, I checked the rule book too. There is nothing that says a competitor cannot ride an Arabian horse. What's your problem with that?"

"Well, we all know there's no place in Rodeo for Arabian horses. So why are you hanging out with Katie like that?" Heather snapped.

"I'm at every event you are. I know how much time it takes. You'd have plenty of time to work as hard as we do if you wanted to," Karen snapped right back. "What is your problem?"

"I don't like it! It's not right! She shouldn't ride an Arabian horse and try to represent Rodeo! That's just wrong on so many levels!" Heather spat out.

Karen took a minute to gather her thoughts. That left Heather sputtering in the background. "Heather, I think you have it all wrong. Arabian horses were part of the foundation for the breeds you mentioned. They are part of the foundation of every light breed of horses. I don't know what you have against them, but maybe you should get to know them before you mouth off like that. I did, and I was impressed. They are really sweet horses."

"No, you don't!" Heather raged. "You are not going to push that garbage down my throat. I know better. Rodeo is for Quarter horses only. The Arabians need to get the heck out. They don't belong. If you are sticking up for her, I can have your crown."

Karen was shocked at the anger Heather showed. Then she got mad about what Heather said. "You go right ahead and try!" Karen shouted into the phone. "You go ahead. As Queen, you are supposed to support the rest of the court. If you try to take my crown because of who I am friends with, I will make such a stink; you won't be able to come within 50 miles of it!"

Karen heard the click as Heather hung up the phone. Karen was incensed about it. Who did she think she was anyway? She didn't work half as hard as Katie did, or she did, for that matter. Heather tried to skate along on her looks alone.

The phone call upset Karen. She thought about it. Then she dialed the Queen Coordinator for her area. Miss Michelle answered the phone on the second ring. Karen told her she wanted to talk to her about a problem.

"Sure, what's on your mind?" Miss Michelle asked.

Karen relayed the conversation she just had with Heather. "Miss Michelle, she told me she was going after my crown. What should I do about that?"

"Let me handle it," Miss Michelle said. "Did you know that you were one-thousandth of a second from breaking the first record in Leona Valley, and you were three-thousandths of a second from breaking the second one? They didn't announce that because you were close, and didn't actually break the records. I'm so proud of you; I could just burst. You and Samantha did better than anyone expected and all the work you've been doing shows. You've never missed an event or a meeting. You've done better than anyone since Katie."

"I had no idea," Karen said in surprise.

"If I had to pick my Queen's Court again, I'd include you and Katie. Don't you worry about anything. You've done your part. You've earned your place. I will take care of this."

Karen left with her parents for Hartley Ranch feeling much better. She wondered why Heather mistreated her, but it didn't seem to matter as much. With the news from Miss Michelle, she felt on top of the world.

CHAPTER THIRTY-FOUR

The young people hung out in the main barn aisle while the tri-tips cooked on the grill. They talked about Tevis with Nathan. They talked about Cutting with Brody. They talked about the big fire and the canyon that protected them in Colorado. They talked about many things. They also talked about Rodeo.

"I have a great idea," Todd suggested. "Why don't we put together a little horse show presentation for Katie's parents.? Prince Ali could do either Native Costume or English Pleasure. La Duquesa can do Country Pleasure. Desperado can do Arabian Reining and let Desert Rose show Arabian Cutting. We can also let Prince Ali do Liberty. If we groom the horses, polish up our tack, and get ourselves cleaned up in show clothes, I'd bet we can make a good impression on Katie's and Karen's parents. What do you guys think?"

Maryann spoke up, "I think you left Freedom out. He could tack him up in his endurance equipment and show how fast that horse can trot down the rail."

After more discussion, they reached a decision. The "show" would be under the lights in the evening when it was not so hot outside. The group planned a ride the following morning. They would get together tomorrow afternoon to bathe and groom the horses and clean the tack. The riders planned to bring what show clothes they could plunder from Maryann's or Brody's closet and Aunt Ginny's, or borrow from one of Aunt Ginny's other students. Maryann would make those phone calls. Aunt Ginny could announce the discipline, horse, and rider. Becky made notes about everything so she could copy it for everyone. They decided to end the lineup of "classes" with Desert Rose's cutting demonstration and turn Prince Ali loose in the arena for his Liberty Class at the end.

Just as they finished planning, the dinner bell on the patio rang to signal the meal was ready to serve. Those in the barn headed back to the terrace. Karen's phone rang again. She looked at the caller-ID and was surprised again. "I'd better take this call," she told the group. "I'll meet you on the patio in a couple of minutes."

Karen answered her phone. It was the Princess on the Queen's Court. Shelly was eleven years old but mature for her age. "Karen, I tried to call Heather, but she had no suggestions. I just heard the City Council is planning to shut down the Equestrian Park five days each week because of budget cuts. That only leaves it open on Monday and Tuesday. We need that park! I live three blocks away and ride over there almost every day. It's the only place I have to practice. My parents have a large lot for our home. After they put in a back patio, the barns and paddocks, there's not enough room to put in an arena large enough to practice for the barrels or pole bending. Our arena just isn't long enough for all those poles and not wide enough for barrel practice. What are we going to do?" Shelly was almost in tears. "I can't ask my Mom to haul my horse and me somewhere else to practice every day."

Karen understood the problem immediately. She used to live in the same neighborhood as Shelly. She used the Equestrian Park all the time. Since her parents bought the new property close to Katie's home, they had enough room for her to practice at home, and she was close enough to ride to Katie's and ride there.

"Lots of people use that park. They have that arena for jumping. They have the dressage court. They have the arena for riding, and they have the one just for pole bending and barrel practice. They are busy every single day. This is really sad. There must be something we can do," Karen told her. "Give me tonight to come up with some ideas. I'll call you tomorrow. Don't worry. We'll figure something out." Karen stuffed her phone back in her rear pocket and walked up to the terrace for dinner. She knew just who to talk to. Katie would have some ideas.

Karen thought about the situation. She knew many people used the park to get their horses ready for Rodeo competition and Horse Show competition as well. There was a local group who used the large arena to put on open horse shows nearly once a month from February through October every year. She'd seen the Dressage Court used for competitions too. The area had unusually large lots with each home, so many equestrians kept their horses at home and used the park for exercise and practice. She wondered if the City Council planned to shut down the baseball/softball diamonds, tennis courts, soccer fields, or picnic areas too.

After dinner, Karen mentioned the problem to Katie. Katie's eyes popped open in surprise. "Is she sure?" Katie asked.

"Shelly told me her mother saw it in the newspaper. I guess we better get a copy and read the article. Once we know what it says, maybe we can form an action plan."

"Yeah, shutting down that park will hurt a lot of people who live near there. We also need to find out who uses the park, how often they use it, and when they use it. Maybe we can find someone who lives there to help with that leg work."

"Shelly might be a good person. She's this year's Rodeo Princess. She's cute, mature for her age, and I'd bet she would be very willing to help out," Karen told her.

"Why don't you give her a call. Ask if she and some of her friends can keep an eye on the park for a full week. We need to find out how much use it gets and when? If it really is being used a lot, we have something to take to a City Council meeting and discuss with them," Katie suggested. "One more thing it would be helpful to know is how much maintenance does it need to keep the Equestrian section open. The girls who are watching for use might also watch to see who comes to maintain it, what they do, and how often they do it."

"Those are great ideas," Karen said. "We need to gather information before making any kind of plea to the City Council about keeping our part of the park open."

"Yes, and if the numbers show it's used a lot, we'll have to make a presentation to the City Council. It wouldn't hurt to get the entire Queen's Court there in their outfits and have each one make a presentation. I can wear my outfit from last year. We've all had to write speeches and do presentations to get on the Court. This is a great way to use what we learned from that. This could be a community service project," Katie told her. "Let's use what we know."

"I didn't tell you," Karen began. "I got a call from Heather just as we were leaving to come over here. She ripped into me and threatened to take my crown because I associate with you and Kashmir."

"What?"

"Yeah, she was nasty about it. She also didn't like the fact we beat her. She told me right out that 'You don't beat the Queen!'"

Katie laughed at that. "Well, if the Queen doesn't practice, she can't expect to win. What is she asking you to do, fall on your sword to keep yourself from beating the pants off her?"

"That phone call upset me," Karen snickered. "I called the Queen Coordinator after I hung up on Heather. I told Miss Michelle about the call. She said she would take care of it. Maybe we should include her in this project. She's also in that community, so she would be affected by the closing. If we coordinate with her, we can make this a better-publicized community service project and maybe get it in the newspapers too. We need neighborhood support."

"Great idea!" Katie agreed. "On another subject, I think we should leave our horses here tonight so we can all get an early start tomorrow morning. We'll need that if we plan all the "horse love" in the washracks, and "tack love" in the aisle later. I have never seen some of the disciplines they plan to demonstrate. I'm excited about seeing that."

"I am too," Karen said. "Do you know what a Liberty class is all about?"

"I'm not sure, but I think they turn the horse loose in the arena. The idea is for the horse to show off its best moves with no restraint. Prince Ali is such a beautiful horse just standing in his stall. I can't wait to see his moves!"

"Maybe we should check with Aunt Ginny about leaving our horses here tonight and find out from the others what time they want to ride out. I can get a ride to your house when my dad goes to work. He leaves at 6:30 a.m. Would your Mom or Dad be able to drop us off here at Hartley ranch after that?"

"Sure, my Dad feeds early when he's home. I'll check with him. I think that will work."

CHAPTER THIRTY-FIVE

The early morning ride in the desert was cool, with a slight breeze crossing the desert from the West. Brody decided to take the group up one road that terminated in dirt trails about 5,000 feet above sea level on the north slope of the San Gabriel Mountains. Pinon Pines grew in the area and provided some shade on the trail. The group saw something slink behind a large boulder. "I think that was a bobcat," Brody announced. "They won't hurt you. I think they are more afraid of us that we are of them."

"You sure that wasn't a mountain lion, Brody?" Becky asked with a shiver up her spine.

"Positive. Do you know how big my dog Clyde is? He weighs between 105 and 110 pounds. A mountain lion is even bigger than that. The females, the smaller ones, weigh around 150 pounds. What sneaked behind that boulder was just a cat on steroids."

Nathan agreed with Brody. "I saw one on the Tevis Ride. They look like big kitties. They don't look like lions. They just have stubs for tails, but their ears are cute."

The group reached a promontory point with a fabulous view of the high desert. Brody pointed out where Hartley Ranch was and several other points of interest, including a great view of Mt. Whitney, the highest peak in the continental United States. "That peak is 275 miles from here, as the crow flies," he told the others. They watched the raven families soar on thermals above the desert as they searched for food. "Uncle Mike calls them the garbage men of the desert. They eat carrion when they find it," Brody mentioned. They stood side by side and looked at the beautiful scene below and in front of them for several minutes.

Finally, Maryann suggested they head back to the barn. "We have six Arabians to bath and groom, and a pile of tack to clean up."

On the way back, Karen and Samantha happened to get in front of Brody and Desert Rose. Brody commented, "You sure are the standout in this bunch. You have the widest butt on the ride." He realized what he said the minute he said it. His face flushed bright red clear up to his hairline.

"And just what did you mean by that?" Karen frowned and looked over her shoulder to ask.

"Ah, oh, boy, I, ah, I meant your horse," Brody stammered.

The other six laughed out loud. Karen was the only one riding a Quarter horse. Everyone else rode Arabians. The laughter and the joking continued back to Hartley ranch. The kids dismounted and began the washing process, two at a time in the wash racks. By the time they scrubbed the six Arabian horses, no one could tell for sure who was wetter, the freshly bathed horses, or the young people doing the work. Four horses dried off on the hot walker while the other two waited their turn in the wash rack.

Brody and Todd ran up to the ranch house for soft drinks and ice while the girls dried off their clothes seated on a bench behind the barn in the sun. Karen talked to them about the Equestrian Park closing. Everyone had ideas on how to stop that. Some were crazy, and some were practical. Katie and Karen listened carefully.

When the first two horses were dry enough to work on with the clippers, the girls put the final two on the hot walker. Maryann and Becky showed Karen and Katie how to clip the bridle path for Arabians. Becky gently pushed one of Ali's ears backward on his neck. "See, we use the length of one ear as a measure. You clip from just behind the ears for the length of one ear. We clip longer bridle paths on Arabians to emphasize the arc of their throatlatch," she pointed to the area at the bottom of Ali's neck where it met his head."

"Thanks for showing me that," Katie said. "I was only cutting about two inches on Kashmir, just enough for the bridle to fit. I see how that works."

Becky and Maryann made short work of the face and bridle-path clipping on Prince Ali and La Duquesa while Katie and Karen brushed the two horses down. Nathan, Todd, and Brody watched until the girls finished the first two horses. Todd and Brody put them in their stalls while Becky and Maryann brought the next two in and cross-tied them. The girls finished the clipping in a few minutes. Once all of the Arabians were back in stalls, the kids grabbed tack and portable saddle racks, saddle soap, neatsfoot oil, and rags and brought them into the barn aisle. Two hours later, saddles gleamed, bridles, reins, and girths shined. The kids were starving! They hadn't eaten since breakfast before their ride that morning.

Aunt Ginny rang the dinner bell on the back deck. All seven kids trooped to the back terrace. Aunt Ginny passed out bags of chips, sandwiches, and pointed to the cooler of soft drinks. "Looks like you've had a busy day," she said as she handed out the last sandwich.

"This was fun," Nathan said. "I like working with horses. I like riding them. I like being with kids my age who like them too."

"I heard you are going to Cal Poly this year," Todd said. "How does that feel to you? Are you excited about it?"

"Oh, yes!" Nathan grinned, looking at his sandwich. "I talked to the Director of the Kellogg Center. He's going to put me to work there for part of my education. I can hardly wait for school to start."

"You'll have to keep us up to date on that school," Todd told him. "My mom and dad went to school there. That's where they met. Didn't your mom and dad go there too, Becky?"

"Yes, my dad went to the school of architecture. My mom was in the equine section. She got to ride the Cal Poly Arabians in the shows for a couple of years. That's where my mom met Aunt Ginny," Becky told them. "She was going there and showing horses for her parents."

"Aunt Ginny met Uncle Mike there too! He came from Montana to study agriculture. His folks owned some kind of Dude Ranch. He wanted to work with cutting and reining horses, but they insisted he go to college. He met Aunt Ginny, married her, and bought this ranch. I think his brother runs the Dude Ranch now. Uncle Mike likes this much better," Brody filled the other in.

"Does this mean I'm going to meet a girl there?" Nathan asked.

"Well, you could," Becky laughed. "But most of the girls at that school now are a bit older than you. You might have to wait a couple of years."

"Good. I can concentrate on learning then," Nathan sounded relieved. Socializing with other young people was new to him. He still felt awkward and didn't have much to say. It was different with this group. They had a shared love in their lives – their horses.

CHAPTER THIRTY-SIX

After another wonderful barbecue dinner at Hartley Ranch, the adults pulled their folding chairs out on the lawn in front of the main arena for the show the kids planned. Katie and Karen's parents sat in the middle for the best view. The young people all headed for the barn and closed the front door of the barn so the parents couldn't see their preparations in process. Grandpa Carnegie walked to the barn to see if anyone needed extra help. The kids promptly chased him out and asked him to stay with the adults this time. The young people wanted to do this by themselves.

The first horse up was Prince Ali. Becky and Maryann tacked him up for an English Pleasure class. When he was ready, Becky pulled on her day coat, pulled her derby hat on, and climbed into the saddle. The kids left the arena gate wide open. When Becky was ready, Todd and Brody opened the main barn door long enough to let the pair out and closed it behind them.

Prince Ali knew something was up with this display because of the particular grooming and fancy clothes Becky wore. He put on his best English Pleasure attitude. He blew through the gate into the open arena at a beautiful, strong English trot. Becky sat up straight, holding the reins while Prince Ali circled the arena. Once she passed the gate, Becky halted Ali and turned him around to trot the other

190

direction. She trotted him halfway around the arena and cued him to a canter. As he passed by the adults on the lawn, Katie's mom gasped. "He's so beautiful. I've never seen anything like this before."

Chris O'Neal, bursting with pride, told her, "I've ridden that horse to several National and Canadian National Championships. Becky has, too, in the Youth Division. He's one of the best you'll ever see. But at home, he's just a horse, and he's Becky's best friend."

Becky finished her final pass in the arena and trotted out the gate. She took Ali down the side of the barn to the rear entrance, just as the front barn door opened enough to let Maryann and La Duquesa out.

La Duquesa floated into the arena like she was dancing on air. Maryann sat upright, holding the reins as Quesa trotted once around the arena. Maryann halted Quesa and turned her around so they could trot halfway around the arena and switch to the canter. Maryann sat so still on Quesa's back she never budged an inch up or down, so smooth Quesa's canter was to ride.

Shanna asked, "What is the difference between what this horse is doing and the first horse?"

Aunt Ginny explained, "Prince Ali is a true English horse. You can tell that by how high he lifts his knees at the trot. Prince Ali breaks above level, or parallel to the ground. La Duquesa is a Country Pleasure horse. She looks like more of a pleasure to ride. Her knees are just a tad lower than level with the ground when she breaks over at the trot. She's another National champion."

When La Duquesa and Maryann finished their pattern, they headed out the gate and went down the side of the barn to the rear entrance just as the front barn door opened again. Todd and Desperado jogged to the arena gate. They began their first pass, doing a complete large circle in half the arena at a fast lope. When they reached the starting point, they did a smaller circle inside that at a controlled lope before they reached the center of the arena. They switched back to the fast lope and made another large circle in the opposite direction, followed by a smaller circle inside of it at a slow lope. They returned to the end of the arena and charged as fast as they could toward the other end of the arena. Todd cued Desperado to put on the breaks. He slid to a perfect stop, no hops on the back end. Dirt flew several feet in front of them. Todd asked him to back up three steps and halt. Then Todd asked him to spin. Desperado did three full quick rotations around one rear leg before stopping again in the same position they started. Todd asked Desperado to lope to the far end of the arena and made one faster sprint to a sliding stop on the opposite side of the arena. Desperado halted and backed up three steps, halted, and did another three complete rotations at the spin. He looked gorgeous with his long black mane and tail swinging in the wind. The cues Todd used were subtle. If one didn't know what to look for, it appeared Todd just sat there for the ride. He did smile the whole time and took off his cowboy hat for a bow before jogging out of the arena.

Katie's dad was impressed. "I've never seen this before," he said. "That was a remarkable display. That horse has a lot of talent. I don't think I've seen any horse spin like that, or stop from that speed either. Wow! I'm liking it! Too bad they don't do reining like that in rodeo. I can see where all those moves, including the flying lead changes in the middle of the arena, come into play. I have to push my horse to rush after a steer. I've never had my horse stop quite like that on purpose. I didn't even see his cues!"

Todd rode Desperado out of the arena as another horse and rider came out of the front. This horse and rider were in hunter tack. The rider looked strangely familiar to Shanna and Clint as they watched her and her horse enter the arena at a hunter trot. It wasn't until she was passing them at the top of the arena; it finally dawned on them. They were looking at their daughter, Katie, and her Arabian horse, Kashmir.

"How the heck did that happen?" Shanna asked no one in particular. Clint was equally confused.

"This is a little surprise we had cooked up for you," Aunt Ginny said. "While you and Clint were gone, Katie talked to me. I went over and saw the horse. I told her I thought he'd make a great hunter. She'd never ridden a hunter before, so she rode him over here, and I gave her lessons. She wanted a reason to keep Kashmir. If you two refused to let her show him in the Rodeo events, she wanted a back-up plan. This is it. Katie learned to post, how to sit on a hunter saddle, and she took to it like a duck takes to water. She impresses me!"

Shanna couldn't keep her eyes off Katie as she rode her pattern on Kashmir. She and Clint were astonished. Shanna felt terrible she'd ever said something to Katie about selling the horse. She must have worked night and day while they were gone. She worked Shanna's training horses. She worked Kashmir in three disciplines. She coached Karen. She took care of the house and barn. And, she did all her schoolwork. Tears formed in her eyes and threatened to spill over. She reached out for Clint's hand and squeezed it. "I'm so proud of our daughter," was all she could say before one tear finally escaped and trickled down her cheek.

"So am I," Clint nearly choked himself.

Katie finished her pattern and left the arena as the barn door opened for Nathan and Freedom.

Freedom streaked in the arena at his best ground-eating trot. The tack for endurance was not so fancy as the show tack the other horses wore, but Nathan's skill at riding was as impressive as the others had been. They did two complete passes in the arena at the fast pace Nathan and Freedom used in endurance riding. They switched up to a single pass at the gallop before they disappeared down the side of the barn.

The barn door opened once more to allow Becky and Prince Ali out. Becky led him to the center of the arena, wearing just his show halter. When they reached the center, she stopped and pulled it off of him. Prince Ali was free to do what he pleased. Someone in the barn turned on the music. The sound wafted over the arena from speakers near the barns. Prince Ali picked up the pace. Becky walked to the gate and closed it behind her. Ali began to dance. He trotted along the rail with his tail in the air. Ali stretched out his neck and flung it side to side, tossing his silver mane around. He snorted and blew like a powerful stallion, which he really was. He put on a show for the guests for five minutes. Then he walked over to the rail and nickered. He hoped for a scratch, a pat, or a treat, and he would be happy with anyone of them.

"I understand this is a stallion?" Clint asked.

Walter Howard beamed. "Yes, we bred him several years ago. We didn't expect what we got, nor did we expect him and Becky to become such good friends. Caroline and I would trust him with Becky anywhere, anytime. He loves her and looks after her."

Chris O'Neal walked to the arena rail and gave Ali a good scratch on the withers. "This horse helped make my ranch, too. He began winning when he was just a year old. He hasn't stopped yet. It was exciting taking him into international competition. I'd never been to the Salon du Cheval in Paris before. You wouldn't believe the people you meet there, especially when you take the best two-year-old stallion in the world into that arena."

"Wow, he won in international competition too?" Shanna asked. "That's amazing."

"What did you think of Kashmir today?" Aunt Ginny asked.

"I didn't recognize him. I thought there was something familiar with him but couldn't put my finger on it until they got close to this end. What did they do to him?"

"The kids groomed him like an Arabian is all," Aunt Ginny said. "We don't do a lot of things different, just a few. A good bath and grooming certainly can change the look of any horse."

Uncle Mike stood up. "Ladies and Gentlemen, we need to get ourselves over to the other arena. That's where the cows are. The kids have one more demonstration for you today."

The group walked down to the cattle area and leaned on the rail. There was one nice fat steer in the arena, about a year and a half old. He was walking around looking for something to nibble on when Brody rode up on Desert Rose. "Uncle Mike, can you open the gate for us?"

As Brody rode Rosie into the arena, Clint and Shanna shared a look. The horse looked like it was smaller than that steer. Clint started to say something to his wife about it when Rosie went to work. She pushed the steer to the opposite side of the arena and chased it down the length of it. She stopped the steer before he reached the end of the arena. She turned him around and chased him down the arena again. Rosie never let up on the steer. She moved him as far as she wanted to, and she turned him at will. When the steer tried to bolt across the arena to get away from her, Rosie pinned him to the rail and forced him to move forward again.

Clint finally said something. "Mike, that steer is bigger than that horse. Aren't you worried the mare could get hurt?"

Mike grinned at him. "Nope. It's all about attitude. She has the attitude of a Percheron size horse. She's always been that way. She loves working cows. She makes them do what she wants them to do. It doesn't matter what size the cow is."

"Mike, Ginny, my wife and I got an education here today. Those Arabian horses are spectacular, and they seem to do anything and everything. The one that stands and eats in our barn did not look like himself today. Neither did our daughter. Those two looked like fancy equestrians. I wouldn't have believed it if I hadn't seen it with my own eyes. I will never look at an Arabian horse the same way again."

"I was proud of my daughter today. I realized all that she's accomplished in just a couple of months. That horse seems like the catalyst for that. I'm very grateful to Kashmir. I want to see him live a long and happy life with Katie and her friends. Thank you so much for the education," Shanna added.

Aunt Ginny smiled, "Don't thank me. Thank those kids. They did the work. This was all their idea. I think they did a great job, don't you?"

"I've always thought "horse kids" are the "best kids," and this proves it right again," laughed Shanna. "Yes, those kids did a fantastic job showing us two old Rodeo people something new and exciting. I will never look at an Arabian horse the same way either."

Clint and Shanna went home alone that night. Katie stayed at Maryann's house with Maryann and Becky. They planned to get together with the boys again in the morning for another ride. Karen was riding over to meet them. Clint and Shanna had the house to themselves when they got home. Clint poured them each a small glass of wine, and they sat on the back porch in the cool of the evening. Occasionally they would hear one of the horses in the barn shuffle around or snort. Other than that, they heard nothing but sounds of nature. They sat in near silence and listened to the crickets.

"So, what do you think?" Clint asked Shanna

"I think we have a wonderful daughter. I think she's going to do whatever she sets out to do. If she wants to be a Rodeo Queen, she will be. If she wants a college education, she'll get it. If she wants to be a dog-catcher, I wouldn't get in her way. We gave her a good, solid foundation, and she's a great kid. I'm proud of her."

"I'm not going to stand in her way with that Arabian of hers either," Clint said. "Those two make a great team. If any of my brother-competitors suggest anything different, they'll have to take that up with me. They won't win."

Shanna smiled over her glass at the love of her life. He turned out to be a great father too.

Katie spent one more night at Maryann's so she could hang out with Becky, Nathan, and Todd until they went back home. The kids spent the time riding, playing games, and talking about horses. Uncle Mike and Aunt Ginny hosted barbecued hamburgers and hot dogs the next night. Shanna and Clint Barclay hosted the entire group of kids for lunch that day. Every one of the kids had to have a try at pole bending and barrel racing with limited success. Katie and Kashmir set the bar pretty high.

Before Becky and Nathan went back to San Juan Capistrano, they left their phone numbers with Katie and promised to stay in touch. Todd O'Neal did the same as his parents loaded Desperado for the long haul back to Colorado.

CHAPTER THIRTY-SEVEN

Karen called Shelly about the Park situation that night. Shelly put together 15 girls and mothers that would help monitor the use in the Park and the maintenance schedule. Karen was surprised she'd been able to get so many people so quickly.

"The newspaper had general information, and all these people live in the neighborhood around the park. Most of them use it almost every day. They are not happy about closing it except for two days a week. One of the mothers called the paper. She talked to the reporter who wrote the story. It was her information that the park would only be open Mondays and Tuesdays, so the city doesn't have to pay extra to have people there over the weekends," Shelly told her.

"What about the horse shows they have on weekends?" Karen asked.

"I don't know about that. If the park is only open on Mondays and Tuesdays, the horse shows would have to find someplace else, I guess," Shelly said. "We've already started counting people and watching the maintenance people. It looks like they grade the arena every morning. They send in sanitation people to take out the trash twice every day. They have someone in the office to make sure everyone who uses the park signs a liability release form. We had 101 different people using the equestrian part of the park on the first day and 117 people the second day so far.

Karen called Katie and gave her the update. Katie was with Maryann and Becky. She talked to them about it.

"More than 100 people a day use that park, and they want to close it down to only Mondays and Tuesdays?" Maryann asked.

"When Karen lived by the park, she used it every day. That's over 700 riders a week using that park. We must be able to do something," Katie said.

"Why don't you and the Rodeo Pageant people get together and go to the City Council meeting. Wear your outfits and hats with crowns. Let the newspaper know you are going to be there. That might get some attention with the people who use the park."

"Do you mean someone from the group should speak to the City Council?" Katie asked.

"Isn't that part of what you do as Rodeo Princesses and Queens?" Maryann suggested. "I know you have to give some kind of speech after your interviews. Maybe you should tackle that yourself. You give great speeches."

"What in the world would I talk about?" Katie asked.

"Talk about how the park means so much to the kids who need to practice for the Queen Pageants. Talk about how the practice arena helps to get ready for competitions. You can talk to some of the girls who do horse shows and see how it will affect them. You already know how it affects those who compete in Rodeo events. There are other things you can mention, too, about how riding helps kids and makes them disciplined and do better in school. Do some research on that. Talk to someone who works with equine therapy for some information. You could put together a great speech. Maybe they will listen to you. Also, you can maybe estimate how much time the city spends maintaining the park and how you can get volunteers to do some of that work. You will have to set up meetings in the area to speak to local residents about what they are willing to do to keep the park open," Becky suggested. "I have some connections at the Shea Therapeutic Riding Center that may be able to give you some information."

Katie went to bed with her head spinning. She knew Heather, the current Queen, wouldn't be interested in helping out. She might show up at the City Council meeting though, if she thought someone would be there to take pictures. She'd be the one smack in the middle of that. Katie vowed to work with Karen and Shelly and get something moving. The horse people, and especially the young people, in the area, needed that park.

When Katie woke up, she had breakfast with her mom. Katie told her mom about the possibility of the horse park closing. She explained her concerns plus the concerns of some of the girls who lived in that area. Shanna thought about the problem seriously for a minute.

"I have horse friends from that area too. I'm going to give them a call this morning. Maybe we should try to get a community meeting in the Equestrian Park to discuss it. Perhaps we can come up with some ideas to give the City Council that will keep the Park open. Why don't you check in with Karen to make sure Shelly and her friends are keeping a close eye on the usage of the park and what the city maintenance people have to do there. That would be important information, even if it isn't a full week, to discuss with the community."

"Great idea, Mom!" Katie said. "I'll call Karen after breakfast and see how Shelly and her group are doing on the counts. Maryann and Becky are rounding up some information for me about how equestrian activities affect children and young adults. I will need that information if I give the speech to the City Council."

"Katie, that's a wonderful idea. I may have something you can use too. I saw an article in one of the women's magazines I saved. It was about a study done in Japan with children and academics. You'll love this one."

"Great, Mom. Anything that will help our cause is welcome."

Katie spent the next couple of hours on the phone with Shelly, Karen, Maryann, and Becky, before she called Michelle, the Queen Coordinator. She took notes from the girls. Katie checked the Civic Calendar and found the next City Council meeting was two and a half weeks away. She reported to Michelle what she discovered. Katie told her that her mom thought they should get a community meeting together at the Park to discuss options. She mentioned there might be things the community could do to offset some of the costs to the City.

"Wow, Katie. I'm impressed. You girls are sure taking the bull by the horns on this. I'm proud of you all. Yes, I agree about the community meeting. I can reach the reporter who wrote the original story for the newspaper. He might be able to help as well. If we set a date for the community meeting, he can get that in the newspaper, so we get better participation from the neighborhood surrounding the park. They are the ones who use it most. I love the information you've put together, showing the benefits of horseback riding as well. That's great stuff!"

"Michelle, I would like to write and give the community opinion before the City Council myself. Would I be permitted to wear my Young Queen outfit? I know the other girls are wearing theirs. Mine has last year's date on it. From what I could see in the Civic Calendar, they won't be taking a lot of discussion from citizens, so I'd like to represent them."

"Katie, are you sure you want to do this? We can find one or two fathers who can talk to the Council members, maybe one of the mothers too."

"Miss Michelle, I thought about that. The people who benefit most from the Equestrian Park are the young people because we use it more than the adults generally. I thought one of us young adults might have more impact on the City Council than somebody's dad or mom."

Katie, let's present that idea at the Community Meeting. You can give your speech there and let them decide if they want to let you represent them. And, yes, you can certainly wear your Young Queen outfit to the City Council meeting. Honey, I'm proud of you!"

Katie met her mother in the barn when she went out to work with Kashmir. She filled her mom in on her conversations while she brushed Kashmir down and saddled him. Rather than just working barrels that day, Katie decided to go on a short trail ride, so she had time to think. Katie needed to write a speech that would grab the attention of the City Council members and get them to agree to leave the Equestrian Park open seven days per week. She began to have some doubts.

"I can hear what you are thinking," Kashmir told her.

"Oh, yeah," Katie muttered under her breath without thinking.

"Yeah. What you propose is a good thing. You will help a lot of horses and people if you succeed. I can feel your heart light now. You are honestly thinking of others first. You could also mention the benefits for the horses. Most of them would be standing for long periods of time. If they don't have room to stretch, they can't increase their speed. If they try to do that in smaller spaces, there is a high degree of risk for injury for them. Bathing and grooming are wonderful, but horses need room to move to stay healthy. You could also mention that."

"Kashmir, thank you. I never thought about it from the horse's perspective. That's a great idea."

"Horses need practice too. They do better in all kinds of events. They also do better in life when they have proper exercise."

"I can see it now. We came up with over 100 riders in the park each day. If those riders had to walk the neighborhood instead of using the Park, there would be a lot of horse poop on the sidewalks. I don't think the neighbors would be happy about that either," Katie laughed. "Horses aren't like dogs. You can't scoop that up and carry it home with you easily."

"Only you would think of that," chuffed Kashmir.

"I have a great idea. Why don't I bring you along when we go to the meeting? If we get there early, you and I can ride around and look things over. You may be able to come up with some other suggestions from a horse's perspective, you know?"

"Sure, I'll look around and tell you what I think," Kashmir offered. *"At least we can try a new place to ride for an hour or so."*

After the ride, Katie gave Kashmir a fresh bath, rebraided his mane and tail, and put him back in his stall with a handful of hay and two horse cookies she'd made that week. "I'm going to work on my speech for a while. I'll come see you before I go to bed."

"Thanks for the ride, and the opportunity to offer advice," Kashmir said as he crunched his cookie. *"By the way, these are really good. Thank you."*

CHAPTER THIRTY-EIGHT

Katie worked on her speech for several hours, crossing out words, rewriting sentences, and practicing some of it out loud as she worked. "Ladies and Gentlemen, Members of the City Council, I'd like to speak with you about the Equestrian Park, and its effects on riders young and old, and the horses as well." That sounded pretty good to her so far.

"The Equestrian Park was built where it is in the master plan of the community located around it. The lots for homes are larger, so the owners can have their horses at home with them rather than having to board them somewhere else. That reduces the cost of horse ownership. Most homeowners in the community own horses. Many own the horses to benefit their children, others for their enjoyment. Most of them moved into the neighborhood because of that, and the central location of the Equestrian Park, which gives them space to ride and exercise their horses." Okay, that sounded good so far. Katie knew she could deliver that part without a problem.

"I'd like to talk to you about some of the benefits horse riding bring to the people who ride. There was a study done in Japan several years ago. Young people from age eight to fourteen took academic tests covering language skills, math skills, and general history knowledge before riding. Those children spent the next hour and a half with a horse. They had a trainer to work with their riding skills. They also spent time grooming and prepping their horses before and after their ride. As soon as they finished the time with a horse, they tested again with different questions on language skills, math skills, and history knowledge. The testers compared each child's scores from before and after riding. In every single case, the young person scored higher after the time of working with their horse. Most scores were 10% or more higher after riding, and in one case, it was 37% higher. The benefit of riding horses translates to high academic achievement with young people." That sounded pretty good to Katie. She didn't think there was much to fix in that section. She continued on.

"Equine Therapy is used for young and old. Older people find their ability to concentrate improved with riding. They also develop core strength and gain better physical condition from the exercise. People who have PTSD find help with exposure to horses, both in the saddle and on the ground. Many service members have a difficult time rejoining regular society after serving in a war zone. They find horse therapy very helpful because it is soothing to jangled nerves. Horses never judge. Young children with neurological, psychological, or motor skill problems can develop their cores and partnerships with a horse and therapist. They learn to move around better after riding. They relate to others better after riding. There are so many benefits. I can't list them all. Horses are some of the best natural healers on the planet."

Maybe this section needs a tweak or two, Katie thought. I'll come back to it. She needed to get accurate counts from Shelly and her group as soon as they could provide them. They also needed to talk with the community members to see what, if any, of the workload the city maintenance people did could be done by community volunteers. That would have to wait until the counts were complete and the community meeting held. She also needed to find out how long the City Council would permit her to talk to them. Did they have a two-minute rule, or would she be allowed to speak for up to five minutes? By this time, Katie's eyes were tired. She needed a trip to the barn to see Kashmir; then she was off to bed for the night.

Her cell phone woke her up the next morning. She grabbed it off the nightstand and saw it was almost 8:00 a.m. She'd slept in. She jerked awake and answered her phone.

Heather was almost screaming at her. "What in the world do you think you are doing?"

"I have no idea what you are talking about," Katie snapped back.

"Why are you giving a speech before the City Council about the Equestrian Park? That should be my job, not yours. You are not even in the Queen's Court this year, remember!"

"If you were the Queen you should be, you'd be doing this yourself, but you have done nothing for the girls who depend on that park. Someone had to, so I stepped up. I have Michelle's permission. As a citizen, I don't need permission, but I asked. Don't worry, the reporter and his cameraman will be there. You will get your photo opportunity. I'm sure that's the only reason why you would show up for the meeting anyway," Katie spit back, clicked off on the call, and dropped her phone back on her nightstand.

Heather, practically foaming at the mouth, called Michelle. Michelle was not available, and her voice mail came on. Heather left a hateful message as she stumbled over her words before clicking off the call. Michelle had a difficult time figuring out who the caller was until she checked her caller ID. She couldn't understand much of the message, either. She decided to ignore it for the moment. She had work to do and no time for a silly, privileged girl's rant.

Karen called Katie a few minutes later. "You sure put some burrs under Heather's saddle blanket," she laughed when Katie answered. "I got a call from her about the City Council meeting and you giving your speech to them. Holy cow, that girl can go on and on. She's going to have her Daddy do something, she says. They don't even live in town. I can't imagine what her Daddy is going to do if he doesn't live or work here, can you?

"Heather likes to throw her "Daddy-Big-Bucks" around a lot. I feel sorry for the man. It must be awful living with a spoiled brat like her," Katie snickered. Katie thought for a minute, then continued,

"On second thought, I guess we shouldn't make fun of her. Maybe she's lonely. She lives way out there from everyone else, and she's just now old enough to drive. I know she's an only child. I heard her Dad works all the time. I don't know much about her mom except she has friends in the Los Angeles area with lots of money, and she spends time down the hill with them all the time."

"I heard her mom is in one of those TV shows. It comes on during the middle of the day. I don't watch those shows. She probably stays down the hill while they film. She also does movies on occasion. I heard Heather has a governess that takes care of her and the house."

"What in the heck is a governess?" Katie asked.

"I think that's just a fancy name for a Nanny," Karen said. "My guess is people worth a lot of money don't use Nannies. They hire Governesses for their kids. It sounds better."

"What do you think we should do about Heather? I don't want her going off while we're trying to help keep the Equestrian Park open. Got any suggestions?"

"One. Why don't you call Heather and ask for her help?" Karen suggested. "She was very nasty the last time she talked to me because I hang out with you and your Arabian. It might come from you better than it would from me. I'm the Young Queen on her Court. You are not on the Court at all this year."

"Okay. I'll be the bigger person. I'll ask her for help. Maybe that will calm her down, especially if she thinks she can play a part in this. Perhaps that's what makes her mad in the first place. She lives so far away, maybe she feels like she can't help. She may even have some resources we've not thought of. That could work," Katie agreed.

Katie talked with her mom over breakfast about Heather. She told her about the phone call from Heather than morning and what Karen had to say as well. Shanna did know a little about Heather's parents. She explained what she knew to Katie. "Her dad is an international businessman. He travels between here and Europe and South America on business all the time. He owns companies all over the world. Her mom is a successful actress in Hollywood. She does movies and has been on one of those long-running TV soap operas for years. Neither parent is home much. I think Heather has grown up not seeing her parents often at all, and rarely at the same time. She might get one or two days over Christmas and New Years with them before they take off again. I think you are right. I think Heather's problem is she is lonely. Inviting her to participate in your project is a wonderful idea. Just don't let her give you a hard time when you ask. Be patient with her."

Katie came in from the barn with her mom for lunch. After lunch, she picked up her cell phone and asked her mom to cross her fingers for her. She dialed Heather's number. Heather answered right away. "What do YOU want," Heather snapped at Katie.

"I called because we need your help," Katie said evenly. "Would you take a few minutes and let me explain?"

"Why would you need MY help?" Heather snapped again.

Katie took a deep breath to hold her patience in check. "It is a big deal for many people if we can help keep the Equestrian Park open more than two days a week. I thought it would be a great community service project to work on that. That park benefits so many people in the community who can't afford acreage with enough room to work their horses. I know that's not a problem for you or me, but it is for so many others. Would you help us, please?"

Heather was silent on the other end of the phone call for nearly a minute. "Katie, what can I do to help?" Katie almost sighed out loud. The sound of Heather's voice completely changed. She was no longer talking to the angry young woman that answered the phone. This Heather was more like herself.

"Let me fill you in," Katie said and began to do just that. After talking to Heather for about 15 minutes, Katie asked if she had any other questions.

"What is the biggest size arena most of the homeowners in that neighborhood can have in their back yards?

"From what I understand, taking out for housing your horse, you could probably build an arena about 72 feet by 48 feet. That's not wide enough for a standard barrel pattern. You'd have to increase that to twice that size to put in a pole bending pattern with six poles 21 feet apart. That is also square. There's not enough room for an oval arena, and it's not large enough for the girls who show their horses in three gaits. The jumpers are plain out of luck with small arenas. If they don't have the park for practice, the only options open are to take their horses to a boarding facility with large arenas or put them with trainers who do. That's not a financial option a lot of them have," Katie told her.

"So they want to close down the Equestrian Park to only Mondays and Tuesdays because of budget cuts?" Heather asked. "Has anyone looked at the budget? My dad is a wizard at that sort of thing. If we could get our hands on the budget for the Equestrian Park, he might be able to help a lot with where cuts happen and how community volunteers can help keep costs down. Do you know if the reporter could get his hands on that budget?"

"I'm so glad I called you," Katie smiled. "None of us thought about that. That's the core of the problem. You are a genius! Michelle has been in touch with the reporter. Do you want to make that call, or should I?"

"Ha! It's something I can do!" Heather said in a gleeful tone. "I'll call Michelle and see what we can get. I will give my dad a call about it too. He may know someone on the City payroll somewhere that can get him a copy. He probably knows the Mayor. I'll ask him to rip through that budget and see where we can save the city money and still keep the park open. This is going to be a fun project!"

"I'm so glad you are on board with this, Heather. Thank you!" Katie said. "You do plan to come to the community meeting, don't you? I think you need to be there so we can talk about what the community members can do to reduce costs. By that time, you might even have something back from your dad that tells us how much needs cutting to keep the Park open. Will you need a ride in? If you do, my mom and I can pick you up."

"My new car was delivered yesterday. I got my driver's license in the mail last week. I get to drive in by myself. Thank you anyway."

"Oh, you have to tell me. What did you get?"

"Dad bought me a new Jeep Wrangler. It's bright red with black trim. It's pretty, and it's rugged. Dad wanted me to have a four-wheel-drive vehicle out here in the desert."

"Heather, I never pictured you as a Jeep girl. Didn't you want a Porche or a Lexus?"

"Katie, remember I'm a Rodeo Queen! What do you think they drive?" Heather laughed.

Katie did too. All Rodeo Queens needed Jeep Wranglers or big Dodge trucks. How were they supposed to get around without one? Katie laughed with Heather this time.

Katie thought about the whole "Medicine Woman" thing. Had Karen called Heather, she didn't believe the call would have turned out nearly as well as it did. Maybe there was something to it after all. Heather was an angry girl. Katie almost saw her as a wounded animal. She spit and hissed at everyone around her. What Heather needed was someone to pay attention to her. Heather needed someone else to help so she could feel validated and worth something. Katie had endured her own struggles with self-worth. She understood that. Katie felt great giving Heather some support. She thought it was interesting that when you help someone else, you also help yourself. She would keep that in the back of her mind for later.

CHAPTER THIRTY-NINE

Heather Madison's dad did know the Mayor. He called and talked to him. The Mayor had the entire budget sent electronically to Heather's dad. He spent two days going through the city budget. Bill Madison found more than enough cuts in that budget to keep the park open and still save the city money. He talked to the mayor about it and went over it line item by line item. The Mayor agreed with him but needed him to come to the City Council meeting and make a full presentation to them. They were the ones who would ultimately approve the city budget. Heather's dad made several changes in his schedule so he could be at the meeting. He didn't tell Heather. He figured he would surprise her. He knew his daughter was going to be at that meeting with her group attempting to keep the Equestrian Park open.

In the meantime, there was another competition coming up. This one was out of the area in Santa Barbara County. All of the Queen's Court planned to attend, as well as many of the High Desert competitors. Katie was excited about running barrels with Kashmir again. They did well in Leona Valley, as did Karen and Samantha. Katie and Karen spent the better part of the week before the event tuning up and getting the trailer packed to go. On the spur of the minute, Katie called Heather and asked if she wanted to go with them. Heather was surprised. There was nothing she wanted more than to feel like part of the group. She gladly accepted the invitation. She brought her outfits to pack with Karen's in the trailer. Her governess dropped Heather and her horse off the afternoon before Katie's parents planned to leave. Heather would spend the night at Katie's house with her. Heather could hardly contain herself. She'd never been invited like this before.

Katie kept in contact with Maryann and Brody. They were almost as excited about the Santa Barbara event as Katie was. It was a big Rodeo. Her dad was also competing. Since it was a "family affair," they decided to bring the living quarters trailer with room for four horses along. Shanna planned to go with her family, and they would bring Samantha with Kashmir and her dad's horse and Heather's horse. Karen went with them. Her parents couldn't make it this time because of her dad's work schedule. Heather, Karen, Katie, and Shanna had the trailer packed so they could pull out on Thursday evening for the two and a half-hour drive north to Santa Barbara.

Maryann talked her grandparents and her mother into driving up for the event too. Brody worked on Aunt Ginny. They had the motorhome parked at Hartley Ranch. There was plenty of room for everyone. They met at an agreed point on the road and followed Katie's dad with their trailer to the Fairgrounds in Santa Barbara.

As soon as they found stalls for the horses at the Fairgrounds, the group gathered at the trailer and motorhome and set up camp with tables, chairs, and the pop-up shelter. Grandpa pulled the barbecue out of the motorhome, and they began dinner for the humans that night.

The events in the morning began early, so everyone had their fill of dinner and went to bed early. They would be rising before the sun the next morning. There were horses to feed and bathe before the Opening Ceremonies. Heather and Karen needed to get into their outfits, so they were ready for them. The girls chose to sleep in the motorhome, so Brody slept in the travel trailer with Shanna and Clint. He got more sleep. The girls were too excited to sleep that night.

Before dawn, Clint woke Brody, and they began washing horses. The girls were the next to awaken and were there to help while Shanna, Celeste Carnegie, and Aunt Ginny got breakfast ready.

By 7:00 a.m., the girls were at the show office to check-in for their events. They got a similar reaction from the office staff that they got in Leona Valley. The office staff laughed about an Arabian horse in the pole bending and barrel racing events. The news spread through the competition. "What is an Arabian doing here?" people asked. "Who does she think she is bringing one of them to a Rodeo?" Curiosity sent other competitors by the barns to check it out. People began whispering the news throughout the line-up of competitors. Some had heard about the Leona Valley Rodeo and were curious. Some were darned near angry about it.

Clint and the others knew what Kashmir and Katie were capable of. They simply smiled when others asked them. They refused to offer any opinions. Heather and Karen stayed silent on the subject and quietly got ready for the Opening Ceremonies. Katie and Maryann helped each of them get into their costumes. Grandpa Carnegie, Clint, Shanna, and Rose Wilcox helped get the horses ready.

At 8:30 a.m., Heather took her place behind the Santa Barbara Queen. Karen got behind the Santa Barbara Young Queen, and the Opening Ceremonies began with them running around the arena with their flags flying, followed by the younger girls. The National Anthem played on the loudspeakers as the audience in the stands clapped, cheered, and stomped their feet. By the second pass, the Anthem finished playing, and the Rodeo officially opened for the first event.

As in the Leona Valley Event, Katie asked for the final number in the line-up for both her events. Karen asked for second to the last place.

When the announcer called the pole bending event, the girls lined up in their order. Katie was behind Karen. They spent most of their time watching other competitors run through the poles. A few poles were knocked over in the process. The announcer called every girl's score according to their times. Karen and Samantha were ready. They ran a perfect race with no poles down and the fastest score to that point. Katie met Karen at the gate and slapped her a high five on her score. Then it was time for Katie and Kashmir's turn. She walked Kashmir to the start position and waited for the signal. Kashmir exploded in a flash of speed that shocked the audience. He turned between the poles with the grace of a ballet dancer. He made the spin around the final pole without overshooting it. He charged back so close to the poles, the air moved them slightly, but none fell over. Kashmir hit the finish line with the same exuberance he showed passing the first pole. It was a joyful thing to watch. Kashmir really liked what he was doing.

The audience went silent briefly as the timer checked and re-checked the time. The timers couldn't believe it themselves. Finally, the time was accepted, and the announcer announced it with a flourish. "Ladies and Gentlemen, we have a special announcement on this event. The final run, which you just watched with your own eyes, broke the Santa Barbara County Rodeo Association record in Pole Bending. That record was set over 30 years ago. Our congratulations go to Katie and her horse Kashmir. They set a new record here today, and you just witnessed it! Let's give a big hand to Katie and Kashmir!"

Katie could hardly believe it. Another record-setting run. She hugged Kashmir around the neck and stroked him while they sat facing the timing clock at the end of the arena. His time was even faster than the time he got in Leona Valley. Did this horse have a bottom? Was there a time he couldn't beat? She felt on top of the world right then. Kashmir did as well. The whole thing was fun for him. He knew he had more in him. He could do this again. He could do even better next time. He would do it for Katie. He would do it with Katie. Katie pulled her hat off her head and bowed to the crowd from her seat on Kashmir's back. The crowd cheered louder.

Karen and Heather were waiting for Katie and Kashmir outside the arena. They both had high fives for Katie. "Wow! Another record for you two!" Karen said as they walked back to the barns.

"You are making a believer of me," Heather said as they walked side by side. "I've never seen anything like that. Kashmir was like greased lightning in that event. Does he have a sister or a brother available? I'd like to get scores as good."

"I think Kashmir is a one-up. I don't think there is anything like him," laughed Katie. "He's special. I love him. I think it might be something between us. You might have to find something like what we have. It may be another Arabian, but it could just be the connection between you and your horse," she admitted. "If you think pole bending is great, wait until you see him on the barrel runs."

The three girls walked their horses back to the stables so they could rinse them off and put them back in stalls to relax. Katie wanted to watch her father compete, so she headed off to the grandstands to wait for the team roping competition. The barrel racing wouldn't be until the next evening.

Katie looked around for the others in the grandstands, but people packed the seats, and she couldn't find them. She took an empty seat she found near the exit gate of the arena. The whispering got louder and more vicious. People noticed her and commented about her bringing an Arabian horse into the competition. She turned bright red over some of the comments.

One cowboy from Oklahoma finally stood up and turned to face the crowd. "Y'all should be ashamed of yer selves! This young lady here just went out there and whipped butts. Y'all are talkin' about the horse she rode. How dare y'all! That horse she rode has a head an' tail an' four feet just like any horse. Who cares what breed it is? She did something y'all didn't do. Stop yer gripin' and do it better'n she did if ya can or shut yer dang pie hole! Her daddy is comin' up. She'd like to watch him. But she can't if y'all are goin' to talk trash about her and her horse. Stop already or walk out back and have a go at me. I admire any young lady that can do what she done with her horse. Y'all should be too. I'll be waitin' for anyone who wants a challenge. Come see me out b'hind the cattle pens. I've got a punch in the nose for any o' y'all!"

The crowd got quiet after that. Katie reached across and took the man's hand to thank him. "It's nothin' ma'am," he told her as he settled back in his seat. "Congratulations," he said to her while tipping his hat before turning back to the action in the arena below. Katie wondered if all real cowboys were so polite.

Clint and his partner won their event easily. Katie was as proud as a peacock. She couldn't wait to get back to the barns to congratulate him and his partner – and ask him if he knew the cowboy from Oklahoma who stood up for her in the stands. She finally found out his name was Wesley. She adored his accent, and she was grateful for his intervention. He was a hero for her.

CHAPTER FORTY

The barrel racing competition was an evening event. Some of the best Rodeo events were done then because of the draw they had for audiences. There were more people in the stands watching. That put even more pressure on the competitors. Heather would compete on her fancy and expensive quarter horse. Her horse came from a breeder in Texas. Her horse was as "blue-blooded" as they come. The horse trained with a well-known trainer in the same state. Heather flew to Texas to meet the horse, then flew to Texas for training from the man who trained the horse. Her parents spend a lot of money on both the horse and horse training, as well as her training.

The pressure on Heather was immense. After all the money they invested, her parents expected her to do well. The only problem was Heather. She liked what she did, but she didn't love it. She liked her horse, but she didn't love it either. She didn't know what to tell her parents. Heather would rather paint her horse than ride it. She'd always had a talent for arts and crafts. She dabbled in art privately. Heather was afraid of what her parents might say if she told them the truth about her real passion. Here she was at another competition, and she had no enthusiasm for it.

She grabbed her sketchbook and walked to the arena. She hoped to catch some of the action on the arena floor as events took place.

That was where her enthusiasm was. She was a good sketch artist. She wished she could learn to paint her subjects in oils or watercolors. She never told anyone about her passion for the arts. She hid it instead. She kept her sketchbooks hidden from everyone. That was sad because her sketches were incredibly good. She managed to capture action, character, and feeling in the same quick drawings.

Heather was on her knees, resting her bottom on her bootheels with her sketchpad clutched on one hand, and her pencil in the other. She stared at the calf, running directly at her with a man on a horse chasing it. His lariat was in the air circling just above the calf's head. The calf's eyes were open wide in fear. The look on the man's face was determination. The horse also had wide-open eyes as he watched the calf in front of him. The horse ran flat out. Flecks of spittle hung off its lip. The calf's movement cast a cloud of dirt behind it. The horse's movements cast an even bigger shadow behind him and the man. Heather's pencil made short, quick strokes on the paper.

In front of her, the man's lariat circled the calf's neck and pulled it up short when the man halted his horse. He lept off the horse and ran to the calf, pulling it over on its side as he tied three legs together with quick motions of his wrist. He stood with both hands in the air while the calf struggled to free itself from its bonds. At the eight-second mark, the announcer called the man's time over the loudspeakers. The crowd cheered. One of the Rodeo employees rushed over to the calf and untied its legs, setting it free. The calf saw an open gate and charged toward it and freedom.

Heather's pencil continued the short strokes on white paper until she had a good likeness of the calf, the horse, and the man. Her eyes shifted up and down from her sketch pad to the scene in front of her. Now she concentrated on the sketch. She began to fill in the details from memory. She drew in the yokes on the front of the man's shirt. She filled in his dark-colored hat. She finished the blazed face of the horse and left the white marking on the forehead of the calf. Her drawing caught the emotion and the action of the moment. It made her feel a little sorry for the calf.

"Wow! I had no idea you could draw that well. That's beautiful work!" Katie said in a soft voice over Heather's shoulder as she stared down at the scratchpad.

Heather almost fell over in her haste to close up the scratchpad, tuck the pencil in her pocket and stand up. Her face turned bright red. "I didn't mean for anyone to see that," she mumbled.

"Heavens! Why not?" Katie asked her. "I had no idea you were such an artist. You could make money on pictures like that."

"Promise me you won't tell anyone," Heather begged her. "I just do this for fun. I don't want my parents to find out. They think starving artists are a disgrace."

"Heather, you are not exactly a starving artist. You have a real talent. You should develop that talent. Good artists can make money, you know. Western Art is very popular. I just watched that roping run. I can't believe how well you captured it and how fast you worked. That's unbelievable."

"Thanks, but please promise me. I can't let my parents find out. No one else knows. I've never shown my work to anyone. I try to catch action scenes quickly so I can move away and not get caught. You sneaked up on me."

"I didn't do it on purpose." Katie looked her in the eyes. "But I'm glad I did. That is impressive work. I'm glad I got to see it. How would you feel about doing one of Kashmir and me in the barrel event? I'd love to have that one. I promise not to tell where I got it."

"Sure, I can do that as long as I don't have to sign it, and you promise not to tell who did it," Heather smiled back at her. "You've got to keep my secret."

Katie reached out with her pinky finger. Heather hooked her pinky finger around Katie's. "That's a pinky promise!" Katie told her as they turned to walk around the booths at the event.

Katie and Heather walked around the Rodeo grounds and found something to eat at one of the stands. They sat down to eat their meal. "You know, you are not what I thought you were," Katie said. "I like you. You are more down to earth."

"I'd hate to know what you really thought of me before, then," laughed Heather. "You are not what I thought you were either. I like you too."

"What, besides being a stuck up rich kid?" Katie giggled.

"Well, all that lovely money comes from my parents. They make ridiculous amounts of it, but I hardly ever see them. My mom checks in with me every day to two. I hear from my dad when he is in a time zone where he can call me after school. That doesn't always happen. Mom comes home for a few days when they stop shooting a season for the TV show, but she generally leaves right away for some location shooting for a movie. Dad's schedule is more erratic. He takes a day or two between trips sometimes, but he's usually so jet-lagged he sleeps most of that away. They do make time at Christmas, so they are both home for a few days then. The rest of the time, I'm with Cassidy. She's only ten years older than me. Mom found her through an ad in the London papers. Cassidy finished up her education and was at odds. She thought it would be fun to visit America, so she posted the note that she was available as a governess. My Mom was in London at the time and saw the ad. She met Cassidy and hired her. Cassidy got here without either of my parents. Our maid, Maria, showed her around and introduced us."

"Don't you ever wish your parents had normal jobs, not so much money, and more time at home with you?" Katie asked.

"All the time," Heather sighed. "I've been with nannies or governesses all my life. I'm closer to them than I am with my parents. My parents aren't even close to each other. They only stay together a few days a year over Christmas. Dad sometimes visits Mom on a movie set in Europe if he's close by. Other than that, they probably don't even talk to each other much. I think that's sad. I found pictures of them when they were first married. You could tell in the pictures they loved each other. Does that happen to everyone after years and years?"

"No, I don't think so," Katie said. "My dad travels a lot because he competes and he's found a way to make a decent living moving livestock around the country. He's on the road quite a bit, but he's so happy when he gets back home with Mom and me. I've seen parents of other friends like that too. I'm sorry you don't get to spend more time with yours."

"If I ever find my Prince, I think I'll take some time before jumping into marriage. I don't want to bring a child up alone. I want to be sure," Heather said.

"I think we all need to do that. I have lots of things I want to do before I find my Prince. I want to wear the Queen's crown. Then I plan to compete for the State Queen's crown. I would love to go after the Miss USA Queen's crown too. My mom did that right up to the national crown. I'd love to wear that one before I find the love of my life," Katie admitted.

While they ate, Katie and Heather talked about other things. Katie suddenly had an idea.

"I know what you can do. Don't you graduate this year? You should have the summer off before your parents ship you off to college, right? Why don't you take some art classes? You can get them at the community college right in town, I think. You can keep your work at my house, so your governess doesn't know what you're doing. You can always tell her you are taking lessons from my mom. That gives you an excuse to visit me, and we can hide your practice pieces, so no one else knows," Katie suggested.

"Katie, I'd love to do that. I'll check with the college when we get back home. I hope they have classes in oil and watercolor painting. That's what I'd love to do."

"Heather, don't give up on your pencil drawings. The one I saw over your shoulder was great. I loved that one. I can't wait to see how you do with Kashmir and me. I guess we'd better figure out how you can do that. We compete in the same event. I asked for the final spot on that one. Where are you on the list?"

"I got the second run in that event. I'll be going in early so it shouldn't be a problem. I can rush right back to the barn and should have time to untack my horse and rush back with my sketch pad before you make your run."

"Just a suggestion, why don't we bring Karen and Maryann into our little secret. Karen's got the run just before mine. She can stay at the trailer until you get back. She and Maryann can give you a hand with your horse before Karen has to rush to the arena. Would that work for you?"

"Can Karen and Maryann keep a secret? I don't want too many people to know about this. They won't blab this around, will they?"

"No. I guarantee Maryann and Karen are not gossips. If we ask them to keep it themselves, they will."

"Okay, then. Let's go find Karen and Maryann and set it up," Heather suggested. They dropped their lunch trash in a trash can and went looking for the two girls.

CHAPTER FORTY-ONE

The evening activities began with the Barrel Races. The first girl did a respectable job, but she left room on the table for better scores. Heather was the second contestant and set the bar a little higher for the next competitors. As soon as Heather's run was complete, she dashed back to the trailer to untack her horse. Karen had Samantha ready to go before Heather got there. Karen and Maryann helped Heather untack her horse. Maryann took it from there and tied him to the trailer, and provide him with munchies to keep him busy. Karen hopped on Samantha and charged off to the arena to find her place in line. Heather dashed into the trailer and pulled her sketch pad from under the mattress of the bed, grabbed two sharpened pencils, and hurried back to the arena with Maryann. Maryann went to find the rest of the group. Heather had plenty of time, so she looked for a quiet place along the outside rail, away from the grandstands.

Heather flipped her sketchbook open to a new page and watched the next competitor do her run. The horse was a beautiful Appaloosa with a gorgeous blanket across his rear. Heather began sketching the horse and rider as they rounded the second barrel. Her pencil strokes were quick, with varying pressure applied to deepen the color in areas. She also made another quick sketch of the pair on the same page, as they made their way to the finish line. The rider was standing in the stirrups, leaning over the horse's neck and encouraging him home. She continued filling in details on both sketches after the time for the run was called. It gave her something to do while she waited for Katie's turn. The rider had long thick hair braided into a single tail. On their dash to the finish line, her braid streaked straight behind her head, matching the tail of her horse. Her expression was one of serious concentration. Her hat brim flipped up in front because of the speed they were going. Small details like the fringe on the rider's chaps and the squared-off toes of her boots were easy to touch up later, so she roughed them in, paying more attention to the expression on the horse and rider's faces.

Heather worked on some of the fine details on the two sketches while other riders took their turn at the barrels. She flipped the cover over her work when Karen and Samantha stood ready to make their run. She watched Karen and her horse move swiftly and gracefully around each of the three barrels. They came close to the barrels but did not brush against them. When Karen turned Samantha toward the finish line, Heather appreciated the speed and fluid movements of those few seconds. She wondered if she and her horse looked like that. She didn't think so. She thought about taking real lessons from Katie's mom. She was sure she could improve and thought it would be fun taking lessons and working with Karen and Katie rather than always doing it alone. Heather was not surprised when Karen took the top spot with the best time of the night. There was only one competitor left. Katie sat waiting for the starter.

Heather flipped open her sketch pad to a clean sheet of paper, holding her pencil poised. She wanted to watch at least the first barrel before she began working on this sketch. Heather watched as Kashmir turned into a streak of lightning on the starter's signal. He was there one second and somewhere else the next. Heather changed her mind into "video" mode so she could capture the movement like a roll of film in her mind she could replay as needed while she worked on this sketch. Her pencil didn't touch the paper until Katie and Kashmir reached the second barrel. She watched as Kashmir leaned into the turn, placing his feet in the right place, so he didn't tip over. Katie leaned with the horse more like a part of the horse than a rider sitting on it. Heather was mesmerized watching. One second they were rounding the second barrel, and the next second they were halfway around the third one. They completed the final turn in the blink of an eye and headed for the finish line. Kashmir's expression was pure joy. Katie was almost the same with a dash of concentration mixed in. She didn't need to encourage Kashmir. He was running because he loved it. Heather could see the difference. It was suddenly so obvious to her and her artistic eye.

When the pair streaked across the finish line, the crowd in the stands began cheering and screaming and stomping their boots. Everyone was on their feet. It took the announcer several minutes before he announced Katie and Kashmir's run at the barrels. The time flipped up on the screen, and the cheering got louder than ever. "Ladies and Gentlemen, you've just seen the fastest time ever recorded for a barrel race in the history of the Santa Barbara County Rodeo Association. Katie and Kashmir didn't just break the record; they smashed it! Their times count in the Junior Division, but I was just informed their time beat the all-time record for this event set back 22 years ago in the Adult Division by Miss Sandra Harris and her horse Jacks On Fire, a direct son of Two Eyed Jack. Congratulations, young lady!"

Katie was stunned. Two events and two more records broken. How did that happen? She was weak in the knees. She climbed off Kashmir and stepped back into the arena from the outgate with Kashmir beside her. She wasn't sure she could walk on rubber legs, but she managed. She pulled her cowgirl hat off and bowed to the crowd, then turned around and nearly collapsed into her father's arms. He and her mother helped get her back to the trailer. She sat on the fender of the trailer, stroking Kashmir's neck. "What a great horse you are, my friend. We make a great team together, don't we?"

Kashmir whinnied softly in her face. *"Yes, we do,"* he told her.

The others in the group came back to their encampment, excited and wanting to relive that barrel run. None of the others had seen anything like it. Grandpa and Grandma Carnegie had never been to a rodeo in their lives before. They were as excited about it as children. They couldn't stop talking about the different events they'd seen, but especially that final barrel run with Katie and Kashmir. Uncle Mike made it a point to pull out a fresh apple from the motorhome for Kashmir. He hand-fed it to the horse while stroking his neck and telling him how great that race had been to watch. Aunt Ginny was stroking the other side of his neck at the same time. Maryann, Brody, Karen, and Katie talked nonstop with Heather about it. Heather made another decision then and there. She was going into training with Katie's mom. Heather decided to call her dad and mom the next day and let them know where to send the checks. She made arrangements with Shanna and Clint to take her horse, Twister, directly to their ranch for training as of the next day. Clint and Shanna took a closer look at Heather's horse. He was everything he should be from his breeding. He needed a little tune-up from Shanna first, then schooling for Heather and Twister from Shanna to get them ready for the future. Shanna encouraged Heather. "He's a really solid horse. There is no reason why you shouldn't be in the top three in your division. We can fix that! He's also a handsome devil. Let's get out there and make our Queen competitive!"

Other spectators began pouring in. The last event of the evening was over. The Queen's Court made their final ride around the arena to the National Anthem. That's when Karen and Heather realized they missed that presentation completely. They were so busy back at the encampment; they forgot they were supposed to be dressed up and riding in the finale. Neither of them ever forgot before. They felt a little sheepish when the Queen of the Santa Barbara County Rodeo Association came by for a visit so she could see the Arabian too.

Many people stopped by for a look at the famous Arabian horse who was fast as greased lightning. Most had very complimentary things to say about him. Many had questions about Arabian horses. Aunt

Ginny, Maryann, and Brody were happy to answer their questions. Then there were a few with an obvious bias against Arabians who showed up. One group of three girls, about 14 years old, made rude comments while standing back looking at Kashmir. Heather heard some of the comments. She went into full "hair on fire" mode and approached the group. "I've listened to what you've been saying. It is obvious you know nothing. What is your point? Why are you here? Why don't you grab your teddy bears and let your mommies sing you a lullaby to sleep? You could try to learn something before you open your mouths. Go to the National Rodeo Association page on your computers. Ask for the rule book. Memorize it. You will find there is nothing in it that says an Arabian horse can't participate in Pole Bending or Barrel Racing. No where does it say that! Before you shoot your mouths off again and show your ignorance to the entire world, I would advise you to know the facts first. You've clearly not done that. If you can't say anything nice here, don't say anything at all."

The girls looked sheepish, like children caught with their hand in the cookie jar, and walked away. Heather hoped they learned something. Gossips like them did not like being called out in public on it.

Shortly after her altercation with the group of young ladies, the adults in the group began tearing down the encampment so they could head for home. It was time. Heather realized how tired she was and was thankful to leave. She hoped she could find time to finish up the sketches she'd begun. She wanted Katie to like them.

CHAPTER FORTY-TWO

Katie and Heather sat in the back seat of Clint's truck on the way home. They chatted amicably between themselves as the miles flew by until they both settled into shallow sleep from exhaustion. Competing could be very tiring. When Clint turned off the highway onto the dirt road leading to their ranch, both girls woke up, somewhat refreshed. They watched as the truck pulled up to the barn and hopped out to unload the horses. Karen went home with her parents. The four of them were left with four horses in the trailer to put away for the night. Heather and Katie took care of that. Samantha was the first horse out. Kashmir followed her. Twister and Clint's roping horse waited their turn and settled into their stalls, tired from the weekend as much as the others. The girls distributed half flakes of hay to the four horses before closing the barn and shutting down the lights.

Heather faced the prospect of a 40-minute drive home. She was exhausted and wasn't sure she could do that safely. Katie solved the problem by asking her to stay the night. Heather gladly accepted and called her governess to let her know where she was and how to reach her. She changed into nightclothes and dropped on the couch in Clint and Shanna's living room seconds before her eyelids slammed shut. She was done for the night. Katie did the same thing in her bedroom.

Clint and Shanna had a glass of wine on the back porch before turning in. They talked about the Rodeo their daughter competed in. They both burst their buttons with pride in how well she'd done. They spoke about the Arabian horse angle and decided it wasn't an angle at all. Kashmir was entirely acceptable to both of them as their daughter's mount for as long as she wanted him. They talked about Katie's new friendship with Heather. They spoke about Heather putting her horse in training with Shanna. They were happy with the prospect. Shanna could see the potential in the horse and hoped she could improve the partnership between him and his owner.

Clint had also done well at the Rodeo. He handed over his winnings to his wife to bank for them. They talked about Clint's schedule for the next couple of weeks. Unless something came up, he would be on the road most of the time. They finished their glass of wine and went to bed.

The following morning, Katie was the first one up. Heather was right behind her. They climbed into "barn dress" and went out to feed the horses. Katie went into Kashmir's stall to check him over and make sure he was no worse for the wear from the weekend.

"Can we talk for a minute?" Kashmir asked her.

Katie answered with her mind. "Sure. Heather does not know about our special connection. I'm not sure this is a good time to tell her."

"Okay, I wanted to talk to you about Twister. That's Heather's horse. He wants to connect with Heather. He wants to be her partner. He's not sure that's what she wants. He loves her, but he thinks she just likes him because her parents paid a lot of money for him. He feels guilty about that."

"I hope you did reassure him that's not why she likes him. That would make anyone feel bad. I think she had a few minutes to think about their relationship. That's why he will be staying here, and my mom will work with him for a couple of weeks, then work with the two of them. I think Heather saw a different side of horses this weekend. I'm encouraged about that."

"I know Heather is a lonely girl. Her parents are not around. She misses them. I think she tries to push that off with an aloof attitude, but

I know she's sad inside. I can see it in her heart. I hope a better connection with Twister will help her be less sad."

"You are so right, Kashmir. She and I had a chance to talk. She is lonely. She doesn't know how to handle that. I was happy to see her talk to my mom about leaving Twister here for training. I think she would like to be here working with Karen and me. We are a poor substitute for her parents, but we won't judge her, and maybe it will help make her happier with herself."

"I liked your suggestion that she follow her heart and take lessons in art. She has the eye of an artist and the heart of one too. She would be wasting her time doing anything else. She was born to do that."

"How did you know about that?"

"You forget that I can hear through your ears and see through your eyes. I could see the heart she puts in her work. She has a passion for it. That's what she was born to be. Your encouragement and suggestions will help her develop as she should. She will be much happier now that she's found a friend in you."

"Kashmir, how do you know all this? I get confused, sometimes. I know you and I have a special relationship, and I know others have special relationships with their horses. But how is it possible you can know all that you know?"

"Katie, I thought we discussed that the first time we met. YOU are a Medicine Woman. You are a healer of people and animals. I am a Medicine Horse. I am also a healer of people and animals. We have something unique in common. Your aptitude for the work has improved quite a lot since we first met. You are learning more lately. And you knew a lot intuitively, to begin with. I see now how your aura glows brighter than it used to. It becomes a witness to those who need your help, without them even knowing. Do you realize how much you've helped Heather just in the last few days? You probably have no idea. But it has been more than what she's received from her parents for her entire life. Your encouragement for her artwork soothes her soul in a way they can never understand. She's being made whole by your encouragement. There are many others in need of your support. I trust your kindness will find them when they need you the most."

"You give me too much credit, Kashmir."

"No, I can't give you enough. You are a special soul. Look at what you are attempting to do for so many others with the horse park situation. Yes, I know about that. Please remember to include the benefits for the horses. That pulls some heartstrings. You can make such a difference for the people in that area, all the people, and their horses. Please let me know if you want a horse's perspective."

"Kashmir, Heather doesn't know that we talk. I don't tell anyone about this because some people will think I'm crazy. I need to get on with the morning feeding as usual. I need to step away from our conversation right now. I love you, and thank you for the weekend we had. That was so exciting for me. You are extraordinary."

"Please tell Heather that she needs a farrier to look at Twister's right front foot. The farrier who set his shoes clipped him, and one nail is causing him pain. He's tried to tough it out and not show lameness, but it is becoming difficult. That second from the last nail on the inside causes him pain. He won't be able to hide the lameness for much longer. She needs to use your farrier. He knows what he's doing. He won't drive a nail into soft tissue like that guy her parents hired."

"Thank you for telling me, Kashmir. I will have that checked out today. I can't stand for a horse suffering over the incompetence of a human, regardless of what he charges. That makes me mad."

Katie walked over and hugged her horse. There were so many things extraordinary about Kashmir; she couldn't list them all. He was unusual, and she loved him dearly.

Katie walked out of Kashmir's stall and latched the door. She walked down to Twister's stall and felt his right front leg. She did find a little heat in the leg. She called Heather over. "Twister's right front leg is a little warmer than it should be. I would like to call our farrier over to check it out. Maybe we just need to reset that shoe. If we leave it alone, he could go lame, and we can't work with him that way."

"How did you know to do that?" Heather asked.

"I thought I saw something the way he was moving when we put him in the barn last night. I don't think it's serious right now, but it could become a problem if we let it go."

"Please call your farrier. I don't want my horse lame from neglect," Heather frowning slightly. "We should probably leave him in his stall until then. Will you let your mother know? I think she planned to ride him this morning."

"Yes, I'll be sure mom knows. I have to get the phone number from her anyway."

"Do you mind if I stay here until he gets here? I need to call my governess and let her know I won't be home for a while. I don't expect my parents will call anyway."

"Sure. After we finish feeding, I planned to call Shelly and see how those counts are going at the Equestrian Park and how many people they've talked to about the community meeting this week. I hope we get a good turn-out for that, and I hope the park use numbers are solid. I've got some information I wanted to put into the speech for the City Council. Maybe you can help me organize that," Katie suggested.

"Katie, you do such a great job with that sort of thing. Honestly, I don't like giving speeches. I'm sorry I gave you a hard time about doing this. I don't mind helping put things together, but I think you should be the one who talks to the City Council at their meeting. I know you'll do the best job. What I'd like to do is work on that sketch for you. That's what I enjoy doing."

"Well, thank you. I appreciate your confidence in me. If you want to work on the sketch, you can work at my desk in my room if you'd like."

"That would be great! Do you happen to have any colored pencils? I have an idea I'd like to try with this one," Heather asked. She looked away with a dreamy look on her face that evaporated when she looked back at Katie. "Yes, I definitely want to try something different with this one."

CHAPTER FORTY-THREE

While Shanna worked horses, Katie called Shelly and took notes on the conversation. Heather worked in silence in Katie's bedroom. Katie sat at the kitchen table, working on her speech for the City Council meeting. She had a full week of data the volunteers gathered about park usage and the city's maintenance schedule. She learned the city did not attempt to recycle plastic bottles or aluminum cans. There had to be money in that. If the city would put separate bins out in the area of highest traffic, the volunteers offered to help with the recycling effort. That was a good point for them. The volunteers collected the weeks' worth of bottles and cans before the city maintenance workers emptied the trash. They took them to a recycling plant. It was close to $30 for that one week. Katie multiplied that by 52 weeks and arrived at an estimate of $1,560.00 per year that the city threw away. And it wasn't good for the planet either.

Volunteers found the arena lights in the park stayed on until 11:00 p.m. There was never anyone in the park using the arenas past 9:00 p.m. Volunteers suggested 9:30 p.m. during late June, July and early August while the kids were out of school. They also suggested shortening that during the winter. Katie could see how the city might save considerable money by putting the arena lights on a timer to shut them down according to the usage of the arenas by the length of daylight during each month. It was beginning to look to Katie like the city could save money and still provide daily access to the Equestrian Park. She couldn't wait to talk to the community members at their meeting and see if there were any other suggestions like that.

Katie organized the counts for the various arenas. She added the numbers up, then multiplied them by 52 weeks to show how consistently the arenas were in use in the community every single day of the week.

She went over the park maintenance schedule. City workers came to the park early every morning and removed trash bags from all the outside trash containers. They replaced the liners and left within 30 minutes. The same team of city workers returned every day around 4:00 p.m. and did the same thing again. The volunteers said there was not a single trash bag full of refuse anytime during the week they observed the procedure. They felt, if the city provided recycle bins in the park for plastic bottles and aluminum cans, one visit per day would be more than enough to keep the park clean.

A city worker drove to the park, unlocked a garage, and drove the city's tractor out to each arena. He graded it to smooth the surface. He took the tractor back to the garage and checked fluids and diesel fuel. If the tractor needed anything, the worker added it from the supply stored in the garage. He parked the tractor in the garage, closed the door and locked it before leaving. It took him about two hours to do all four arenas and the routine maintenance on the tractor.

Seven different people in the community said they could take over some or all of the grading of the arenas. Three of them were retired, but all of them had extensive experience driving heavy equipment for a living. They all said they would be happy to demonstrate their ability and knowledge to the City to show they were capable of doing the work required. That could eliminate the use of a city worker for two hours every day. Katie wished she knew what the salaries were for city workers. She would love to extend the savings out into real dollars before meeting with the City Council. She knew talking to them in real money might sway them better than any other way. She would need to speak to an adult about that. Katie organized her paperwork and stuffed it in a folder. She also had horses to work that day.

Heather came into the kitchen for a glass of water. She checked the time. "Wow, I didn't realize I'd been working that long," she told Katie. Katie stood up from the kitchen table with her folder in her hand. "I didn't realize I'd been working on this stuff this long either. I wish I knew someone who could help me pull it all together in dollars and cents."

"My dad has a copy of the City Budget. Maybe he can help you. He does that kind of thing all the time. He owns companies all over the world. Why don't I talk to him and ask him to call you? With the information the community came up with, I bet he can help you," Heather offered.

"Do you think he has time to talk to me about this stuff?" Katie asked.

"For him, it would be fun, I bet," Heather laughed. "It's not his money this time." She picked up a single sheet of heavy white paper from the counter, turned it over, and handed it to Katie. "What do you think?"

Katie looked at the drawing, and her mouth dropped open. She couldn't think what to say for a few seconds. "I LOVE this!" was the best she could do. Katie continued to stare at the beautiful, detailed drawing of her and Kashmir. Heather added color into portions of the picture to highlight Katie's clothes, the color of the barrels, the deep brown of Kashmir's coat. Every detail showed, from the tooling on the saddle to every strand of hair on both her and Kashmir. The set of her mouth matched the set of Kashmir's. The eyes were the best feature in the picture. Katie's blue ones and Kashmir's brown ones looked real enough to blink at any second. Katie couldn't take her eyes off the drawing. It looked so real. It showed her how much of a team she'd become with Kashmir. Their bodies matched in the action at that split second, and they both looked happy doing it. Heather roughed in the balance of the picture. The arena rails, the grandstands, and the crowds of people she loosely sketched in for perspective. Heather spent her effort on the horse and the young girl in the center of the drawing.

Katie finally took her eyes off the picture and grinned at Heather. "Wow. I've never known a real artist before. This is beautiful work. We need to get you in those courses at the Junior College this summer. I like your use of color in this. It's not entirely a color drawing, but you used enough color to bring it out and make it pop. I'd love to see what you can do with that calf roping one you did over the weekend. If you can make that calf's eyes look as real as these, you could make money selling that one."

"I've loved drawing since I first picked up a pencil. I wish my parents knew how much I love doing this. They want me to go to college. Dad would love me to get a degree in finance so I can take over his businesses one day. Mom would love me to go to medical school. She'd adore telling her friends her daughter is a doctor. I don't think they've ever asked me what I want, but I've heard enough comments about "starving artists" from them, I've never brought it up. If it were up to me, I'd be heading for Chicago to study art there."

"I wish you could talk to your parents about what YOU want," Katie said. "What good would it do you to go to school for four to eight years and be unhappy? You should follow your heart and do what you love. You have real talent. You are a great Western Artist. I can see you in a few years with an art studio in your barn so you can spend time with your horses and do your paintings there too."

"That sounds wonderful to me!" Heather laughed. "I still love my horses. I might even think about trying an Arabian someday. I'll have to get a decent size barn so I can have horses in one end and a studio with great light at the other end. I'll probably have to spend my inheritance on tack, horse feed, and art supplies."

The two girls were giggling over that thought when Shanna came through the back door into the kitchen. "Whatever are you two up to? The farrier just got here. He's pulling Twister's shoe off right now. I came to get you so you can see what he finds," Shanna told them.

Katie and Heather sobered immediately. Heather headed for the back door. Katie set the drawing down on the end of the counter and followed her to the barn. They were both out the back door dashing to the barn when Shanna saw the drawing on the counter. She picked it up and stared at it for several minutes. Shanna noticed Heather's signature at the bottom. She was stunned. She knew exactly where her daughter and Kashmir were in that drawing. It was just the past weekend. What stunned her more was the skill and talent shown in the drawing. It was as good as any artist she'd ever seen. She would have to find out about this later. She laid the picture back down where she found it.

The farrier just finished pulling the shoe off Twister when the two girls got to the barn. "Did you find any issues?" Katie asked him.

"Look at this nail," he said and pointed to one that looked like it had blood on it. "I think the nail was set wrong. It should have been in the hoof, but it looks like part of it was inside the tissue of his foot. That would be like you having a splinter underneath your fingernail. Those hurt like crazy. These shoes weren't on long. I can reset this shoe and get the nail in the right place. It will be a little sore for a day or two, but he'll be right as rain after that."

"Thanks, Rex. I'm glad we caught you when we did. I'd hate to think of walking on a splinter under my nail," Katie told the man. "I know Twister appreciates it too."

"Yes, thank you for finding the problem and fixing it. What do I owe you?" Heather asked.

"These folks are some of my best customers. You don't owe a thing. I'm happy to help out," Rex told her. "If you need a good farrier, I'll leave one of my cards with you."

Heather took the business card he offered. "I will give you a call when he needs shoes the next time. I hope you don't mind driving to Apple Valley."

"Heavens, no. I live there," Rex smiled at her. "If you need anything, give me a call."

Katie and Heather brushed Twister down, working on both sides of him at once after Rex picked up his tools and left the barn. "What school did you want to go to if you had the choice?" Katie asked Heather.

"I've dreamed of going to the School of the Arts Institute in Chicago since I was little. They have a fabulous fine arts program there. Many incredible artists from around the world have studied there. But it doesn't have a medical school or school for financial analysts either. I could get a medical degree in Chicago, but Mom and Dad both insist on one of the Ivy League colleges on the east coast. They cost more, but they think they have more prestige."

"Have you ever thought about someplace other than Chicago?" Katie asked.

"There are two other schools, both on the east coast. One is the Savannah College of Art and Design, and the other is the Rhode Island School of Design. But, I don't want to do illustrations. I don't want to design wrappers for bread or canned peas. I don't want to do graphic design. I want to paint! I want to learn both oil/acrylic painting and watercolor. I like the crispness you can get with oils and the softness you can get with watercolor. I'd like to experiment and see if I can get both with one medium. I've been dreaming about that for years while I do pencil sketches. Those I can hide under the mattress."

"Maybe those art classes at the community college this summer will help you make up your mind which medium you like," Katie suggested.

"Believe me; I can't wait. I'm so glad you suggested them."

"Have you ever thought about talking to your parents about your wishes?"

"Yeah, sometimes. I know they would never approve, so I keep it hidden away. I don't want to disappoint them."

"Don't you think they would be disappointed with you if they knew you were unhappy doing what they want instead of what you want?"

"Katie, I don't even see my parents very often, like I told you. I know my dad would be happier if he had a son instead of a daughter. I'm not sure why my mom wanted a kid at all. Maybe they were different when they were younger. They seem to be happy enough with their lives now. They each want something different for me. I get confused sometimes. Should I be the doctor my mom wants, or should I be the jet-setting business owner my dad wants? I don't want either of them. I would love to find a tough but gentle man to fall in love with and marry. I want to keep my horses, have children I raise myself with my husband, and I want to paint. I don't know how to talk to them about it."

The girls finished up with Twister and put him back in his stall. It was time for lunch. Katie offered to make sandwiches for them both as they walked back to the house.

CHAPTER FORTY-FOUR

The girls walked into the kitchen just as Shanna finished placing sandwiches on three plates next to a pile of potato chips. Three glasses of iced tea already sat on the kitchen table.

"Mom, you didn't have to do that. I was going to make lunch today," Katie said when she and Heather walked into the kitchen.

"It's okay. I knew you two were in the barn with Twister. What did the farrier find?"

"My farrier set one nail wrong. It was sticking him in the soft tissue of his foot. Rex pulled the shoe and reset it for me. Twister does seem relieved, doesn't he, Katie?"

"Yeah, I wouldn't want a splinter under my nail like that either."

"After you two went to the barn, I found this on the counter and wanted to ask about it," Shanna said. "I know what it is and who did it, but I'd like to know more." Shanna held up the pencil sketch for the girls to see.

Heather's face turned bright red, and she stared at the toes of her boots. "I forgot to put that away before we went to the barn, Mom," Katie explained. "I caught Heather sketching the Rodeo last weekend. You should have seen it, Mom. She was squatting on her bootheels, drawing a picture of one of the calves from the calf roping event. It was perfect. She had a scared look in the calf's eyes, the rope just about to drop out of the sky around his neck, and that cowboy had a look of determination on his face. It was such a nice sketch. I asked her to do one of Kashmir and me. She gave that to me."

"Heather, this is beautiful work. I didn't know you were an artist. I love this sketch. Where do you think we should hang it, Katie?"

"Mom, Heather doesn't want anyone to know about her sketching," Katie explained.

"Why? You are so incredibly talented. You could be holding your own art shows at the Apple Valley Gallery, and who knows where else. Why would you hide a talent like this, Heather?"

Heather didn't respond. She felt tongue-tied and didn't know how to answer. Katie spoke up for her. "Mom, Heather doesn't want her parents to know. She thinks they will disapprove. She thinks they want her to be a doctor or a business wizard or something like that. She believes they would be ashamed of her as an artist."

Shanna sat down at the kitchen table, thinking for a minute. Katie and Heather joined her, although Heather didn't meet her eyes and stared at her plate.

"Heather, could you do this sketch in a larger size for me?" Shanna asked.

Heather nearly choked on a sip of her iced tea. She coughed then asked, "Would you like me to do that?"

"Yes, I would. Definitely! I will frame it and hang it right there," she pointed to the wall behind the kitchen table. "I would love to look at that picture while I'm in the kitchen. It would be my favorite work of art in the house. Your composition is wonderful. The way you've done the eyes of the horse and my daughter draw you right into the picture. I really love it."

Heather smiled shyly at Shanna. "Would a 16" by 20" be big enough? I don't think I've done a sketch larger than that. They are too hard to tuck under the mattress in my room."

"What in the world do you have stashed under your mattress, young lady?" Shanna asked. "Please pull them all out. I'd love to see every one of them."

"I don't have that many right now. I've dumped a lot of them in the trash cans at school. They started piling up, and I was afraid someone would find them. I'll sneak them out of the house and bring them over when I come tomorrow to see Twister. Oh, Rex said he would be okay to work the day after tomorrow. Katie and I plan to give him an Epsom salt soak today and tomorrow to be sure. I can't wait to get started working with you."

The conversation over lunch changed abruptly to horses. The three talked happily as they polished off their sandwiches, potato chips, and iced tea.

"You have the technique down," Shanna told Heather. "I can't fault you there. You've done the practice, and you work hard. What you are missing is the bond with your horse. That's the stuff you and I will work on together, okay?"

"Yeah, after watching Katie and Kashmir last weekend, I see what you mean. I would love to develop that between Twister and me. He's such a great horse. I'm not giving him what he needs from me. Do you think we can improve our standings with that?"

Shanna laughed. "He is a great horse! With a better bond between you and him, I see you rising to the top of the standings. I'm not sure he's quick enough to beat Kashmir, but I see you coming very close. Would that make you happy?"

"I'd love it! I don't think there is a horse out there right now that could beat Kashmir. He's so fast and so tight rounding those barrels, I've expected them to twist in place from the momentum," Heather laughed. "Boy, anyone who says Arabians don't do rodeo hasn't seen Kashmir do a barrel run!"

The three laughed over the idea Kashmir ran around the barrels so close and so fast they might just screw themselves into the ground as he passed by. They sure weren't going to tip over.

After Heather left to go home that afternoon, Shanna talked to Katie. "I got a phone call from Heather's dad. He wants to come here the first of next week so he can talk to you about your project with the City Council and the Equestrian Park. He did manage to get his hands on the current budget for the city, so he's got some information you can use in your speech. He also wants to talk to me about Heather and Twister's training here."

"Mom, that's great!" Katie said. "I wondered how I could reach him and talk to him about the park situation. I'm really happy he's willing to sit down and help me with this."

"I have something else up my sleeve," Shanna admitted. "I really want that sketch from Heather, and I want it matted and framed and hanging on the wall before he gets here. I'm a parent. I think I understand more about how a parent thinks than Heather does. I'm going to bet when he sees that sketch and finds out his daughter was the artist who did it; he will change his mind about what he'd like her to do after high school."

"Mom, I talked to her about taking some classes in oil/acrylic and watercolor painting from the community college here this summer. I checked. They offer them, and I'm sure we can help get her enrolled. She thinks it may be her last chance before she heads off to some Ivy League college on the east coast. She is so not looking forward to that."

"Maybe my plan will work. I'm willing to bet it will. What school does Heather want to go to?"

"She's had her heart set on the School of the Arts Institute in Chicago. She also mentioned a couple of other colleges on the east coast, one in Savannah and one in Rhode Island, I think. But the one in Chicago was the one she wants to go to. I think her dad is a graduate of Yale, so that's the one he wants her to go to. She dreads the idea."

"Yale also has a Fine Arts Degree, I believe," Shanna said. "But I understand why she wants to go to Chicago. If it were me and I had her talent, I'd go there or the one in New York."

When Heather arrived at the ranch the following morning, she brought a stack of sketchbooks with her. Shanna insisted they go inside and look at them right away. Heather's subjects varied from flowers with butterflies and birds to the action of people and horses. Every one of the sketches took Shanna's breath away. When she got to the sketch of the calf roping event, she stopped and looked at Heather. "I will give you $100 for this sketch. I can give you cash right now, or take it off your bill, your choice. I want it for Clint. His birthday is coming up. I'd love to give him this matted and framed, and I know just where I'd like to hang it."

"Really?" Heather was flabbergasted. "You want to pay me $100 for this sketch?"

"Really!" Shanna said. "This reminds me of Clint. I love this one!"

"Mom, I knew that one would be your favorite. It reminded me of Dad too." Katie added.

"I'm not sure it's my very favorite," Shanna said, "but it's a close second to the one of you and Kashmir."

CHAPTER FORTY-FIVE

At 12:30 p.m. the following Monday, a new, shiny black Mercedes sedan pulled into the drive and stopped next to the ranch house. A tall, handsome gentleman stepped out and looked at the coating of dust on his car. "Boy, those dirt roads are murder on black cars," he smiled as Shanna walked over to greet him. "I'm Bill Madison. I assume you are Shanna Barclay?" he said as he extended his hand to shake. Shanna took his hand and said, "Yes, but please call me Shanna."

"Then you must call me Bill," the man smiled and released his grip from her hand. He reached into the back seat of his car and grabbed his briefcase. "I think I'm here to discuss my daughter, Heather, and your daughter, Katie, I believe?"

"Yes, why don't we go inside. The girls are in the barn bathing their horses right now. You don't look like you need to get horse shampoo and conditioner all over you right now. We can talk better inside. May I offer you a glass of iced tea?"

Bill smiled at Shanna. "I'd love that. Lead the way." He followed her through the back door into the kitchen. She pointed him toward the kitchen table. "I'll fix us some tea. Why don't you make yourself comfortable there?"

Bill sat down, placed his briefcase on the table, and opened it. He pulled several files out of the briefcase before closing it and setting it on the floor beside his chair. He set the files down in front of him. "Heather told me she sent her horse to you for some additional training. How is that working?"

"Twister is a fine animal, one of the best. He's very well trained for what Heather wants him to do. Your daughter works very hard at what she does. I told her there's nothing wrong with their training or practice. The missing piece is a bond between the horse and the rider. It's not there yet. The riders who win have developed a bond with their horse. They work as a team or two partners. I'm helping Heather develop that partnership with her horse. I know it will improve their performance and improve their standings."

"Okay, I'm glad to hear that," Bill said. "Marilyn and I paid quite a bit for that horse and his training. We also paid for Heather to fly to Texas and work with the trainer there. I'm glad to hear we didn't waste our money."

"You absolutely did not waste your money. You got what you paid for. What I am working with Heather on is something you don't learn as a technique. She needs to learn to trust her horse, and her horse needs to learn to trust her. They are coming along quite well in a short time. Heather has seen the difference. I'm pleased with their progress," Shanna told him. "I don't think Twister needs to stay here much longer for this work. I know Heather likes having him here because she has Katie and Karen to ride with. They also have other friends that meet them for trail rides. Horse kids like to hang out with other horse kids."

"Common interests create stronger bonds," Bill said. "I remember hanging out with the other jocks in school. I was one of those. It only seems like a hundred years ago," he laughed.

"I did the whole Rodeo Pageant thing myself. I understand where the girls are coming from." Shanna laughed with him.

"How is it that you began training horses?" Bill asked her.

"When Clint and I discovered I'd be on the road for most of a year if I continued to the Miss USA Rodeo Queen Pageant, we were young, so we got married instead. Katie came along. We decided one of us should be at home full time with her. Clint still competes on the circuit. I train horses and take care of our daughter. Now she's in the pageant thing with your daughter and their friend, Karen."

"Do you mind Heather's horse staying here after you finish the training?" Bill asked. "Heather has her license now, but I'm not sure I'm comfortable with her hauling her horse around too much so she can spend time riding with her friends. We have a great set up at home for Heather's horse, but it is isolated. I hadn't given much thought about her wanting to ride with friends for fun. I'm certainly happier with her doing that than some other things she could be doing. I don't mind paying you to board the horse if you have the room and the time for it."

"I have no problem with Twister staying here. We have room, and the girls pitch in extra help with feeding and cleaning. I'm happy to have him here," Shanna said. "By the way, what do you think of my newest acquisition? Have you looked at the drawing right there?" she pointed at the framed and matted sketch Heather did of Kashmir and Katie.

Bill turned his head and stared at the sketch. He looked long and hard at it before he spoke. "That is a wonderful piece. I love how the artist did the eyes of the girl and the horse. They draw you right into that arena. I can almost smell the horse from here. Who is the artist? I don't think I've seen any of his work before."

"Would it surprise you to know that you know the artist?" Shanna asked him.

"No way. I would remember that kind of talent," Bill said

"Take a look at this one I just bought from the artist. It's a little smaller and a little different from the one there on the wall, but I love it," Shanna told him as she handed him the framed drawing of the calf roping scene.

Bill held the framed sketch and stared at it for several minutes before saying anything. "This is fine work. You can see the emotions in this sketch. The calf is desperate to get away. The horse is not going to let that calf outrun him. The cowboy is determined to stop the calf. I can feel all of that here. It is some of the most amazing work in graphite on paper I've seen."

Bill looked at the sketch again. "Who is this artist that you think I already know?"

Shanna reached over the pulled the sticky note paper she used to cover the artist's signature off the glass in the frame.

Bill gasped when he saw the signature. He looked at the sketch and looked up at Shanna. "Is this my Heather?"

Shanna shook her head up and down in the affirmative.

"We've never seen any suggestion Heather was artistic. We've never seen anything she's done before. I'm astonished. How could she develop this much talent, and Marilyn and I have no clue?"

"Katie caught Heather working on the calf drawing at the last rodeo. Heather has been keeping her drawings under her mattress at home. She feels you and your wife would disapprove, and she didn't want to upset you. She's been throwing her work away, so nobody sees it until Katie caught her in the act. The picture on the wall was something Katie asked her to do after she saw the calf drawing. She wanted a picture of her with her horse. Heather does not know I'm talking to you about this right now. She thinks we are talking about Twister's training."

Bill shook his head. "I don't know what to say. Had we known; we would have encouraged her. I feel guilty we didn't catch on long ago. This kind of talent needs developed and strengthened, not thrown away. That makes me feel a little bit sick. Do you have any suggestions?"

"Bill, if Heather were my daughter, I'd feel the same way. She is worried you will be disappointed in her if she doesn't go off to one of the Ivy League schools on the east coast. Heather told me you are a Yale graduate, so I assume you've already talked to them about admitting your daughter. She told Katie she would love to go to the School of the Arts Institute in Chicago for a degree in Fine Art. She wants to learn to paint. If I were in your shoes, I'd send her there. You will get a much happier kid when she finishes her degree there than if she goes off to Yale for a business degree."

"Phew, that changes a lot of things," Bill said. "I hoped she would take over my businesses when she's older, so I can retire. Maybe I should plan to sell them instead. I can't imagine an artist running them. It doesn't sound like she'd be happy doing it. I want my daughter to be happy!"

"I was hoping you'd say that," Shanna smiled at him. "I know she'll be happy too when you tell her."

"Let's put this aside for right now. I'm going to have to think about this before I talk to Heather tonight. But, I planned to talk to your daughter about the horse park situation. I have some facts and figures to go over with her. I want to help her with her presentation to the City Council later this week. I brought some information for her," he said, as he patted the stack of folders on the table. "I'm ready anytime."

Shanna went out and called the girls in. Bill sat down with both of them and went over the plan for the community meeting and the City Council meeting. "What you need to do, Katie is prove there is real value in keeping the park open seven days a week. That's easy." Bill pulled a couple of sheets of paper out of one folder. "These statistics show the equestrian sports improve academic achievement in students. You should make copies of this for all the City Council members. Horseback riding also enhances the quality of life for older riders too. Here's a handout for the City Council members to cover that. You should read this so you can quote a fact or two from each one in your speech."

Bill opened another folder and pulled a couple of sheets of paper from that. "The next thing you need to do is show the value of the volunteers, and show the City Council members in real dollars and cents how much they can save the city's budget. Let's take the tractor work first. I happen to know heavy equipment operators earn at least $28.00 per hour. You say it takes about two hours per day to maintain the arenas. Let's take that $28.00 and add one third more to it for benefits."

"What do you mean by benefits?" Katie asked.

"The city pays workers for the time they work. They also pay for a portion of their medical insurance. They also pay them for holidays when they don't actually work. They give each employee so many days each year for sick-pay and vacation pay. The City also contributes something for every employee in their retirement accounts. Generally, if you add up all the extra stuff the City pays their workers beyond what they pay for actual work, it amounts to another one-third of their hourly wages. Does that make sense to you?"

"I think so. The State pays the same stuff for teachers, right?"

"Yes, most employers do. All we need to do is come up with an average to show the City Council. We take that $28.00 and add $9.34 to it for benefits. It would cost the City $37.34 per hour, times 2 hours per day, times 365 days per year to maintain the arenas for everyone. If we add all that up, we come to a total of $27,258.20 to keep the arenas ready for everyone to use. If you can get volunteers to do that, you will save the City $27,258.20 each year. Do you understand how we got to that number?"

"Wow! Yes, I see how you came up with that. That's incredible. If we can come up with savings for electricity on the lights, maybe they will pay attention to us and keep the horse part of the park open," Katie said with excitement in her voice.

Bill, Katie, and Heather went over facts and figures for everything the volunteers could do, and reductions the city could take and found nearly a hundred and fifty thousand dollars in savings for the City and keep the horse park open seven days per week.

Bill, Katie, and Heather slapped high fives all around. Bill reminded Katie he would be there at the City Council meeting to help support her with her speech. He wished her good luck and told her he was proud of her taking the task on in the first place. "Katie, you won't be affected by the park closure one way or the other, but I am certainly proud of you for standing up for those who will. You put together quite a team. I will also be at the community meeting to help you if you need it. I've got some things to do, so I'll be on my way. Heather, I'll talk to you when you get home." He reached over and kissed his daughter on her forehead before picking up his briefcase and leaving.

Shanna met Bill on his way to his car. "That was the School of the Arts Institution in Chicago, right?" he asked her after dropping his briefcase on the back seat.

Shanna smiled at him and shook her head up and down in the affirmative. "Yes. That's the one."

Bill climbed in his car, lowered the driver's window, and told Shanna, "I'll be checking that out. You have a great kid too!"

The following night, Katie, Shanna, and Clint drove to the Equestrian Park for the community meeting. Katie dashed off the minute the truck stopped. She wanted to meet Mr. Madison again and check one or two more facts before the meeting started. She walked to the podium with Bill Madison. He introduced himself and opened the meeting. He introduced Katie Barclay and let her give her speech to the crowd. Katie presented nearly the same speech she planned for the City Council meeting. Bill Madison took the microphone several times to explain points to the community. He brought copies of some documents that were passed out by volunteers in the crowd.

When Katie finished talking, the community members stood clapping and cheering. Bill Madison retook the microphone. "One point I need to emphasize to everyone here is that the City will require an iron-clad Release of Liability from any community member who volunteers to do tasks the city maintenance people have been doing. I've asked my attorney to draw up several versions of those. I can't overstate that the City will require one of these from every person who does maintenance in the Equestrian Park. Please look these over. If you have questions, you can call my attorney or your own. We are pledging work in exchange for keeping this park open for the enjoyment of adults and our children. The City must have protection from unnecessary lawsuits. Those will wipe out any savings we can give to the City by doing those jobs ourselves, and the Equestrian Park will probably go back to the two days per week they initially proposed. Think it over carefully, folks. We'll see you on Thursday at the City Council meeting.

Many community members swarmed Katie to thank her for working so hard on this project and speaking for the community. Many people wanted to volunteer to help out. Katie realized they would have to appoint one or two of the homeowners to coordinate all of the work. It was not something she could do. She told Bill Madison about that idea when she finally pulled free. Bill went among the crowd talking to people about it. They decided on a phone chain to contact every homeowner in the community and promised that someone would be elected or volunteer before the City Council meeting.

When Katie got home that night, her parents went into the house. Katie went to see her horse. She walked into Kashmir's stall and put her arms around his neck and hugged him.

"How did the speech go tonight?"

"I guess it went okay. The people in the neighborhood seemed to like it. I had lots of them come up to me afterward and tell me how much they appreciate me doing this."

"You are doing them a great favor. You are also doing their horses a great favor. Many creatures stand to benefit from the work you are doing. That is why you are a Medicine Woman."

"I don't understand Kashmir. I'm giving a speech. I'm hoping that speech will open the eyes of the City Council members, so they keep the horse park open for more than two days a week. How does that make me a Medicine Woman?"

"Katie, look at what you've already accomplished. Look at Heather. She was dreading leaving High School. She didn't want to do what her parents wanted her to do. She spent years hiding her true talent. Thanks to you, her life will be what she wants. You've healed her heart and given her something to look forward to. You are a Medicine Woman."

"Kashmir, that was my mother. She's the one who showed Heather's dad what an artist his daughter is. I can't take credit for that."

"Katie, you were the first one to discover the talent she hid so carefully. You brought it out in her so your mother could see it. You are ultimately the one who put things in motion to help your friend. You are a Medicine Woman."

"I still don't get this whole Medicine Woman thing. I don't feel any different than I did last year. What's so special about me now?"

"Nothing. You were special last year too. The difference is you didn't know why you are so special. Look at me. I was an angry horse. I wanted to stomp every human I could see. I hated them because I thought all humans were cruel. Now, I am free from the burden of hatred. If you had turned on me that first day, I would still be the same angry horse. You didn't. Don't you remember treating my wounds? You didn't have to do that, but you did. You healed my skin at the same time you healed my heart. I will always love you for that."

"Kashmir, I would have done the same for any horse. I don't like to see anything in pain or watch anything, or anyone suffer. What I did was not special."

"Katie, you miss the point. You don't like seeing anyone or anything suffer. You do what you can to alleviate pain and suffering of all kinds. You are a Medicine Woman."

"Kashmir, I didn't do anything special!"

"Katie, everything you do is special. I didn't have a job. You gave me one that I love more than any job I could dream of. You set Heather up on the path she wants to travel. You are helping an entire community get something they need. You don't personally benefit from any of those things. How can you believe that is not special?"

"I guess I have to think about it. I'm tired and should get some sleep." Katie stroked the soft hair of his neck tenderly. "You probably need some sleep yourself. I'll see you in the morning, my friend." Katie kissed Kashmir on the end of his nose before she left his stall. "I love you too," she said to him before leaving the barn.

CHAPTER FORTY-SIX

Michelle, the Queen Coordinator, met with the entire Queen's Court and Katie outside the auditorium doors before the City Council meeting. She checked each girl over to make sure their sashes were straight, their collars were correctly turned, and their crowns were polished and gleaming. When she was satisfied, she ushered them inside. They stood at the back of the room until the City Council President called the meeting to order. Michelle contacted the local newspapers ahead of time, so there were reporters and cameramen in the auditorium to take still photos and video. Many of the young people that accompanied their parents to the meeting came in their show clothes. Western hats, velvet hunt caps, top hats, and derbys graced heads all over the room. Katie was impressed at how many young people showed up for the meeting dressed up. Every seat was full. People stood several deep along the sides of the room and across the back of the room as well.

The City Council President called the meeting to order right on time. There were several other matters to discuss before the Council tackled the Equestrian Park issue. Those topics were discussed, voted on, and set aside.

The City Council President brought up the topic of the Equestrian Park. He explained to the other council members that the recommendation made was to close that part of the park except for Mondays and Tuesday. That was to eliminate some of the costs for maintenance because of the budget crunch. "I understand there is someone here that will speak for the community on this topic. I would appreciate that so we can shorten the amount of time we spend on this one issue. Would that person please come to the podium and tell us who you are."

Michelle walked with the entire Queen's Court to the podium with Katie right in the middle of the group. Cameras flashed, and video focused on the group. Bill Madison stepped behind the group of girls next to Michelle when they reached the podium.

Katie adjusted the microphone for her height and began, "Ladies and Gentlemen, I am Katie Barclay. I will speak for the community on the subject of the Equestrian Park. I have some handouts I would like to have you see. I will pass them down to the secretary so she can get them to each of you if that is permitted."

"Of course, Miss Barclay. May I ask how old you are?" the President of the City Council asked.

"Sir, I am 16 years old," Katie smiled at the man and glanced at the other members of the City Council.

"Miss Barclay, how much time do you spend using the Equestrian Park yourself?" the President asked her.

"Sir, I don't use it at all. My parents have a large 20-acre ranch just outside of town. I'm here to speak for those who do use it and need it open seven days a week."

"What makes you think you should be speaking to us about this if you don't use the park at all?" the President asked her.

"Sir, I grew up in an equestrian home. My parents are both equestrians. I've ridden since I was a few weeks old. I understand the needs of equestrians and horses. There were many volunteers from the community that worked together to gather information for this presentation. It is a community effort. I volunteered to present it to you as part of my community service objectives. I've been on the Rodeo Queen's Court since I was five years old. Community service is part of being on the Rodeo Queen's Court. We don't always look so pretty.

Sometimes we get our hands dirty, helping others in need, " Katie smiled at the City Council members as she stepped back into the line of the Queen's Court group of girls. Cameras flashed at the group.

"You may proceed," he smiled back at her.

Katie closed her eyes for three or four seconds and took one deep breath. She opened her eyes and smiled at the man. "Sir, I'd like to speak to you about the many reasons we would like to see the Equestrian Center open for community use every day. I would also like to speak to you with suggestions on how the community served by the park can help reduce the costs of keeping it open. Our proposals may eliminate some of the budget challenges you face today."

Katie met the glance of each member of the City Council as she spoke. She hoped she was engaging each of them equally as she continued with her speech. She passed handouts to her right, and they passed to the right until they reached the Council Secretary. The Council Secretary walked behind the members, placing each one in front of the City Council members. Katie remained relaxed and poised through her speech. She spoke confidently and from her heart to theirs. Katie didn't stumble over any point she made. When she finished her speech, she thanked the City Council members for allowing her to address them.

One of the Council members asked Katie where she got her figures. Bill Madison put his hand on her shoulder and asked her to let him answer that. Katie stepped away from the podium and let Bill approach it. He adjusted the microphone for his height and introduced himself. "I am an international businessman. I have an accountant in Los Angeles. He knows accountants out here in our area. They put the salary numbers together for us. My accountant gave us a range of salary and benefit package costs for the city. We used the lower number in the range, so if the numbers are off, they should be understated, not overstated. I'd also like to let you know that we had volunteers, both young people and adults, who monitored park usage and your city maintenance people for two full weeks. They counted usage in the number of riders and length of time in all four arenas. They also watched the city workers for the amount of time each day of the week they spent doing maintenance of any kind. They noticed nothing was recycled. The community went through the trash for recyclables during those two weeks and weighed them. The numbers we used we extrapolated from that. You are throwing money away by not putting recycle cans out in the park. We didn't check the other areas. There may be more recycling if we include the baseball/softball area, the tennis courts, the basketball courts, the soccer fields, and the picnic and swimming areas. My accountant also gave me the energy cost numbers we used in calculating the reduction in energy costs by setting the lights on timers and changing them monthly. I also talked to an electrician friend of mine for the cost of those timers. It's all in the handouts. He's also included an override code. If you need the park as a staging area for firefighters, as we've seen in the past, the override code will turn on and off lights in the park as needed. That cost is minimum."

The City Council President looked at each of the other members of the City Council. "I think we are all in agreement that we are not going to vote on this issue tonight. We have some reading to do. We need to evaluate and double-check the numbers you've given us. I'm going to stick my neck out here, but if your numbers are close, I think we will all agree to keep the park open seven days a week. Let us do our homework. We'll get back to you and the media by this time next week. We'd like to thank you, Miss Barclay, for your impassioned plea on behalf of the equestrians in our city. I can see you running for Mayor in a few years. I would not want to run against you," he laughed. The other members of the city council laughed along with him.

"Mr. Madison and Miss Barclay, would you please stick around after the meeting. We need to get your contact numbers so we can let you know our decision, and we may need additional information before we come to our conclusion. With that, I'd like to adjourn this meeting. Do I have a second?"

One of the other members of the council seconded the motion to adjourn. The clapping and cheering started all over again. Members of the community were happy the City Council was going to consider their plea. Some of the kids were jumping up and down, knocking their hats askew in the process. The Queen's Court was busy hugging Katie.

Many of the young people who showed up for the meeting in their show clothes were the ones who would be most affected by the park closure. Their parents could not afford the cost of putting their horses in full training with a professional trainer. They didn't have enough room in their backyards for arenas the size needed to work the horses properly. They could afford to pay for a coach to come to the park once a week and give their youngsters coaching and tell them what they needed to practice. The kids would practice on their own in the park. If the park reduced hours to only two days each week, those kids had nowhere else to go and would be out of horse shows by default. Many of those youngsters idolized Katie Barclay for standing up for them. There wasn't one little girl in the bunch who didn't want to grow up and be just like her someday. They told their mothers, their dads, and the Press.

The reporters began catching young people as they left the auditorium with their parents. The kids had a lot to say. News photographers and videographers were busy snapping pictures and catching people on video in the hallway outside.

Katie collapsed in a chair. She was tired. The City Council secretary came to get her phone number and chased after Bill Madison to get his. The tension of the moment exhausted her. Her parents both came to her side. "I'm so proud of you," her mom whispered. "I am too," her dad whispered in her other ear after he planted a kiss on her forehead.

"Mom and Dad, all I did was tell them what other people found out. All I did was deliver the message. I didn't write it. So many volunteers did that."

"Yes, Katie, you delivered the message. But you made them pay attention. I think they are really considering what you had to say. That took guts. There's no benefit for you. They also know that now,"

Shanna said. "When I received the State Queen's crown, my speech wasn't nearly as important, or as long, as the one you just gave. I am more proud of you than I can say."

"I agree with your mom," Katie's dad said. "I was there when Shanna gave her Queen's speech. I loved it, of course, but I loved this one more. I'm glad I was home to hear it."

"Speaking of home, I'm tired. Can we go now?" Katie asked.

The trio got to their feet and walked uphill to the auditorium doors. The minute Katie stepped into the hallway outside the auditorium, the flash from cameras almost blinded her. She staggered and nearly fell. Shanna and Clint held her arms and steadied her. Clint spoke up. "Hey, guys, can you hold off on the flash for a second. My daughter almost fell. We need a minute."

The news reporters came over to talk to Katie. They began peppering her with questions. She couldn't answer them fast enough. She finally turned her face into her dad's shoulder.

Shanna saw how upset Katie was. "I have an idea. Why don't you come to the ranch in the morning at10:00 a.m.? We'll have a mini-press conference then. You can ask your questions one at a time. Katie will be available then. I need to get her home. She's tired." Shanna gave their phone number and address to the reporters. She and Clint whisked their daughter outside to their truck and drove straight home. Katie fell asleep in the back seat.

CHAPTER FORTY-SEVEN

Shanna called Bill Madison that night and asked if he and Heather could be at the ranch the next morning for the meeting with the press. He agreed and was there a half-hour before the newspaper and TV reporters showed up. His daughter, Heather, was about 10 minutes behind him. Shanna, Clint, and Bill had a cup of coffee together while they talked about the previous evening.

"I have to go along with the City Council President," Bill told the Barclays. "I can see her running for Mayor or Governor, or President someday, and I wouldn't want to be the one running against her. She has a way of speaking to people that draws them in. She's quite the young lady!"

"Yes, she does, especially if it is something she's passionate about," Clint commented.

"I'm not sure she'd want to get involved with politics, but she can be pretty persuasive when she wants to."

"I have a daughter, too. I understand," laughed Bill. "Speaking of which, here she is."

Heather's car pulled into the driveway. Right behind her was a convoy of cars and media vans. The parking area clogged with vehicles in minutes.

"Where's Katie?" Heather asked when she found Shanna, Clint, and her dad on the patio.

"She was fixing her hair," Shanna told her. "Why don't you go see if you can help so she can get out here. It looks like we have lots of company."

Heather dashed to the back door and ran into Katie in the kitchen. "You ready?" she asked.

"Are they here already?" Katie asked Heather.

"Yes, and it looks like a crowd. I saw TV people there too."

Katie took a deep breath and let it out slowly. "I guess we'd better get out there," she said as she pulled open the back door and stepped outside.

Bill had a stack of copies of the handouts from last night in his hand. "I made extra copies for today," he whispered to Shanna. "I hope I have enough. If not, do you have a printer so we can run a few more?"

"Yes. Let me know. I can make copies and get them back out here for you," Shanna whispered back.

Katie and Heather walked out to the waiting group of news people. "Hi, thank you for coming. I'm Katie Barclay, and this is my friend, Heather Madison. She's the current Rodeo Queen for this area. We can take your questions now, but can you please ask one at a time?"

The questions and answers flew for about 20 minutes before slowing down. One of the newspaper people asked how they came up with the water savings numbers.

"We found out from one of the mothers in the volunteer group that the city provided four fifty-gallon water tanks by the arenas to water horses," Katie explained. "Those tanks had to be dumped every two days, scrubbed out because of algae, and refilled again. That was time-consuming work we found at the last minute. Once we realized we were wasting 200 gallons of water three times a week by dumping and refilling those tanks, it was easy to see how replacing them with automatic waterers would save precious water resources and lots of time in wages. We saw that if we installed automatic waterers at one end of each arena, it would save hundreds of gallons of water every week, along with hours of labor. Mr. Madison helped with the calculations on that, but it amounted to significant savings."

"Couldn't you have dumped the water onto the lawns or trees and saved water that way?"

"Nobody could pull a 50-gallon tank of water over to the trees in the first place. The trees and grass are already on water timers set for nights, so the water has time to soak in and not evaporate away during the daytime. That water ended up making a mudhole near the tanks and benefited nothing at all." Katie explained. "Every time someone dumped the tanks to clean them, they had to rinse the algae and dirt out before they could refill the tanks with drinking water. That created an additional loss of water. A City Worker had to stand over each tank with a hose to fill it, so it took a lot more time because there was only one hose and one water spigot to hook it up to. Automatic waterers only hold about a quart of water in the bowl and only refill as the horse drinks the water. Cleaning them will cost a quart of water every couple of days. They don't get as much algae as the big tanks do because the water isn't sitting stagnant for days at a time. It recirculates every time a horse takes a drink. We have lots of horses using them every day."

One of the reporters for the local paper stepped forward. "I just got off the phone with my office. The City Council is asking for a meeting with the volunteers at the Equestrian Park this weekend. It sounds very much like they may be taking your suggestions seriously, Katie. How do you feel about that?"

"Wow, I'm excited! I really hope they keep the Equestrian Park open all week long. That will help so many people and so many horses," Katie sputtered. "That's wonderful news!"

"If this works out, and the City Council takes your advice and keeps the Equestrian Park open seven days a week, what are your plans for the future, Katie?"

"I plan to compete again in the next Rodeo Queen Pageant. I want to finish high school with a solid 4.0-grade point average. I want to go to college, but I haven't made up my mind where yet. I'm thinking about UC Davis, Fresno State, or Cal Poly. I want to take my horse to school with me. He and I want to continue competing. At some point, I want to compete in the State Rodeo Queen Pageant, and I'd love to compete in the National Queen Pageant. Someday, I would love to be Miss USA Rodeo Queen."

The reporter chuckled. "I have no doubt you'll get there, Katie. You seem determined, and you know what you want. I'd like to ask you one more question. I've heard that you compete in Rodeo events on an Arabian horse. Is that true? Isn't Rodeo the sport for Quarter horses?"

Katie looked exasperated for a second. "I tell you what. I do compete on an Arabian horse. We've broken records at both Rodeos we raced in so far. I have a horse who loves to run, and he loves me. We are a team. I don't care what his breed is. He's my best friend. He's my partner. We win events together. We're going to keep doing it. There are no rules against it. If you could feel what I feel when we are racing together, you would never question why I ride him. I feel pure power, pure speed, and pure joy. I don't think many people can say that about their horse in competition, and if they can, they should continue at all costs."

The reporter smiled at her. "This has nothing to do with the Equestrian Park, but can we meet your horse?"

"Sure. Please give us some room at the barn door, and I'll bring Kashmir out for you." Katie answered as she and Heather walked into the barn. Katie haltered Kashmir and walked him out in the sunlight for the reporters to see. Lots of cameras clicked at the beautiful bay horse walking proudly beside Katie. "Would you like to see a barrel run?" she asked the group.

"Absolutely!" "Yes!" "Please!" Many heads bobbed up and down in agreement. They all wanted to see it up close.

"Give us a couple of minutes to tack him up, and we'll show you what we do," Katie told the group as she walked Kashmir to the cross ties. Shanna came in with Heather to help tack the horse up for a ride. Katie led Kashmir back outside in the sunlight and mounted him. She walked him toward the arena set up for barrels. "Someone call "GO" when you're ready," she said, then hung on to the reins and waited for everyone to find their spot around the arena.

At "GO," Kashmir turned into a bullet. He was outside the gate one minute and beginning his turn around the first barrel almost before the reporters knew what happened. He flashed by the second barrel on his way to the third before they could catch their breath. He was on his final dash to the finish line split seconds later. Katie glanced at the timer on the side of the barn and pointed it out to the reporters. "See that time. That time would earn me money for college, and we are not even warmed up yet. I know he loves his job. Do you love yours as much as he loves his?"

Kashmir was a little antsy after that run. "Tell you what. I need to work him down a bit after that exhibition run. My parents and Heather's dad are back at the house. If you have any questions, I'm sure they can answer them. Heather's dad was the one who helped put the numbers together for the presentation." She clicked at Kashmir, and he trotted back into the arena for a couple of passes to stretch out and calm down. She walked him to the barn, untacked him, and handed him an extra carrot. "You showed them again! Thank you for that run. They now have something to write about," she laughed. Katie stroked his neck as he chewed on the carrot. *"That was fun,"* Kashmir said between crunches.

At 5:00 p.m. that night, Michelle, the Queen Coordinator, called the Barclay house. Shanna was in the kitchen and picked up the phone. "Quick, turn on your TV to the news. Your daughter is on right now. If you miss it, it will be on again at 6:00 p.m."

Shanna turned the TV on and rushed to the back door, calling for Clint and Katie. "Get in here, Katie! You are on TV right now."

Shanna rushed back to see the tail end of the cut. It was a portion of the barrel ride Katie did for the reporters that morning. The reporter read over the video, "…and this young barrel racer stood up to the City Council this week to convince them they could save money keeping the community Equestrian Park open. More on that story in our 6:00 p.m. coverage." The scene on the screen changed to a political speech someone in Washington DC was giving. Katie and Clint missed the clip of Katie, but the family sat in the living room with their eyes glued to the TV until the 6:00 p.m. report started.

The report began with a photo behind the reporter. It was a photo of the Queen's Court taken in the auditorium the night Katie spoke with the City Council. The Little Miss, Miss, Princess, Young Queen, and Queen flanked Katie. The girls were all beautiful and looked their best in their Queen's Court outfits, hats, and crowns. Katie's stood out because her outfit was from the prior year, but that only seemed to help her. The edited clips of her presentation played, including the City Council President's comment about not wanting to run against her for Mayor. The video switched to the ranch earlier that day with Katie talking again and ended with Katie's run around the barrels with Kashmir. The woman newscaster said, "The City Council has announced the Equestrian Park in their city would remain open seven days per week. They are working with the community to set up the structure recommended by this 16-year-old barrel racer. The President of the Homeowner's association had this to say." The video changed to the man who was the Homeowner's Association President. "Thank you, Katie Barclay. You saved the Equestrian Park for our friends and neighbors. The baseball, softball, soccer, and tennis associations are also looking into cost-cutting and volunteerism they can provide to the city to keep their areas open as well." The news rolled right into another story while Katie sat on the couch with her mouth open.

"Wow, Mom, that was Aimee's dad. I didn't know he was the President of the Homeowner's Association. He's a super nice guy. He helps out with a lot of the events the Queen's Court does."

"Well, now you're famous. How does it feel?" Clint chuckled.

Katie threw a pillow at him in his recliner. "Dad! I didn't do much. I just gathered information, worked with Heather's dad to crunch some numbers, and stood up and gave the presentation. It's not like I got dirty doing that or anything."

"We haven't talked much about your education after high school. I heard you rattle off UC Davis, Fresno State, and Cal Poly as possible schools. Do you want to talk about that?" Clint asked her.

"I want to take my horse with me. I know Cal Poly is Arabian territory, but Kashmir is an Arabian, so I thought that might work. Fresno State has a Rodeo team, so I thought that could work. We should be able to get on that team. UC Davis is crawling with horses, so I figured I might be able to sneak one more in there. I know we haven't talked about it. That just came off the top of my head," she grinned at her dad.

Shanna interjected, "Cal Poly is close enough to drive. If you went to Cal Poly, you could take all your classes in two days and have five days a week to get your studying done and live at home. You can keep your horse right where he is and have weekends to compete. I'm sure Cal Poly has a Rodeo Team somewhere on campus. Their mascot is Broncos."

"Fresno State has a great Rodeo team. I used to compete against them. They get kids from Texas, Oklahoma, Nebraska, the Dakotas, Wyoming, Utah, basically all over the West," Clint said. "Those are the kids who grew up with Rodeo, the same as your Mom and I did. With your times on the barrels and poles, I'm sure you will be snatched up for their team if you apply there."

"Are you interested in becoming a veterinarian? UC Davis is the closest school in the country if you are looking to become a vet. You would never be out of work if that's what you decide to do, and you specialize in large animals. There doesn't seem to be enough large animal vets around," Shanna told Katie.

"Mom, no way. I don't want to spend eight years in college, then do a residency that could be two more years before I could earn a living. I would have to apply for student loans to do ten years of education, even if I got the Miss USA title. The scholarships only pay for about six years of college, so I'd have to come up with the money for four more years. I want to be a horse trainer like you. I can stay right here and work next to you. Even if I got married, my husband and I could build another house on the ranch, and I'd still be here next to you. You guys wouldn't mind, would you?"

"No, sweetie, we wouldn't mind one little bit," Clint said as he got up and hugged his daughter. "…as long as I get to pick your husband!"

CHAPTER FORTY-EIGHT

Michelle was looking over her current Queen's Court, trying to see who would likely apply for the position for next year. She had a couple of candidates she thought might apply for the Queen's position Heather would be leaving. Neither of them excited her much. They were pretty girls but never had much time to spend on community service projects or the usual Queen's appearances. Neither of them showed much leadership.

Then she looked at the girls she knew would apply for the Young Queen's position. She was sure Karen would apply again. She also thought Katie would. Of the two, she felt the job should go to Katie, but that would leave Karen entirely out. Karen put in a substantial amount of work on community service projects and showed real leadership skills in several areas. She never missed an event that invited the Court.

Michelle went on down her list, looking over each position, and the girls most likely to apply for them. She had several strong ones for each spot right on down to the Little Miss position. It was looking like a great year, except for the Queen's spot.

Michelle pulled out the applications for the Young Queen position last year. She reviewed each one to see if the young lady would still qualify for the Young Queen spot, or would she age up to the

Queen's position. Michelle was hoping one of the Young Queen candidates from last year would be old enough to apply for the Queen's role next year. She looked at Katie's application, saw her name at the top, skimmed it briefly, and set it aside. The next one in her pile was Karen's. Karen wouldn't work. She looked at each application in the pile.

Something was screaming at her to review Katie's application again. She set the paperwork down and picked up Katie's application one more time. She looked at the birthdate again. There it was! Katie was 17 days too young to apply for the Queen's position on the court. Seventeen days? Was that enough to keep her from becoming the Queen? How hard and fast did the deadline have to be. If she were allowed to compete for the Queen's position for next year, Karen could re-apply for the Young Queen position. She could serve there for one more year and should be ready to take over the Queen's place the following year when Katie left for college. That would be perfect in Michelle's judgment.

Michelle picked up the phone and began making calls. She needed to talk to the Rodeo Queen Association members for the High Desert. She required them to stretch the Queen's birthday cut-off date by 17 days, and she would have the perfect court for them for the next three years. Michelle worked it with all her might. She stressed the amount of community service work Katie had done, even though she was not in the program the current year. She reinforced the positive impressions Katie made on the Southern California community at large with her plea to keep the Equestrian Park open seven days a week, even though it didn't affect her personally. Three hours later, she had the complete agreement of all members of the Rodeo Queen Association, even the old stick-in-the-mud, Miss Harrington. Miss Harrington had never authorized anything that was not positively, 100%, according to the written rules.

Katie could apply for and become the next Rodeo Queen in the area. Michelle looked at her watch. It was too late for her to call Katie. She'd have to call her in the morning.

When the next morning arrived, Michelle thought it would be even better to deliver the news in person. She called Shanna at home and asked if she could come by for a cup of coffee. Shanna thought the inquiry was strange but agreed. Michelle then asked if her daughter would be home at that time. Shanna thought that was even stranger, but knowing Michelle, she said she would make sure of it. Over breakfast, Shanna told Katie they were expecting company for coffee soon. Shanna didn't have any more information, so she didn't offer it. Katie rushed through her breakfast and cleaned up a bit more than she usually did for going to the barn.

Michelle arrived right on time. Shanna invited her into the kitchen and pointed her to the kitchen table. She poured Michelle a cup of coffee. "Need anything in this?" Shanna asked before bringing the cup to the table.

"No, I take it just like it is, thank you," Michelle said. "I have some news I'd love to share with you and Katie, though."

"She will be here in a minute," Shanna told her. "She went out to say good-morning to her horse. That generally doesn't take all that long," she laughed.

"Well, before she gets here, I was going over the Court for next year. I discovered Katie is only 17 days early for the Queen position. I talked to the entire Association and got their agreement, even Miss Harrington, to waive those 17 days and allow Katie to apply for the Queen's position for next year. I'm certain she will be accepted, hands down. That would give her two years she can hold that position if she wants it before she goes off to college."

"Are you kidding me? You got Miss Harrington to overlook 17 days? I've heard she won't overlook 10 minutes on an assignment in school before she issues a D grade. That's incredible. That will make Katie so happy! She knew she was going to have to run against Karen for the Young Queen position next year. Katie didn't want to win and take it away from Karen. Now she doesn't have to. That's great!"

"I'm pleased about this myself. Katie has gone to events as the former Young Queen and done as good a job as any of the current court. Not only that but with the work she put into the Equestrian Center with the City Council and the interviews on TV and all, she's the best representative we've had in years. I'm excited about this. Karen does a great job and will make a great Queen when Katie goes off to school. She's getting better all the time. I give Katie a lot of credit for mentoring her. Katie has even mentored the present Queen. I've seen so much improvement in Heather in the past few months too."

"Heather is getting ready for her education too. I know she's taking a few courses at the community college this summer before she flies off to Chicago. I'm hoping she does well there," Shanna said.

"I thought she was off to Yale," Michelle questioned. "What changed her mind?"

"Katie had a hand in that too," Shanna admitted. "Take a look at the portrait on the wall beside you for a minute."

"Isn't that Katie and her Arabian?" Michelle asked. "That's a beautiful portrait. I don't think I've ever seen that artist's work before."

"Heather did that," Shanna said. "Katie caught her at one of the rodeo events sketching the calf roping event. She asked her to sketch herself and Kashmir. Isn't it impressive?"

"Heather? Really?" Michelle was shocked. "I never thought Heather was interested in art much. That surprises me. She's excellent. What classes is she taking at the community college this summer? Art classes?"

"Heather has done sketching since she was little, she told Katie. She thought her parents would be disappointed in her if she wanted to become an artist instead of what they wanted for her. Heather has been throwing her work away, so her parents didn't see it. I showed this to her dad just before the City Council meeting. Her parents are not disappointed with her talent. They are thrilled by it. Heather will attend the School of the Arts Institute in Chicago next year. She wants to be a painter, and she loves the western style. I'm looking forward to buying some of her work. I'll show you the first piece she ever sold. I bought it for Clint for his birthday," Shanna walked down the hall and pulled the calf roping sketch off the wall and handed it to Michelle. "What do you think of this one?"

Before Michelle could answer, Katie stomped into the mudroom. "Sorry I'm late. I had to give my horse his goodie bucket."

"You're just the person I wanted to talk to," Michelle smiled at Katie. "I have some great news for you. And, Shanna, I don't blame you. I would buy this myself if you hadn't already bought it. Do you think she has others?"

"Definitely," Shanna said. "We'll have to get a showing together for her before she leaves."

"What did you need with me?" Katie asked, taking a seat at the kitchen table.

"I've spoken with the entire Rodeo Queen Association for this area. We are going to allow you to compete for the Queen's position next year. You could be taking Heather's place when she leaves if you want it. Karen can compete for the Young Queen's position for next year. I'm pretty sure you will both get those spots if you want them."

"You are kidding me, right?" Katie asked. "My birthday is off a few days. Are you telling me that Miss Harrington was willing to ignore that?"

"That's exactly what I'm telling you," Michelle looked directly at Katie. "Do you want that spot?"

"Oh, man, you bet I do! That means I wouldn't bump Karen out for the Young Queen spot if I applied for that. I'd love to be the Queen. Yes! I want it! I'd be honored!"

"Get your paperwork in on time. You have two and a half months to get ready to be our Rodeo Queen. Think you can do that?" Michelle laughed.

"Watch me!" Katie nearly shouted as she offered her palm for a high-five from her mom and Michelle.

The next two and a half months flew by for Katie. Karen was thrilled she had the opportunity to be Katie's Young Queen. Heather took her classes at the community college seriously and learned the rudiments of painting with oils/acrylics and watercolors. Her paintings got better and better. Shanna and Michelle helped set up a showing of her work at the Apple Valley Gallery. Her sketches sold out entirely, and her paintings usually sold within a day or two.

Shanna helped Heather find a stable near Chicago for her horse. They had rodeos in Illinois and several states around, as they found out. Heather was thrilled. She could get her art training and still ride her horse in the rodeo events they loved so much. Her partnership with Twister improved by the day when they worked with Shanna. They became a team worth watching. They also became a team between themselves. The only tighter bond Shanna ever saw was the one between Kashmir and Katie.

The big event for the year came over Labor Day weekend. The Wranglers from their area joined with the Sheriff's Rodeo people to put on a Labor Day spectacular rodeo for three days. Cowboys and cowgirls from all the western states came to this one event every year. The prize money, based on ticket sales and entry fees, was higher than usual and drew more competition. The new Queen's Court for the area was introduced at this event every year. The Queen opened every session, from morning, afternoon, and evening every day with her entourage. Queens from other areas joined the party. This year, Queens from Washington, Oregon, Northern California, Arizona, Nevada, Colorado, New Mexico, Utah, Wyoming, and Montana planned to join Katie in the opening ceremonies.

Katie felt lucky she was at her home base for this event. She didn't have to trailer in for miles to get there, and she and her horse could sleep in their own beds at night. It was the first time it ever occurred to her how nice it was to open an event near home.

After winning her Queen's crown, life had been a whirlwind of meetings with business leaders, photography sessions, practice at home, and little to no sleep. She was looking forward to the end of the weekend before the weekend even got there. She talked with Kashmir about it when they had private moments together. He was excited about being the mount of a Queen. He soon tired of the events and being on display as well. He hoped they would get a week off after the rodeo to recharge their batteries. He missed the private time he had with Katie.

Katie was up before dawn day of the rodeo. She bathed, fixed her makeup and hair, pulled on her new Queen's outfit, and sat in the truck while her mother and dad loaded her horse. They didn't want her to mess up her outfit. They drove her to the fairgrounds, where the event was taking place. Her mom and dad took Kashmir out of the trailer and tacked him up, so she didn't get her new clothes dirty. She chaffed at that. It was always her job to check the tack on her horse. Now she had to have someone else do it, so she didn't mess up her clothes! She was not sure she liked this. It was early, and she hadn't slept well the night before. Maybe that was making her cranky. It wasn't a good start to what could be the best day of her life. Was it?

She had her first good look at the new tack her parents put on Kashmir. The new Queen's Court outfits consisted of dark blue jeans with a dark blue blouse. Each girl wore a white jacket embroidered with blue flowers around the wrists up to the elbows and on both front and back yokes. The chaps, deeply fringed, were decorated with the same blue flowers around the bottom and up the outside of the legs to her hips. Shanna and Clint had a custom bridle and reins made for Kashmir. They included set blue stones to match the color of the embroidered flowers on Katie's outfit. The stones crossed the browband and up cheek pieces of the bridle. They went from the bit to within six inches of her hands on the reins. The breast collar was studded with the same blue stones. Her dad had the blue stones added to the skirt of the saddle as well. All in all, it was a stunning ensemble for a horse.

"Oh, my goodness," Katie said when she got a good look. "He looks beautiful in that."

"Yeah, if you think he looks good, you should see yourself!" her dad commented. "I think you two are going to be the best looking ones on the fairgrounds today!" he laughed.

"Yeah, but Dad, you're prejudiced. I'm your kid. You can't help it," Katie laughed.

"Wait and see. You listen to the crowd and see what they think," her dad chuckled. "I think they are going to be impressed!"

It was time to mount up and get to the starting gate. Her dad boosted her into the saddle, and Katie checked her gear to be sure everything was right and in working order. Her parents walked her to the gate so she could line up with the other Queens and her Court for the year.

The announcer broadcast his opening remarks over the loud-speakers. He announced the opening of the event and the names of the Queens and the Queen's Court for the year just before the gate opened. Katie took a deep breath and cued Kashmir to a strong trot. The two entered the arena like they were dancing on air. Kashmir trotted the high, floating trot of his breed. Katie carried the Red, White, and Blue flag of her country, snapping in the breeze beside her. Unnoticed by her, but noticed by everyone else in the stadium, was the flag that followed her. It was the jet black tail of her beautiful Arabian horse.

www.ingramcontent.com/pod-product-compliance
Lightning Source LLC
Chambersburg PA
CBHW051541260626
47170CB00003B/1044